Restless
A Finding Love Novel

by Paris Hansen

Alissa,
Thanks for Reading!
xo
Paris Hansen

Cover Design by James, GoOnWrite.com

Chapter 1

Savannah St. James was dying for a drink, a hot bath and her bed, in that order. Or maybe she'd have the drink while in the bath and kill two birds with one stone. She was more than used to long hours, but the day had felt longer than usual. There was so much that she needed to get done, every day she was doing the job of two people, but that morning she also had to cover for one of her employees. She was so beyond exhausted. Every inch of her body ached, even her hair. Ultimately, everything she had accomplished that day had been worth the way she felt as she slowly climbed the four steps to her front door. Savannah knew that she was lucky enough to have made her dream a reality and even at the most difficult times she wouldn't change anything about her professional life.

Before opening the screen door, she grabbed the mail out of the box attached to her Craftman-style bungalow. Aside from her three, soon to be four, storefronts her house was her pride and joy. Savannah had worked long and hard to save up to buy the place and once it was hers, she had slaved over making the house perfect. Between renovations and the interior design that she had done herself, her home had been her first labor of love and all of the work had been worth it in the end. If it hadn't been for working on the house, she may have never realized that she had what it took to open her own cupcake shop. Now five years later, her business was thriving even if it was wiping her out.

Once inside the house, she dropped her keys and purse on the table by the door vowing to move her purse up to her bedroom after she had a minute or two to rest. Flipping the switches next to her, she waited for the light to illuminate her sunken living room and the tiny dining room that was just beyond it. Walking through the now brightly lit rooms toward the kitchen Savannah flipped through the pile of mail in her hands.

Junk mail and a couple of bills were interspersed between the brightly colored envelopes and postcards that she had been getting a lot of lately. For the last year or so, it seemed like there was a never ending stream of invitations, announcements and save the dates; weddings, baby showers, bridal showers and births. Then came the children's birthday parties or the anniversary parties; events that marked significant milestones in the lives of her friends, but often reminded Savannah that there might be something missing from her life.

It didn't happen all the time. In fact, most of the time she loved her life the way it was; she had a successful business and family and friends that loved her. Marriage and children had never really been something that she had much interest in, not even when she was a little girl. She had always been too independent to want someone around all the time and then she was always just too busy to bother.

Over the years there had been dates and occasional hookups to take the edge off, but she was usually far too busy and far too tired for anything else. Relationships were a lot of work and with the frequent 4 am wake-up calls and 12-15-hour work days, the last thing she needed when she got home was more work. Until recently, she had always figured she'd wait until she was settled to think about the other parts of her life, but what if she was never truly settled? What if she never stopped being busy, stopped opening new locations? Would she end up old, alone and miserable like her dad's sister Anna?

Thoughts like that one always had Savannah contemplating giving dating a shot. Sadly, she had no idea where to start and when she started to think about the possibilities she got cold feet and changed her mind. Now standing at the large island in the middle of her kitchen she added the new invitations and announcements to the pile that had come the day before and the day before that.

She tried to picture her life with someone to share it with and she really liked what she saw. Someone to come home to, cuddle with, vent to when she was angry or frustrated, someone to share exciting news with or better than that, create exciting news with. The possibilities were endless and amazing, but the steps to getting there were crazy and scary and filled with horrible first dates and bad pick-up lines. She could practically picture the line of men with horrible body odor, bad breath and mounds of back hair that would likely be waiting for her if she gave dating a try.

A knock at her front door startled Savannah out of her quickly darkening thoughts. Before she could walk back the way she had come, the door was opening, the sound of her sister's laughter filling her silent house. With a muttered curse, Savannah plastered a smile on her face and waited for her mom and sister to meet her in the kitchen.

"You forgot what day it was didn't you?" her sister Brooklyn asked as soon as she entered the kitchen, a bottle of wine in one hand, a pizza box in the other. Even in a pair of holey, faded jeans and an on old Washington State University sweatshirt, Brooklyn was gorgeous. Her face was completely devoid of make-up and her light brown hair was pulled back into a loose ponytail; the natural golden highlights standing out even under the dull overhead lighting.

Savannah had always been a little jealous of her younger sister's flawless, easy beauty. Brooklyn could have been a model and had been approached numerous times as a teenager and in her early twenties, but it was never something that had interested her. In fact, most of the time, Brooklyn couldn't be bothered with make-up, a fancy hairstyle or anything nicer than jeans and a t-shirt.

"No…yes…how did you know?" Savannah grabbed the bottle of wine from her sister before turning to get the bottle opener out of the top drawer next to the sink. She didn't want her family to see the look of shame on her face as they realized that she hadn't remembered their long standing date and then that she had tried to lie about it.

"Because we know you dear," her mother Rebecca said from the other side of the large island. "You work too hard and too much."

Savannah bit her lip to keep from commenting on what her mother said. Instead, she smiled at her mom and watched as she put the bottle of wine and paper bag she was carrying down onto the marble surface. The paper bag had grease stains on the outside and a heavenly garlic scent that made Savannah's mouth water. As much as she had wanted to be alone, pizza, breadsticks and wine with her favorite ladies was definitely a good alternative.

"I just got home about five minutes ago. Gretchen called in sick, so instead of going in at nine, I ended up heading in at six to open the shop out here. I was there until about three when I had to run out to one of the buildings I'm looking at for the new location to meet with the real estate agent. Of course traffic sucked, so I was nearly late and instead of looking like a professional business owner, I had flour and batter in my hair and on my clothes."

"Honey, you still have flour and batter all over you. Why don't you run upstairs and take a quick shower while we open the wine and get everything set up in the living room? We've got time before the show starts," her mom suggested before walking around to her side of the island. She grabbed the bottle of wine and the corkscrew from Savannah's hands before shooing her out of the kitchen.

A hot shower did sound fantastic, especially since the hot bath she had been daydreaming about was not in the cards for that evening. She couldn't believe she forgot it was Wednesday, although her days had been running together a lot as of late. Still, the long standing Wednesday night date with her mom and sister to watch *Survivor* had been a staple in their lives for over a decade. They had vowed never to miss the date, no matter what and so far they had watched every single episode together. Even when Brooklyn was on the other side of the state at WSU they would video chat while they watched.

Remembering the hours of laughter and arguments over who would win made Savannah giggle as she walked up the stairs to her master suite on the second floor. Brooklyn always picked one of the good looking guys, while her mom picked the underdog. Savannah was a little more strategic about her pick and usually waited until the players started to show their game play before picking her potential winner. Of course it was rare that any of them ever actually picked the person that ended up winning the million dollars, but it was always fun to see whose player went the furthest.

Once in her bedroom, she stripped out of her work clothes, shoving them into the separate hamper that she had dedicated to them. While she loved the smell of baked goods, she didn't want all of her clothes to smell like cake. Walking into the bathroom, she looked at her oversized bathtub and sighed. As much as she had wanted to take a long bath and let the hot water melt away her tension, she was also starving and the smell of pizza and breadsticks was making her stomach grumble. Besides her mom and Brooklyn would never let her stay upstairs very long.

After a quick shower, Savannah threw her damp, dirty blonde hair into a messy bun and threw on a pair of flannel pajama pants and a Delectable Delights t-shirt that featured a giant cupcake on the front with the words Lick My Frosting strategically placed over the top. The t-shirt was one of their top sellers with both men and women and it never ceased to make her giggle.

Back downstairs, Brooklyn and their mom sat on the couch directly across from the 55" TV that was mounted over the gas fireplace. Waiting for her on the side table next to her recliner was a glass of her favorite red wine and a plate with a large slice of supreme pizza and a couple of breadsticks. Savannah sighed as she sank into the plush chair and kicked up her legs. The recliner hadn't originally been on her list of must-haves when she was shopping for furniture, but the minute she sat in it she knew that she had to have one in her living room. She immediately bought another one for her upstairs library. The chair was ridiculously comfortable; throw in a good book, a soft throw blanket and a glass of wine and Savannah rarely wanted to get up.

They ate and talked about what they had been up to for the last week while waiting for *Survivor* to start. Brooklyn, with the help of their mom, had spent the week looking for a place she could afford on her own, but wasn't having any luck. She was getting tired of living at their parent's house where she had been for the last couple of years after finally separating from her now ex-husband Frank. The divorce proceedings had been long, difficult and drawn out leaving Brooklyn an emotional wreck for months, but it was obvious to everyone around her that the divorce had been the best thing to happen to her in a long time.

When Brooklyn had first left Frank, Savannah had offered her one of the rooms at her place, but Brooklyn had opted to live with their parents. There she had a mother-in-law style apartment over the garage that gave her the privacy she needed, but it still wasn't as good as having her own place. Brooklyn craved being out on her own, paying her way through life without the help of anyone else, which was yet another thing that Savannah admired about her sister.

"So, Savannah, how are the plans for the new location going?" Brooklyn asked.

The list of things that needed to get done seemed never ending to Savannah even though this was the fourth store that she had opened in the last five years. It should have been old hat for her, but it seemed as difficult and tedious as it had the first time. She needed help, but didn't really have the time to hire anyone as her personal assistant.

"I'm drowning in paperwork and decisions that need to be made. I need help, but I don't have the time to interview a bunch of applicants and there's really no one else I could have do it. Everyone's already constantly busy with orders and the day to day stuff for each store."

"I could do it," Brooklyn offered. "I need the extra money and I've got plenty of free time on my hands with the whole being single and not interested in dating thing. Plus, all of my freelance work has been pretty easy lately. I could actually use something to keep me busy."

"It can be long hours and grueling work, plus I'm not always the easiest person to work for when I get tired and bitchy."

"You don't have to tell me," Brooklyn smiled. "I've been around you my entire life; I know how to put up with your mood swings. I don't think we'll have a problem working together. Besides, I'm not afraid to stand up to you if you're being unreasonable which might actually help your other employees. I wouldn't be surprised to find out that some of them are afraid of you."

Savannah groaned as she took a sip of her wine. "Oh I know some of them are. I don't want them to be, but you know how I get. Everything has to be perfect and done exactly the way I want it done, which is why it's taken me so long to hire someone to be my right hand. I hate giving up control, but there's no other way for me to survive this. Are you sure you want to take on the responsibility?"

"Absolutely! Just tell me when to start."

Savannah should have known by the smile on Brooklyn's face that something was up other than one sister having a new employee and the other sister having a new job; especially when her younger sister looked over at their mother and then back to her. Something unspoken passed between them in the brief moment their eyes met and Savannah knew that whatever it was involved her as soon as her mom turned to look at her with a huge smile on her face.

"Now that you'll have more help, you'll likely be working fewer hours which means you'll have a little bit more free time every day," Rebecca stated the obvious, which was another sign that something was up. "More free time means time to explore situations that you haven't been able to explore lately. You could read more or go hiking. Or…you could start dating."

And there it was; the reason behind everything that happened in the last twenty minutes. Savannah tried to fight the urge to roll her eyes as she took a healthy gulp of her wine, enjoying the burn as it made its way through her chest into her stomach. Noticing that her glass was now empty she got up and headed into the kitchen for a refill and a moment to breathe. The last thing she wanted was for her mother to meddle in her personal life, but the older woman was right. If she was working less, she'd have time for something like dating. As much as the prospect scared her, she didn't really have a choice if she wanted to find someone to spend her life with. She filled her glass once, emptying it again in a single gulp and then refilling it so she could go back into the living room to face her mother.

Might as well get this over with, Savannah thought with a sigh.

"We saw the pile of unopened invitations in your kitchen Savvy. Don't you want someone to go to those weddings with you?

Don't you want someone by your side that will create reasons for you to send out your own invitations and save the dates? If you don't stop and do this now, you'll end up like your Aunt Anna, alone and pissed off at the world."

God, her mom was good. She knew exactly what buttons to push. Bringing up Aunt Anna was a low blow and the pile of invitations was even lower. Why couldn't she have just stuck with the standard, "don't you want to find someone to share your life with like I found your father?" or the more common, "I want grandchildren before I'm too old to enjoy them" ploys that most mothers pulled on their aging single daughters.

Taking a smaller sip of her wine, she tried to do a quick risk and reward evaluation in her head. It was something Savannah had done before she bought her house, before she initially opened her business online and before she opened each of her store fronts. Every major decision in her life was preceded by a risk and reward assessment and if the situation didn't pass, she didn't bother moving forward.

Even though the risks were scary, bad dates, creepy guys, possible broken heart, the rewards definitely seemed to outweigh

16

them. If things worked out she'd have someone to share her life with, someone to love. She would have someone to worship her the way her father had worshipped her mother for over 40 years and someone to have children with once they were ready. Of course, there were also risks to actually finding someone to love. The dating part was just the tip of the iceberg.

Her sister was a prime example of the worst case scenario. Brooklyn fell in love at 21, married at 24, and was divorced and alone by 30. She spent nine not always so happy years with the same man only to end up alone and broken after he continually cheated on her. It took Brooklyn a year to finally move on from the grief of her failed marriage, so in the end it was ten years of her life dedicated to something that was full of heartbreak. Savannah wasn't sure she had it in her to face that possible risk.

"Get out of your head Savannah," her sister scolded. "I know what you're doing and you cannot think about my situation when deciding if you should start dating. There are some amazing guys in the world, sadly Frank wasn't one of them, but eventually I'll use what I learned with him to find someone new. Could you end up with a possible Frank? Yes, unfortunately you could, but you could also end up with the most perfect man in the world for you. It is all definitely worth the risk and I would do it all over again even now that I know that Frank is a dick and not my Prince Charming."

Savannah smiled over at her little sister. She had definitely come a long way in the last year and it was surprising to hear that she'd do it all over again; that what she learned was worth the pain of having her heart broken by the man she loved. But if her sister could do it, then she could too, right? The thought made her stomach do flips. Making the decision to date was by far the scariest and most difficult decision she had ever made. Even deciding to start her own business and then expand it was easier than what she was contemplating.

Losing money and time were nothing compared to possibly losing her heart. From what she could tell from her sister's experience, the pain of a failing business was nothing compared to the pain of a failing relationship and a broken heart. Savannah had only been in love once although it wasn't the all-consuming type of love that she had always heard about and seen when she looked at her parents. It was the type of love that you find in college and when it was over, the split was completely mutual and no one was hurt in the process. The next time she had anything that resembled a commitment was when she was working at a bakery just after graduation. He was her boss and neither of them was in love. The relationship, if it could even be called one, was based on fun and companionship and nothing more. Neither of them had time for anything else and didn't want to try to explain that to anyone that wouldn't understand.

With a sigh, Savannah took another sip of her wine and looked over at the expectant faces of her sister and mother. They seemed to want this even more than she did. Their marriages were two opposite ends of the spectrum and gave her experiences from both worlds for which she was kind of grateful. She hated that her sister had suffered, but her experience had given Savannah and everyone around them something to learn from, even if you couldn't predict who would go from a seemingly perfect guy to a complete dick in a matter of years.

"Alright...fine. You guys are right. There probably isn't a better time than right now to try and put myself out there, but I really have no idea where to even start," Savannah admitted. "I'm not a fan of meat markets so we can cross out the club and bar scenes or any place packed with creeps and horny men looking to get laid."

"That's not a problem. I have a friend…"

"Ugh…" Savannah groaned.

"No…not someone to hook you up with," Brooklyn clarified. "Kerrigan started a matchmaking service a few years ago and it's doing extremely well. It's not online dating or anything like that. She has a whole system that she uses to match people up with potential suitors. I've already talked to her about signing you up for her three-month plan. She'll be meeting you for lunch tomorrow at noon, at that restaurant you love so much, to go over the details and the contract."

"Suitors? Really? What if I had said no, Brook?"

"Then I would have made up a story about you meeting me for lunch tomorrow. No matter what you said tonight, you were meeting with Kerrigan tomorrow whether you wanted to or not. The plan is already paid for, now you just have to make use of it."

Savannah knew there was no point in arguing with her sister or her mother. The women in the St. James family were ridiculously stubborn and always seemed to get their way. Whether she was really ready or not, she was about to enter back into the dating pool after more than a five-year hiatus and she had absolutely no idea what she had just gotten herself into.

****

The next day Savannah tried to focus on her everyday routine, but she couldn't stop thinking about her impending lunch meeting. She was more than just nervous to see Kerrigan again, she was terrified. Not of Kerrigan of course, but of what she represented. Potentially, the man of her dreams was a client of Kerrigan's and in a few short months they could meet and fall in love. On the other hand, her worst nightmares could also be clients of Kerrigan's and in a few short months they could turn her off of dating forever.

She arrived at Arrow at a quarter to twelve knowing that the lunch rush could make getting a table difficult even with a reservation. As soon as she walked in the hostess gave her a huge smile before coming around from behind the podium to give her a hug. Savannah was a semi-regular at the restaurant and knew most of the staff by name. Arrow was centrally located between her house and her first store in the ever growing West Seattle Junction and with her busy schedule she rarely had time to cook any meals for herself. The atmosphere was perfect for a working lunch or for a relaxing dinner after a twelve-hour shift and the food was absolutely to die for.

The hostess station stood in the middle of the entryway behind a large waiting area. To the right was a long bar that spanned the length of the public area. The bar area had a handful of booths and tables to accommodate guests and the bar itself had stools lined along it. To the left of the waiting area was the regular dining room, which was large and spacious. Both sides of the restaurant were usually pretty busy when she came in and today was no exception.

"Savannah, it's been too long since you last came in," the hostess Sylvia said as she stepped back from hugging her. "I didn't see you in the shop yesterday either. I stopped by in the afternoon to pick up cupcakes for the staff."

"I've been craving the stuffed pesto chicken like crazy lately, but the new opening is keeping me way too busy and driving me mad. Brooklyn's going to start helping out so I'll probably be in my office more, which means more opportunities to come by here. Jeanine gave you the discount yesterday right?"

Sylvia smiled as she ran a hand over her sleek blonde ponytail. It was something that Savannah noticed she did a lot when she was talking. The younger woman was extremely pretty and always looked amazing and unique even in the Arrow uniform. She wore the typical crisp white button down shirt and a pair of black slacks that looked like they were tailored to fit her long legs perfectly. With it she wore a pair of coral colored three inch pumps and a chunky coral necklace. From her ears dangled a pair of matching earrings. Most people wouldn't have been able to pull it off or even try, but Sylvia was always very fashion forward, making the standard black and white outfit anything but standard.

"Oh of course. Thanks again for that. We all really appreciate it since we can't get enough of the goodies you sell, even though we have some great desserts here. You know how much Sam hates that we are constantly buying from you instead of eating what he makes."

"Poor Sam. You'll have to tell him I'm sorry that I'm stealing his business, but at least he knows how much I love his tiramisu. It's definitely the best in town. In fact, I'm pretty sure I'll be getting one after my meeting today. I'm gonna need all the comfort I can get after this."

"Well I hope your meeting isn't too bad. When I got here and saw your name on the list, I made sure your favorite table was ready and not open for seating. Your other party isn't here yet, but I'll take you to your table now if you'd like," Sylvia said as she picked up two menus. "Meghan's gonna be your server. She specifically asked for you as soon as she saw you on the reservation list this morning."

Savannah had barely sat down when Meghan approached her table. She wore the same crisp white shirt, but had paired hers with a black knee length skirt. Her shoes were a little more sensible, with a barely noticeable kitten heel. Her long black hair was pulled into a simple bun and her face was devoid of any make-up except for mascara and lip gloss. Meghan was absolutely gorgeous no matter what she wore, but it always surprised Savannah that she never played her looks up at work, despite the fact that it could have landed her better tips from the guys that frequented the restaurant. She was there to do her job. Once that was done, she kicked her look into high gear. Savannah had gone out with her a few times to Heat and Meghan was always the talk of the club.

It had been awhile since she last talked to Meghan. They had both been extremely busy and Savannah hadn't been able to get into Arrow to eat or catch up with her friend. She wasn't surprised that Meghan had a lot to talk about. She definitely never lacked for something to do on her social calendar. If she wanted to, she could have had a different date with a different guy every day of the week for more than a month…probably two if Savannah was honest. That was one of the many ways she and Meghan differed, but they still got a long so well. Although it seemed like Meghan had found one that she was interested in giving a real shot to.

After ten minutes of listening to Meghan talk about the new guy she was seeing, Savannah watched her sister's best friend Kerrigan Foster walk through the front door. As soon as their eyes met, Kerrigan smiled and walked to their table. Savannah took in the other woman's put together appearance as she stood to greet her. Kerrigan always looked so professional, always choosing to wear some sort of power suit whenever she was on the job. That afternoon was no different, even though she and Savannah had known each other for years. The blue knee length pencil skirt and matching blazer she wore looked like it was tailor made to fit her perfectly.

Her dark auburn hair was pulled back from her face in a sophisticated twist. For a minute Savannah wished she had dressed up, or at the very least fixed her hair and make-up. Although she supposed that the fact that her clothes were flour and dough free was a huge concession, especially since she'd started work nearly six hours earlier.

"Oh Savannah, it's so great to see you again," Kerrigan said as she wrapped her arms around Savannah in a friendly hug. "I'm really looking forward to helping you find love. I've been trying to get your sister to go through the process, so I'm hoping that once you become one of my success stories I'll be able to talk her into finally joining."

Savannah smiled as the energetic redhead took the seat across from her. She pulled a folder and a pair of glasses out of her briefcase while Savannah sat back down and immediately grabbed the glass of water that she had been sipping on. Not for the first time since she arrived did she wish the water was actually something stronger. If she didn't have to head back to her office after the meeting she definitely would have ordered a glass of wine…or two.

"This place is as fantastic inside as it is outside and I bet the food is even better if you eat here as often as your sister says you do," Kerrigan looked around the room before putting her glasses on. "So there are a bunch of questions I have to ask you as well as a contract that I need to go over with you, but why don't we order first and then we can start going over that stuff. What would you recommend?"

They spent the next few minutes going over the menu. Savannah pointed out a few of her favorite items which included the ravioli, stuffed mushrooms and a beef and pepper skewer that was so tender it melted in her mouth. She, of course, was getting the stuffed pesto chicken that she'd been craving for weeks and a side salad. Once Kerrigan decided on her lunch, they didn't have to wait long for Meghan to take their order. Savannah had hoped that the whole process would take a while so that she could put off the matchmaking stuff. Unfortunately, as soon as their food was ordered, Kerrigan picked up her folder and pulled out a thick stack of papers. When she said she had a bunch of questions, she hadn't been kidding. The entry survey was nearly 100 questions long with everything from Savannah's religious practices to whether she

27

wanted kids to who her favorite band was. There were even questions about what other people thought of her and what words they would use to describe her.

Savannah had no idea how some of the questions were supposed to find her perfect match, but Kerrigan was the professional, so she answered everything as truthfully as she could. She scanned the restaurant as she named her favorite movie and her first childhood memory. The lunch time rush was in full swing with nearly every table filled. Most of the other diners were like her and Kerrigan, having a working lunch, but there were others that seemed to be on dates or at least dining with their loved ones. Savannah found herself looking toward the bar area so she could sneak a peek at the hot bartender that she'd been checking out since Sylvia had brought her to the table. She first noticed him nearly a year ago when he started at Arrow and she couldn't help but watch him every time she came in. He was exactly what pre-Delectable Delights Savannah would have gone after for a good time; the tattooed, bad boy who didn't seem to give a damn about anything. She had definitely "dated" her fair share of those during college and during the years she worked at a local bakery trying to make a name for herself. They weren't interested in getting attached to someone and neither was she. It had always been a perfect fit when she was younger, but that wasn't what she was looking for now.

He was one of the few people in Arrow that she didn't know by name. Part of her wanted to be friendly, but he was far too tempting to the part of her that just wanted to jump back into the action. Bad boy bartenders did not make for good long term commitments, at least not in her experience. Knowing the type as well as she did, he probably went home with a new girl every night. And she really couldn't blame him or the women. Just looking at him as he pulled one of the beer taps down made her heart race. The muscles of his inked forearm flexed, which led her imagination to run wild with the ways the muscles would flex and move as he touched her. She loved the fact that the long sleeves of his button up shirts were always rolled up to his elbows. She just wished she had the courage to sit closer to him so she could get a better look at the tattoos that covered his arms.

"Now we get to the really good stuff," Kerrigan said, her voice startling Savannah. "What physical characteristics are you looking for in your future mate?"

Before she could answer, Meghan arrived with their lunch. Savannah took a deep breath, grateful for the interruption. Answering the questions had been more difficult than she expected and more demanding. There were a lot of things she either never thought about or never wanted to voice out loud. Now it was all out there on paper and Kerrigan was going to use it to hopefully find her someone to spend the rest of her life with. Butterflies flared to life in her stomach and she hoped that she'd be able to keep her food down when she finally tried to eat.

"Oh my god, this is so freaking good," Kerrigan moaned, once again breaking Savannah out of her thoughts. "I don't even care that I'm going to have the worst breath when I head back to the office. This is absolutely worth it. Thank you for wanting to meet here."

Kerrigan had decided on the beef and pepper skewers which also had onions on it. The skewers were plated on a bed of garlic mashed potatoes which Savannah had to admit were also to die for. They also came with the stuffed chicken that Savannah loved so much. While going through the majority of the questions, they had eaten their side salads, but now the food was too good to talk through. Neither spoke until their plates were nearly empty, although every once in a while Kerrigan would let out a moan after taking a bite.

As she finished her meal, Savannah found herself looking at the bartender again. His brown hair was short on the sides and a little longer on top. It was perfectly styled and looked thick and luxurious. Savannah often fantasized about running her fingers through it or grabbing handfuls of it while he...Shaking her head, she tried to dismiss the thought from her mind. It was definitely not what she should be thinking about while having lunch with her sister's best friend or while discussing her dating future.

"Alright, so back to the final question, what physical characteristics are you looking for in your future mate?"

Savannah smiled as her eyes drifted back over to the bartender. Before she realized what she was doing she was practically describing him to a T, which was not at all what she had planned. Ideally, she wanted a man that was tall, at least 6 feet, preferably with dark hair and in relatively decent shape. She loved a little scruff and didn't mind tattoos. In a perfect world, they'd have a full head of hair, but that wasn't a deal breaker. In fact, when it came

31

down to it, Savannah wasn't really that shallow. As long as he was taller than her by at least a couple of inches, she didn't really mind looks much. She knew that looking at the bartender was clouding her reality. Most men didn't look like him, especially not the ones that were looking to settle down and using a dating service to do so.

"Look, I just really want someone who is stable and fun to be with. My deal breakers aren't really looks related at all. Whoever I date or get involved with has to have a stable job, a stable home, preferably not with their parents, and a stable mode of transportation, that is not the bus or his bicycle. I don't want to end up being someone's surrogate mother," Savannah said. "They have to be self-sufficient, driven, have a great personality and be taller than me. And they have to be comfortable with the fact that I'm a career driven woman. Other than that, if they happen to be smoking hot like the bartender, then bonus. If not, as long as they fulfill the important requirements the physical attraction could come later."

With a smooth, not too obvious, glance over her shoulder Kerrigan took a moment to check out the object of Savannah's lust. When he climbed up onto a step ladder, both women checked out his butt as he grabbed a bottle of alcohol off of one of the higher shelves. Savannah smiled as she heard the other woman mutter the word damn under her breath. It was exactly what Savannah had been thinking in her head, but it wasn't nearly enough to describe the situation. The man was all sorts of gorgeous from head to broad shoulders to forearms to ass and he was exactly what Savannah needed to stay away from.

Kerrigan seemed impressed by Savannah's answer and was certain that she had enough men to make the three months worthwhile. They went over the contract together, which was basic and exactly what Savannah had been expecting. After deciding on scheduling the dreaded first date, for the following Thursday, Kerrigan paid for their lunch, despite Savannah's insistence that she should pay, and then left to head back to her office. Savannah wasn't sure that she was ready to jump right into the dating part, but Kerrigan assured her that scheduling the first date for as soon as possible was the best idea. It was like pulling off a Band-Aid, she said, which made sense, but it still made Savannah's stomach do flips. In a week, she'd be face to face with her first real date in over five years, but in fifteen minutes she was going to drown all of her doubts and fears in some of the best tiramisu she had ever had. She just hoped that the coffee-flavored delight would do the trick.

Chapter 2

"Hey Gabriel, can I get a taster of each of the Hefeweizen we have on tap? Table twenty isn't sure which one they had last time they were here," someone called from the opposite end of the bar.

Gabriel turned around in time to catch Meghan roll her eyes. As he grabbed three of the small tasting glasses he gave her a pointed look. She knew better than to roll her eyes or disparage the customers while out on the floor. Most likely the person at table twenty was looking for some free beer, but there was always a chance that they really couldn't remember what they liked. No matter what, the goal was to get them to come back and if a couple of free tastes of beer did that, then Gabriel didn't mind.

Placing the glasses on her tray with instructions as to which was which, he watched her walk back to her table. Her section was nearly full even though it wasn't even 6 o'clock. Thursday nights at Arrow were getting busier and busier every week, which was surprising and exciting. Without a reservation, a party of two usually had a fifteen to twenty-minute wait, sometimes even longer the later it got into the evening. Over the past three years, business had gotten better and better which had given Gabriel ideas that he wasn't sure he was ready to explore. When he had first taken over Arrow, he had no idea how to run a business, let alone a successful restaurant. After a couple of years taking classes and learning the ropes by being thrown into the fire, he finally felt like he had the hang of it so he stepped out of the office and behind the bar.

Working behind the bar gave Gabriel a better look at the way the restaurant ran and where things could improve. Tweaks here and there resulted in a well-oiled machine, which Gabriel liked to think was one of the reasons behind the large number of regulars that they had. Regulars like the beautiful blonde that currently sat at the end of his bar. She had been in the week before for lunch and up until recently had often come in at least a few times a week for lunch or dinner. Most of the staff knew her by name, but Gabriel hadn't had the pleasure of being introduced to her yet despite the fact that he had noticed her well over a year ago. She had never sat at the bar before and when they were busy he barely got out from behind it.

He poured a glass of the house red as he watched another member of the Arrow staff stop by and say hello to her on their way to the pickup station. She gave Ray a genuine smile and then held up a colorful brochure that she had been going over. They talked for another minute before Ray made his way to where Gabriel stood.

"Hey Ray, who is the blonde you were just talking to? She comes in all the time. It's embarrassing for me not to know her name," Gabriel said while placing Ray's drink order on his tray.

Ray laughed, "That is the bane of Sam's existence. Her name is Savannah. She owns Delectable Delights down the street."

"Oh yeah, the place that Sylvia goes to that has those amazing cupcakes right?"

Ray nodded then walked off with his drinks. Now that he knew her name and who she was, Gabriel knew that he had to talk to her. He'd been putting it off, mostly because he wasn't sure what to say. When she sat in the dining room, she seemed so far out of his reach. Even when she dined alone and he had time to get out from behind the bar, he was intimidated by her, but he didn't know why. It wasn't like he'd never talked to a beautiful woman before. Hell, he talked to plenty every night, flirted with them too if they flirted with him first. Once upon a time, he'd been engaged to a beautiful woman, though that was so far in his past it seemed like a completely different lifetime.

Sucking it up, he checked to make sure he didn't have any orders pending and then walked toward the end of the bar where Savannah was sitting. She had her head down as she looked over the brochure. Part of him wanted to turn around so he didn't interrupt her work, but he also knew that there was no guarantee he would ever get the opportunity to speak to her again. In the year he'd been working behind the bar, she'd never sat there and he worked nearly every day, all day, so he would have known if she had.

"So you're the one that has Sam constantly grumbling that we're all traitors," Gabriel said leaning his hip against the bar, his arms crossed over his chest. He must have startled her because she jumped a little before raising her eyes to meet his. Her eyes were the brightest, most vivid shade of blue he'd ever seen. For a moment they stared at each other. Gabriel knew he should say something, do something other than stare into her eyes, but he couldn't stop. He could easily get lost in the amazing blue depths. She was even more gorgeous up close than from across the room. Most of the time when she came in she had her hair up in a ponytail or one of those messy buns that were all the rage and she wore jeans and a t-shirt or something just as practical. Tonight her blonde hair was down framing her face in soft waves and she wore a simple, yet stunning black dress. Something was definitely different about tonight and Gabriel had a feeling he knew what it was.

"Uh...y...yeah," she stammered. "Sorry about that."

"Oh don't be," he said a smile spreading across his face. "Your cupcakes are freaking amazing. Better than my grandma's, but please don't tell her I said that."

She smiled back at him, laughing at his admission. The sound was intoxicating and the smile on her face was genuine, something Gabriel didn't often see. He wanted to stand there and talk to her forever, but someone was calling his name from the other side of the bar and for the first time he wished he had someone else to tend bar so he could have a conversation. In the last three years he hadn't felt much need for regular conversation which is why he kept himself busy with the restaurant. Less social interaction meant there was less of a chance that someone would ask him about Jonathan or how he came to be the owner of Arrow.

"Um, I have to go, but I'll be right back. My name's Gabriel by the way. Can I get you a drink? Anything you want, on the house."

She smiled again, it was infectious. "You don't have to do that...the on the house part, I mean. I'd love a glass of the house pinot grigio though when you have a moment."

He nodded and then turned to grab a bottle of their best pinot grigio out of one of the bar refrigerators. He poured her a glass and set it down in front of her before heading down to the pickup station where Meghan and Ray were standing. There were more than a few drink orders waiting to be filled. Apparently he had spent more time with Savannah then he'd realized. Quickly, he filled each ticket and checked on the other patrons at the bar before moving back down to where Savannah sat watching him; the look on her face unreadable.

"This is far too good to be the house pinot."

"That's because it isn't. I'm sorry; I don't remember you specifying that you wanted to order the house pinot. That's my mistake, I'll make sure that you don't have to pay for that drink," Gabriel smiled.

"Well, that's a tricky way of getting me to let you buy me a drink. Are you always this nice to your customers?" Savannah asked.

"Only the pretty ones that come in as often as you do. Although, I do have to ask why I get to be honored with your presence tonight? All this time, you've never once sat at my bar. Nor have you ever come in wearing a dress. Special occasion tonight?"

As soon as the words were out of his mouth Gabriel wished he could take them back. He sounded like he spent a lot of time watching her, like he knew her routine. It was creepy which was not at all what he wanted to portray. He watched her face to see if she reacted to what he said, knowing that he had to do something when Savannah raised an eyebrow. This was not the first impression he wanted to make, especially not after a year of wondering about her.

"Sorry. That sounded really bad. I swear I'm not a stalker or anything; I'm here every day from opening to close and it's not always busy back here. I have plenty of time to people watch during

41

my shift and there is no way I could ever forget a woman as beautiful as you."

Gabriel hoped he had recovered well, but he still couldn't really read Savannah. Although the slight blush that was now covering her cheeks was hopefully a good sign. It definitely looked good on her either way and instantly he knew that he'd do whatever it took to make it happen again. Although, he wouldn't blame her if she ran far away from Arrow after his bumbling performance.

"It's kind of embarrassing, but I have a blind date tonight," she admitted then quickly picked up her glass of wine and took a long drink. His stomach sank at her words even though he had a feeling that was why she was dressed up. The fact that it was a blind date was a plus, but blind dates worked out all the time. Of course, he didn't want anything bad to happen to Savannah, but Gabriel silently hoped that the date was a dud.

"There's nothing wrong with a blind date."

"Well...yeah, but...the embarrassing part is that this is just the first of many. It's...uh...been awhile since I've dated, so my kid sister decided to sign me up for a matchmaking service to finally get me to put myself out there so I could 'find the one'," Savannah said, her hands coming up to form air quotes at the end of the sentence.

Her nervous stutter was adorable and was one more thing to add to the list of things he was starting to like about her. When she wasn't stammering, her voice was like velvet, smooth and sexy and he could almost hear her purring his name. God, he couldn't think like that. Not in front of her anyway. Not when they were supposed to be having a normal conversation. Their time together was obviously limited and he didn't want to waste it fantasizing about her. He could do that later when she was sitting at a table with some stranger getting to know him better.

"Well that sounds like it could be fun," he said, trying to sound optimistic.

"And it could be complete torture. Thankfully, I got to pick what we did and I decided that we would come here for all of my dates. Figured it was best to keep things in my comfort zone as much as possible and I love this place. I know that if the date is going bad I can get one of the servers or whoever's at the host stand to help me out since I know everybody. And since I can't go on a second date with any of these guys until the three months is up I'll be the only one who has to eat here repeatedly, which definitely isn't a hardship."

"Well we thank you for bringing in the business. Just for that your next drink should be free too, so can I get you another glass?"

Savannah nodded before looking over her shoulder toward the host stand where Sylvia stood taking names and directing the other staff members to empty tables. Gabriel poured another glass of wine and noticed for the first time that her hands were shaking a little. He supposed she was nervous. Nerves would be understandable if it had really been a long time since she last went on a date. He knew that he'd be nervous if it was him. It had been a long time for him as well, so long that he wasn't even sure he knew how to date, although he knew it was probably time he tried. As he watched Savannah fidget he knew exactly who he wanted to try with. He definitely needed to get to know her better.

"So how many dates are you looking at?" he asked when she looked back up at him.

"Well Kerrigan, that's the matchmaker, said that she could easily keep me busy every night of the week for the entire length of my contract, but I told her that I would go on no more than twenty

44

dates during the three months. Holy crap, that sounds absolutely horrible when I say it out loud."

"Twenty dates isn't really that many dates. It's not like you'll be doing anything else with them except having dinner and a little conversation right? The odds that you'll want a second date with all twenty of them is pretty slim and if it makes you feel better you can think of them as business dinners since dating is kind of like doing business. So really, you're going to have twenty slightly awkward business dinners in the span of three months. At least the food will be amazing."

"I never would have thought of it like that," Savannah said in between fits of laughter. "Thank you so much for saying that. I'm feeling a little better about the entire situation, even though I'm still dreading it."

"Well anything you need, I'm here. If you want you can make sure you're always seated facing me, we can work out some hand signals like in baseball so I know if you need help or if things are going well," Gabriel offered even though the last part made his stomach roll.

"That would be fantastic. Maybe before my next date, I can come in early again and we can work those out," she laughed. "Looks like you're being summoned again. You've been awfully neglectful of the rest of your customers."

Gabriel sighed when he saw that she was right. Three of his wait staff stood at the pickup station and the receipt printer that printed out the drink orders was overflowing with work that he had forgotten about. Without a word, he pulled off the receipts and started to fill the orders. He ignored the dirty looks he was getting from his staff and the other customers around the bar. He worked quickly and diligently until he was caught up with the pending orders and had checked on everyone sitting at the bar.

When their drinks were refilled and those leaving were cashed out, he turned back to Savannah only to find her stool empty. The wine glass she had been drinking out of was also empty, but he could see that there was something underneath it. Immediately, he hoped it was her phone number, but he knew that wasn't likely. Beneath the glass was a piece of the brochure that she had ripped off. Neatly written on the top were a thank you and an invitation to come into the shop for a free cupcake or two whenever he wanted. He looked up and scanned the room until he found her sitting at a table near the front window, which seemed to be her favorite spot. Like they had discussed she was facing the bar while her date had his back to Gabriel. As he found her, their eyes met. He held up the paper and smiled at her, delighted when she smiled back. It wasn't her phone number, but it was damn close. Thankfully, there were at least nineteen more opportunities for him to try and get it from her. And he wasn't going to give up until he got what he wanted.

For the next six weeks, Savannah came in early before her date and sat at the bar. Each night she looked amazing and each night Gabriel liked to think that she was dressing up for him and not the schmuck she was meeting. He watched her during her dates and while she looked cordial and accommodating, she never looked like she was enjoying herself. The smiles she offered her dates weren't genuine; her eyes didn't sparkle like they did when she smiled at him and she never truly laughed when she was with them either. Not like she did during her time at the bar.

He was wearing her down; he could see it in her eyes when they talked. Even before her second date when they worked on the hand signals he had offered, he could tell that he affected her. The

47

signals they had come up with were pretty easy; a brush of the shoulder and things were fine, if she touched her lips she was having a good time and if she threw up her arms in an exaggerated stretch she needed to be rescued. So far, she'd only used the shoulder brush, which was a good thing. Although he definitely didn't want Savannah to find someone that she liked, he also didn't want her to suffer through horrible dates. So far, she'd been lucky and he dreaded the day that she came across a jerk or possibly worse, a really great guy.

"So date number eleven tonight…feel any different now that you're crossing over the half way mark?" he asked as she sat down on the same stool she'd used before every date. He would never admit it to her, but he made sure that no one sat on the stool when he knew she had a date that evening. In fact, even on days she didn't have dates scheduled he left the stool empty just in case she came in for her usual random lunch or dinner like she had before the dates started. So far she'd only been able to come in on date nights, but he wanted to make sure her "spot" was open on the off chance her schedule changed.

The entire situation sounded kind of pathetic, but with every interaction Gabriel felt himself falling for Savannah. She was more than just a beautiful woman. She was funny and smart, compassionate and alive. Her drive and determination was sexy as hell. Knowing that in just five years she opened three businesses and was in the process of opening a fourth made him feel like a slacker. When they discussed her work, Gabriel felt like he could follow in her footsteps and open another Arrow somewhere. She motivated him to be more, to try more.

Having her around made him want to be a better man. While it had been a long time since he'd just gone through the motions, he still hadn't pushed himself too hard since Jonathan's death. There was so much more that he could have been doing with his life in the last three years, but he wasn't because he never felt the need to. Now he realized how much was missing from his life and he didn't want it to stay that way for long. Savannah made him feel things that he never felt before. She made him want to do things he'd never done before. It was a far cry from how his life had been with his ex-fiancée Valerie.

"Well it hasn't been as bad as I thought it would be. None of the guys have been repulsive or complete jerks, so that's been nice, but there hasn't been a single spark with any of them. Not even a hint of the possibility of a spark later on down the road. It's a little depressing until I remember that I still have ten more possibilities to meet," Savannah said as she accepted the glass of wine he held out to her.

Their fingers brushed as he released the glass which was completely by design. He wanted to touch her nearly every second that she sat at the bar. He wanted to reach out and run his fingers through her soft hair as he moved it away from her face. He wanted to trace along the inside of her wrist, her silky skin warm under his fingertips. And he wanted to do things that would definitely cause the beautiful pink blush that he loved so much to color her cheeks, but he was trying to be good. The last thing he wanted was to come on too strong or scare her away, so he kept his looks and his flirtations to a minimum. Instead he let her lead. If she flirted, he flirted. If she gave him a look that made his dick twitch, then he gave her one that hopefully melted her panties. Whatever she dished out, he reciprocated because he wanted her to think she was running the show.

"At least this has gotten you back out there, so if none of these guys work out, you'll be comfortable enough to continue dating on your own. But maybe 'the one' will be one of the final ten or maybe he won't even be a part of the process. You just never really know," he told her, hoping that she would be able to read between the lines and see that he was hoping that maybe he was 'the one' she was looking for.

"Who knows," she said with a wink. "I'm pretty sure the last guy I met had a thing for Kerrigan. He talked about her a lot, about how smart she was and he asked a lot of questions about her. He seemed really nice and was definitely hot, but constantly talking about another woman is definitely a turn off. I'm supposed to give little reviews of each guy, what I liked and didn't like about them and I'm not sure whether or not I should mention his overwhelming Kerrigan appreciation."

"Is Kerrigan single? If so, maybe she'd like to know that one of the guys has the hots for her. I mean, I'm sure she probably has some sort of fraternization policy, but when he's no longer her client maybe something could happen," Gabriel offered as he looked around the bar to make sure that no one needed anything.

Tuesday nights were usually Arrow's slowest night. Savannah was one of only three people sitting at the bar and once she moved to the dining room, she'd be at one of only ten tables in use. He liked nights like this and secretly hoped that Savannah's date stood her up so that he could spend the slow evening talking to her. He needed more time to get to know her better. The half hour conversations they had two times a week weren't enough for him. He wanted to see her outside of Arrow so that he could make more than silly small talk with her. They hadn't talked about family or hobbies or anything of substance in the last six weeks. All they really talked about were her dates and what she thought of them or what she was really hoping to find.

"Thanks. I never thought of that. Jackson seemed like a great guy, just not one for me. In fact, the possible one for me should be walking in soon," she said as she glanced at her cell phone to check the time.

"Well then, I have a question for you."

"Oh you do, do you? Alrighty then, shoot."

Gabriel took a deep breath, willing his voice and his hands to be steady. He was beyond nervous, which was a new thing for him where women were concerned. Usually, if he asked, he knew the answer was going to be yes, but with Savannah he couldn't be certain. In fact, he was actually fairly certain she'd say no at first, but he had to ask her anyway. He had to get her out of Arrow and into a more intimate setting. He wanted to get under her skin the way she was under his and he really didn't think he was accomplishing that with the bar between them and the people constantly around them.

"I'd like to take you out sometime. Nothing big, maybe coffee or dinner somewhere else."

"Gabriel…"

"It doesn't have to be a date date…just two new acquaintances getting to know each other so that they can possibly go from being acquaintances to being friends," he blurted out trying to change directions. His admission was making her nervous and he didn't want that. He wanted her to say yes and he could see in her eyes that she wanted to as well, but something was holding her back.

"Friends? Not a date? But just friends?" she asked hesitantly and he nearly jumped for joy that she hadn't immediately said no.

53

"Not a date, just friends. I like talking to you Savannah. You're the most real person I've ever met and I'd like to talk to you when I'm not working and when you're not constantly looking over your shoulder waiting for your next date to come in. We can do anything you want, you pick the day, the time, the activity. Hell, you can even pick out my outfit if it'll get you to say yes."

He sounded so pathetic; he was practically begging her to hang out with him. But there was no backing down now. The words were out there. The sentiment was out there. He could change things later, make himself seem less needy and desperate, once she said yes. But she had to say yes and her silence was sounding more and more like a no by the second. Gabriel kept his eyes locked with hers hoping that the eye contact would sway her decision.

"Look, Gabriel…I like you too, but I can't have you distracting me from my purpose. I'm looking for stability and commitment, not just a good time. I've been there and done that and it doesn't really work for the long haul. Plus, I can't date anyone outside of Kerrigan's service until after my contract is up no matter how badly I might want to," she said, her voice held a hint of something that Gabriel realized was sadness. "But…I guess we can hang out as friends as long as you are on your best behavior. And…"

"Savannah, your date is here."

Gabriel nearly growled at the interruption. Things were just starting to get good and Sylvia had to make the announcement that Gabriel had been dreading. He'd been hoping there would be solid plans, something that he could hold onto. Now he would have to wait until she came in on Friday for her next date and start the process all over again. Of course by then she would have had more time to think about what a bad idea it was for them to hang out.

"Here's my card, my cell number is on the back. Text me later tonight so I'll have your number and I'll text you sometime about us hanging out. In fact, I'll give you all of the details down to what you should wear," Savannah winked as she slid her card and money for her drink across the bar toward him.

Before he could respond she was following Sylvia to a decent looking guy that stood by the host stand. He was tall, well over Gabriel's six feet two, which he knew Savannah would love. The more Gabriel looked at him, the more he saw what she would like about this guy, at least in the looks department. Thank goodness Savannah wasn't really superficial. It was everything else that would drive her away, so Gabriel had to hope that this guy was a jerk or really lame so that he would finally get his chance with the woman of his dreams.

Chapter 3

She couldn't concentrate. Brad or Dan or whatever his name was kept talking, but she had no idea what he was saying. Her hands were shaking and her stomach was filled with overanxious butterflies. She had given her phone number to Gabriel. Not only that, but she had essentially agreed to hang out with him outside of Arrow. Even though she had insisted that it couldn't be a date and that he wasn't what she was looking for (yeah right), it still felt like she was planning on going out on a date with him. This wasn't supposed to happen, but she knew it would. It's why she never took the opportunity to talk to him before.

Guys like Gabriel had always been her Achilles heel. Usually she could get them out of her system just by talking to them. But he was different. There was more to Gabriel than the tattoos and the sexy hair that sometimes made him look like he just crawled out of bed. And that smile...good god, his smile...it was ridiculous how that smile made her feel.

Even though she knew they had barely scratched the surface during their talks, Savannah knew that Gabriel was more than what he seemed. She could see it in the way he treated the staff at Arrow and the customers that came in, whether they were regulars or people just discovering the restaurant. The first time she had seen an attractive woman flirt shamelessly with him, he had only been nice back and when she handed him her number he politely declined. His actions had shocked her and it was the first time she wasn't sure what she was getting with Gabriel.

For the last few weeks, she never saw him flirt with anyone other than her, not even once. And he turned down a bunch of offers and phone numbers, at least the ones she saw. There was no doubt in her mind that he was offered plenty of other numbers when she wasn't around. Whether or not he took those she didn't know and she liked to try to tell herself that she didn't care, but she did. She knew she shouldn't want anything to do with Gabriel. He was exactly what she was trying to avoid, but he was getting under her skin. It would only get worse the more she was around him. Coming to the restaurant early every date had been a bad idea, but a compromise that she had made with herself. She knew hanging out with him away from the restaurant was an even worse idea, but she had no idea how she was going to get herself out of the mess she was in.

Again she tried to pay attention to whatever her date was rattling on about. She had made the requisite noises to show she was listening, but she wasn't. And now that she was trying to listen all she could concentrate on was the warmth of his stare on her back. For the first time since she had started the crazy dating experience she sat with her back to Gabriel. There was no way she would be able to sit through an entire date without looking at him and once she started she knew she wouldn't be able to stop. It had been hard enough before he asked her out and now…now her resolve was hanging on by a thread. But she couldn't give into Gabriel…could she?

Don't even think about it, she thought as she tried harder to listen to her date. Anything to keep her mind off of Gabriel and what he offered and what she could do with it…with him.

"Savannah…hey Savannah, did you hear me?" her date asked. The use of her name finally broke through to her and she forced herself to focus on him. He was really good looking and from the information Kerrigan gave her, he was smart and accomplished being a doctor and all. On paper and in appearance, he was exactly what she was looking for, but once again there was no spark. Why couldn't there be a spark?

Because you have a spark with the hot bartender that you can't get out of your head even when he's not asking you out, she reminded herself.

"I'm sorry, what was that?"

"I was just asking about your business. I've been talking enough about my work, figured I should learn a little more about you, but you seem a little distracted."

"Oh gosh, I'm really sorry. You're right. I am distracted, but it's about work," she lied without hesitation. "There is so much going on right now because we're opening a new location and I've been working with my sister to get her acclimated so I'll have more help. It's very, very chaotic in my world at the moment."

He asked a few more questions about her business, ones that she was happy to answer not just because she liked talking about Delectable Delights, which she did, but because it helped keep her mind off of Gabriel. As soon as the date was over, Savannah practically ran out of Arrow to head home. She really couldn't face Gabriel, especially not once she made the decision that if he texted her tonight, she was going to text him back. She had also decided that she was going to hang out with him even though she wasn't sure it was such a great idea.

The more she thought about it, the more she realized that hanging out with him might be the perfect way to get him out of her system. In fact, she even thought about maybe sleeping with him just to knock the rust off, not that it had been that long, but since she wouldn't be seeing any of these guys again at least for another month and a half, she needed to do something in the meantime.

As soon as she walked through her front door, she pulled her cell phone out of her purse to see if her sister had called. Brooklyn checked in on her every night she had a date because she wanted all of the details. Her little sister was living vicariously through her and Savannah was usually eager to talk about her dates. Tonight was different; she really wasn't in the mood to talk. Of course, the message Brooklyn left was quick asking for a call before bed after commenting on the fact that Savannah hadn't answered. Usually she was home by the time Brooklyn called, but her date ran over and the walk home had taken longer than usual because she was lost in her thoughts.

Instead of calling, she sent her sister a quick text to let her know she was home safe and that they'd talk in the morning. Savannah knew she needed time to think about what she wanted her sister to know. She was pretty sure she wasn't going to tell Brooklyn about Gabriel, but knew that it was going to be difficult to hide anything from her sister, especially the fact that she had a huge crush on the bartender. Until she was sure what she wanted to do about him, she didn't want her sister to get any ideas.

Since her divorce, Brooklyn had different ideas of what was important in a relationship and she really wanted Savannah to agree with her. To Brooklyn, love and passion should win out over stability and determination every time, but Savannah had a hard time thinking like that. Everything needed to be perfect. There needed to be a spark, but she also needed someone who was stable and reliable.

Ignoring the few text messages she had, she put her phone down on her dresser so she could pull her pajamas out of the drawer. She wasn't tired enough for bed yet, but she was definitely ready to get out of the dark grey pant suit that she'd worn that evening. She had originally bought the suit when she opened her second store and had only worn it a few times over the last couple of years. She figured the suit would be a nice change of pace from the dresses and skirts she'd worn for most of her dates. Kicking off the three inch heels that complemented her outfit, she was thankful that her feet weren't sore. She wasn't used to wearing heels and after walking to and from the restaurant, she figured she was going to be in for some pain once she took them off.

Deciding that a bath sounded fantastic and long overdue, Savannah quickly shed her suit, grabbed her phone and walked into her bathroom so she could start running the water into her oversized whirlpool tub. She still hadn't taken a hot relaxing bath since the night her sister had brought up all the dating stuff, but she'd never stopped needing one. After setting the phone next to the tub, she stripped out of her bra and panties, turned on the jets and then stepped into the nearly scalding water. Sinking down into the tub, her muscles immediately started to relax. The bath was exactly what she needed. If only she had grabbed a glass of wine before heading upstairs everything would have been perfect.

She closed her eyes, letting her head fall back against the cool fiberglass of the tub. Immediately she was inundated with images of Gabriel. Flashes of his smile, the depth of his beautiful green eyes, she even had images of things she had never seen before filter through her head. There was no denying the fact that she was attracted to Gabriel, but there was definitely more to her feelings for him than just a mere attraction. He intrigued her and it was becoming obvious to her that he wasn't the player she once thought he was. And he really didn't seem like he was just some bartender either. She was captivated by him, no doubt, but was he really what she wanted in a significant other. Was being intrigued and captivated by a man enough to build a future on? She wanted stability and being a bartender wasn't very stable. The pay usually wasn't very good and the tips were only good for those who flirted heavily with the clientele.

But did any of that really matter? She was looking for love and wasn't love supposed to conquer all? Did it matter that he didn't have a stable job? He was still a good man and he could make a good husband and father. He made her laugh and obviously didn't mind that she was a career-driven woman, in fact he praised her for it. Wasn't that all she really wanted in the end? A buzzing near her head stopped her from asking any more questions she really wasn't ready to answer. It also interrupted the pleasant cycle of Gabriel images that had made her start asking questions in the first place.

Opening her eyes, she looked over her shoulder at the phone she had set down earlier. The text notification on the screen said that she had 4 text messages waiting to be read which reminded her that she never checked the ones she received while on her date. Scrolling through the messages she saw that the newest one was from her sister and that she had three from an unknown number. She checked Brooklyn's message first knowing that it would be the quickest and then moved on to the others. Her stomach fluttered as she opened up the message thread. She had a feeling that she knew who the messages were from, but the first line confirmed it.

Hey, this is Gabriel. Figured I should text you now so that you could give me instructions as soon as your date is over.

Looking at the time stamp, he had sent his first message right after she left her seat at the bar. His eagerness made her laugh until she read the next text.

Did I do something wrong? I thought we had a plan with the hand signals, but you're back is to me and I'm pretty sure it's because of something I did.

His actions had led her to choose to sit with her back to him, but not in the way he probably thought. Before that night, it had already been almost too difficult to go on a date with another man in front of him, let alone with him being able to see her face. His being able to see every possible emotion or look that crossed her face was too much; especially that night when all she could think about was him. With a sigh, she scrolled down to his last message.

I'm sorry. I don't want things to change between us, so if it makes you feel better I'll rescind my invitation to hang out. I like talking to you Savannah and if I've ruined that, then please let's go back to before I said anything and pretend it never happened.

That last text was giving her exactly what she thought she wanted during her date; he was giving her a way out of spending more time with him. But now, after thinking about things more, she was no longer sure what to do. Deep down she knew she wanted Gabriel, but there was something in her that wasn't allowing her to embrace that. Maybe she just wasn't ready to allow herself to admit that she had been wrong about what she was looking for or to let herself have it. Either way, she knew that she couldn't go back to the way things were. She wanted to hang out with him, to spend time with him away from Arrow. She had to text him back to ease his mind and to satisfy her own.

You didn't do anything wrong. I'm looking forward to our not date. I just couldn't look at you while on a date with someone else. As it was, I can't even remember his name or anything that he said.

With the text sent, she had the urge to stare at her phone until he responded, but she knew he was still at the restaurant and that it could be awhile before he had a chance to text her back. Plus, she didn't want to be the girl that sat around waiting for the guy to contact her. She reached over her shoulder to set the phone back down, but was startled when it started to vibrate again. Her breath caught and her heart started to beat faster.

Immediately she felt foolish. There was a chance it wasn't him responding and even if it was, it was just a text. Except the vibrating wasn't the quick pulsing vibration of a text, it was the constant one that was designated for a phone call. She fumbled the phone, nearly dropping it into the bathtub with her. Looking down at the screen she recognized the unknown number that she had yet to program into her phone as Gabriel.

Holy shit, holy shit, she thought her heart beating even faster. She fumbled the phone again, saving it once again before it fell into the water. Knowing she had to answer it, she still stared at the phone unsure of what to do. For a moment she felt like a teenage girl, a feeling that she hadn't had since she actually was one. Reaching over she turned off the jets so she'd be able to hear him. Taking a deep breath, she swiped her finger across the screen and then put the phone up to her ear.

"Hello." Her voice came out breathy, a little sexy. She didn't think it sounded like her at all.

"Savannah?"

She closed her eyes, shifting her position as he said her name. Her mind started to cycle back through the images of him and in the silence she could hear him breathing through the phone which only added fuel to her fire.

"Yeah. Sorry. I wasn't expecting you to call me. I figured you'd be too busy to even text me back right away so when the phone rang I nearly dropped it into the bath with me," she told him realizing as soon as the words were out of her mouth exactly how much she had revealed.

She heard him cough a little before he spoke, "I get a break every now and then. After your text I felt like I should call. If you're busy, I can let you go."

If you're busy…that was the only mention he made of her being presumably naked and for some reason that made Savannah soften a little. He could have made any number of crude remarks or innuendos. Instead, he offered to let her go, which was definitely not what she wanted him to do.

"That's okay. I can talk. In fact, I need to tell you how sorry I am that I made you feel like you did something wrong earlier. I just…I…well, facing you while on those dates is just hard. And after tonight, I knew it'd be even harder so I made sure I wasn't facing you. I didn't mean anything by it."

"I thought you were mad at me," he said softly. "I thought I had screwed things up by asking you to hang out, which I could tell made you nervous. I don't want you to do anything you don't want to do, so if you don't want to go out, just say so. I'll understand."

She sighed. He really was a great guy, sweeter than she had thought he'd be. She shifted in the bath again so she wasn't at risk of sliding into the water. His voice did something to her that she couldn't explain. She never got tired of hearing him talk, especially since he could make her melt into a puddle or set her panties on fire. Now, his voice paired with the fact that she was naked and wet, made her heart race. The things that were floating through her head at the moment were definitely not of the sweet variety.

"I gave you my phone number didn't I?" her voice again came out breathy, something that had never happened to her before she met Gabriel. In the weeks since she'd met him, a lot of things happened to her that had never happened before. He was awakening things in her and that scared and excited her at the same time.

"That's true. I'd been hoping to get it since the first night you sat at my bar. There are so many things I want to say to you Savannah, but I don't want to scare you."

She hadn't thought it was possible for a man to purr, but she was pretty damn sure that Gabriel had just done so and it sent shivers down her spine and straight between her thighs. Clenching them together, she fought the urge to touch herself, to get off on the sound of his voice, which she knew wouldn't take long at all. But she couldn't do it; she couldn't bring herself over the edge with him unaware of what she was doing. There was no doubt she'd take care of herself later, when she was alone with her thoughts of him, but it would have been so easy to reach down and...

"You already have," she admitted while she fisted her free hand, her nails digging into her palm. "I think..."

"Shit...Savannah, I want to hear what you have to say. I want to know how I've scared you and what I can do to make that right, but there's something going on out front that I need to take care of. Can we talk again later?"

Trying to regain her composure, she shook her head. She had nearly just let him in too far, nearly gave him too much information.

There was no doubt about it, Gabriel was trouble and she needed to be careful with him…around him.

"I've got to get up early tomorrow so I'll be heading to bed right after my bath. Maybe tomorrow or something if things aren't too chaotic," she said even though she knew that she wouldn't be answering the phone if he called her. Text messages were easier and less personal and they did not include his dangerously alluring voice.

"Okay, I'm sorry I have to go. Goodnight Savannah," he said before disconnecting the call. He hadn't even waited for her to say goodnight back and she had a feeling she knew why. Her tone had gone from flirty to all business as soon as he cut her off. Gabriel was a smart man; he had to know what that meant.

The bath no longer held the appeal that it had before the phone call so she stood up and grabbed her towel from the rack. Drying herself off, she pulled the plug on the tub before heading into her room. Things had changed so drastically in that phone call from one second to the next her head was spinning. Pulling on the pajamas she had left on her dresser, she crawled into bed, more tired now than she had been when she got home. Lying down on her side, she curled up into a ball, her arms wrapped around a pillow that she wished was a certain warm body. It was no surprise that she thought about Gabriel as she slowly fell asleep.

****

For the next four days, Savannah avoided Gabriel's attempts at talking. Whenever he'd call her, she would let it go to voicemail and whenever he'd text her, she'd answer with a simple "too busy to talk, sorry". It wasn't a complete lie; she had been extremely busy as they narrowed down the possible location of the new store from six to three. She just wasn't so busy that she couldn't talk to him, in fact all she wanted to do was talk to him, but everything was already a mess and she didn't want to make things worse. As it was she had thought about calling Kerrigan to change the location of her remaining dates, but in the end she knew she couldn't do that. She needed to see him, even if seeing him was pure torture.

Now that she was getting ready for date number twelve, more than anything she wanted to continue to avoid Gabriel. She knew he'd be working, but she also knew that since it was Saturday night, he'd be far too busy to really talk to her.

He was going to unravel her if they spent more time together. She could feel it deep down. It was yet another thing about him that scared her. For most of the day, she had contemplated going into Arrow right on time for her date, but she didn't want to cause any more problems. She was sure that dodging his calls had caused him to worry, but there wasn't anything she could do about that. Although she wasn't ready to talk to him; wasn't ready to tell him what was going on in her head, she still craved him. She still needed to be around him. And more than anything she needed a drink.

Instead of driving to Arrow, she took advantage of the nice Seattle evening and walked. She figured the fresh air might do her some good, maybe help her get her head straight. Ignoring what was going on with her wasn't really working, in fact it was only making her and presumably Gabriel miserable, but what could she do? It was either ignore it or give in and she wasn't sure that she could give in. Being with Gabriel would likely only leave her broken hearted. If not her, then definitely Gabriel if the fear she had of resenting someone like him ever came to pass. She didn't want to be the sole breadwinner in her relationship. She didn't want to be the one with all of the responsibilities. What she wanted was an equal partnership and she wasn't sure she could get that from a bartender.

But wouldn't the time before the heartache be amazing? Wouldn't it be worth it?

Lost in her thoughts, she reached Arrow sooner than she realized. She nearly walked by and probably would have if Sylvia hadn't been outside getting some air. The bubbly blonde stopped her, asking her all sorts of questions about her dates and whether or not she planned on seeing any of them again. After a few minutes of badgering, Sylvia excused herself to go back inside to work. Standing alone on the sidewalk Savannah sneaked a peak at Gabriel through the window. He was as breathtaking as ever as he quickly moved from one side of the bar to the other.

He wore a dark green button up that he had rolled up past his elbows. She had no doubt that the green in the shirt would accentuate his green eyes making it even more difficult for her to look away from him when…if he looked at her. His hair was once again in that stylishly messed up state that made him look like he had run his hands through it numerous times. The constant five o'clock shadow was trimmed to perfection and as always Savannah wondered what it would feel like against her soft skin.

With a sigh, she walked through the door of Arrow and noticed that like every night "her" stool was open. Since that first blind date, every night she came in the stool she occupied that night had been empty. Even when the bar was as full as it was now, with some people standing, her stool had been left open. She had a feeling that Gabriel had something to do with it, but never got up the nerve to ask just in case the answer was no.

She walked past Sylvia, giving the other woman a small smile and a nod of the head letting her know that she'd be in her usual place. Thankfully, Gabriel was at the other end of the long bar, his back to her, as she sat down. She unashamedly checked out his ass as she waited for him to notice her. The black slacks that he wore were tailored to perfection against his backside and his strong thighs. Licking her suddenly dry lips, she let her eyes travel over the rest of his body, taking in every square inch of muscle and tattooed skin. As her eyes reached his beautiful face, their eyes met and she felt her cheeks warm. He gave her one of his dazzling smiles as he finished pouring a drink and then headed toward her. Heart beating faster in her chest, she smiled back at him.

"Hey," she said when he finally stopped in front of her. Inside she groaned at her stellar conversational skills.

"Hey yourself. I was wondering if you were coming in tonight."

His voice was soft and held a hint of uncertainty and yet it made Savannah squirm in her seat. The man could probably recite the alphabet and then sing Celine Dion songs off key and she'd be putty in his hands. Without taking his eyes off of her, he grabbed a wine glass and a bottle of wine out of the refrigerator next to his hip. He poured the wine into the glass and then handed it to her, his hand lingering against the glass even after she had taken it. Her skin tingled where their fingers brushed, immediately she wanted more. Instead of reaching out to him, she pulled the glass back and downed nearly the entire drink in one gulp. She held the glass back toward him and with a raised eyebrow he poured more into it.

"We're about to pick a location for the new store. I'm almost split 50/50 on two locations, although there's a third still in the running," she said suddenly trying to get her mind to think of something other than Gabriel.

She quickly finished her second glass of wine and waited for him to finish with other patrons before he refilled her glass. He looked at her, the uncertainty that she had heard in his voice, now etched on his face. With a shrug she lifted the glass to her mouth and took a smaller sip. It was the delicious pinot grigio that he served her the first night she sat at the bar. She knew it was an expensive brand and here she was chugging it like a teenager. Her nerves were getting the better of her; she probably looked crazy. She knew she needed to calm down before her date showed up. Whether she liked the guy or not, that was definitely not an impression she needed to make right out of the gate, especially since it would get back to Kerrigan and then Brooklyn.

"So, do you think that maybe we could talk tonight after your date?" he asked.

She raised her eyes to meet his, as predicted she nearly became lost in the depth of the vibrant green. With a shaky hand she raised her glass to take another drink nearly spilling the expensive liquid all over her and the wood she leaned against. Was she ready to talk to him? Could she do it face to face, where nothing could hide her emotions?

"Yes, we can talk afterwards. I'd like that," she said before she realized what was happening.

The smile that appeared on Gabriel's face was one she hoped would be etched in her memory forever. It was the same dazzling one that she was used to, but there was so much more to it. She knew it was just for her, which made her stomach somersault. Her heart felt like it would burst from her chest, it was beating so hard. If this was how she reacted to a smile and how he reacted to a simple yes, she was scared, yet excited to see the way they'd react to more.

By the time number twelve showed up, Savannah had finished four glasses of wine and was definitely feeling buzzed. She had only eaten breakfast that morning, opting to skip lunch so she could get some work done around the house. As soon as she was seated, facing Gabriel and the bar, she started to munch on the complimentary bread that Meghan had set on the table when she'd taken their drink order. Despite already polishing off a bottle of wine, Savannah agreed to order a bottle with her date. She needed to keep up the liquid courage so she could make it through her date and then through her talk with Gabriel.

Before ordering dinner, the chit chat between her and Stewart had been nice. On paper he was another one that seemed like a good match for her, but he was nowhere near as good looking as the last few dates had been. Normally she wouldn't have a problem with the fact that his hair was thinning and that he was a tad pudgy around the middle, if his personality had made up for it. But the more he talked, the worse he got.

Not only was he not attractive, but he was a complete jerk. He was demanding and condescending and when he asked her if she would be willing to sell her businesses she nearly lost it. Instead of reacting, she continued drinking until it didn't matter how much she'd eaten, she was so far past drunk she couldn't even see it in her rearview mirror. When Stewart realized how plastered she was, he went into a rage, yelling at her and causing a huge scene. She just stared at him, unwilling to react even though all she wanted to do was kick him in the nuts. She didn't even have the wherewithal to use the signal that she had worked out with Gabriel for when the date went bad.

"I'm sorry sir, but I need you to calm down and quite yelling or I'll have to ask you to leave. You're upsetting your date and the rest of my customers and I can't have that," Gabriel's voice and face were the embodiment of calm, but his body language wasn't. He looked like he wanted to strangle the guy in front of him and he didn't care who watched. His jaw twitched as he waited for Stewart to sit back down, which was interesting since Savannah never saw him stand up.

"Who the fuck are you to tell me what to do? I'm a paying customer and the customer is always right. As for my date…who cares if that drunk bitch is upset? She just wasted my time and my money."

Gabriel's jaw tightened as his hands clenched into fists at his side. Savannah couldn't tear her eyes off of him or his muscles as they flexed beneath his clothes. She wanted to grab onto his forearms, then his biceps so she could feel the strength beneath his inked skin. She wanted to lick his jaw until it relaxed, but instead of any of that, she picked up her glass of wine and drained it not caring that in the morning she was going to have one hell of a headache. All that mattered was that when this horrible date was over she was going to finally have that talk with Gabriel and if she was lucky there might be more than just talk at the end of her night.

"Don't worry sir; you are no longer a paying customer. Please get your stuff and leave. Don't ever come back into Arrow and don't ever contact this woman. If I see you near her or this restaurant again, I will not be accountable for my actions," Gabriel said between clenched teeth.

Savannah watched Stewart grab his jacket from the back of his chair. His red face was covered in sweat. He looked absolutely ridiculous, so much so that she couldn't help but laugh which did nothing to help his attitude. He turned and glared at her before stomping toward the door, she could barely hear his mutters of bitch and asshole as he left, but that made her laugh even harder. Tears started to stream down her face as she laughed hysterically. She couldn't stop, which she figured was probably because of the wine, but also because her life was such a joke at the moment.

"I'm sorry," she said between the hiccups that had started when she tried to stop laughing.

"Oh Savannah."

Gabriel shook his head before kneeling in front of her. He ran his thumb across her right cheek and then moved his hand through her hair. She closed her eyes wanting to get lost in the moment, in his touch. The night so far had been an epic disaster, she wanted him to make things better, to take everything away and give her something good to think about. She pressed her face against the hand that he let rest against her cheek. His skin was warm and he smelled faintly of sweat, beer and something light like fabric softener or cologne. All she wanted was to get closer to him, to wrap herself around him as he pulled her against his strong body.

"Babe, we need to get you home and to bed. You've had a lot to drink tonight and I have a feeling you're going to regret this in the morning," he said

She opened her eyes to meet his. "I'm so sorry this happened. Let me pay for the meal and I'll head home. I walked here. I'll be fine walking back. It's not far."

At this point she couldn't tell if she was making sense although she knew she wasn't slurring her words. She had always been really good at sounding clear even if she was beyond drunk; a particular skill that kept her out of trouble a lot when she shouldn't have been drinking. She placed her hands on Gabriel's shoulders and pushed up so that she was standing. Swaying a little, she steadied herself quickly and then let go of him so he could stand up too.

"I guess you don't want to talk now huh? I screwed everything up, but damn it you make me so freaking nervous. And then he was such an asshole, wanting me to sell my business and be a happy little housewife who did as she was told."

Gabriel grabbed her arm as she swayed again. She watched as he looked around the restaurant. Most everyone had gone back to what they were doing, although Meghan and Sylvia watched them intently from the host stand. The restaurant was still pretty full as was the bar. It donned on Savannah that with Gabriel helping her, the bar was unstaffed, but as she looked over she realized that she was wrong. Ray was behind the bar, pouring a glass of wine for a beautiful older brunette woman that was practically crawling over the bar to reach for him. She started to laugh again as Gabriel led her toward the front door. It felt as if he was escorting her out like some kind of nuisance and suddenly she felt like crying.

"Hey, tell Ray that he's in charge while I'm gone and Meghan I'll need you and the rest of the servers to cover his area until I get back. I'm gonna make sure Savannah gets home safe. Close out the bill and put it in my office. I'll cover it, plus your tip."

Savannah was so confused by his words and what was happening. She hated herself for drinking so much, but loved the way Gabriel's arm felt around her back as he walked her outside. He asked her for directions and she gave them, a part of her excited that he was going to be at her house, the other part ashamed at the reason why.

In that moment she hated herself for being such a coward. She was afraid of how he made her feel and afraid of what it could mean in the long run. They walked in silence until they reached her house. As soon as she was close to the comfort of her home, Savannah couldn't keep it in any longer and the words started to tumble out against her better judgment which was still locked away behind a wall of drunken stupor.

"Why do you have to be so damn hot? And a bartender?"

"I'm sorry, what?" Gabriel asked, shocked by her sudden outburst.

"I mean, I know now you aren't a player...at first I thought you would be considering how good looking you are and what you do for a living. I've had experiences with your kind before and I thought I knew what I was getting with you, but then you turned out to be the nicest guy I've ever met. But you're still a bartender and that…well hell, that's hot, but not stable. I need stable, someone who can help me provide for the household and the potential family that I think I want. Fuck!"

"Sav…"

"No, don't say anything. Your voice makes me go all weak inside and I can't deal with that right now. I'm drunk and horny and I've wanted you since I first saw you behind that bar over a year ago, but I'm looking for someone who's ready to commit and make a life together. Can you honestly say that you are ready for something like that, Mr. Fun Time Bartender? Fuck…do I care anymore? Fighting this…whatever this is that I feel for you is making me crazy."

"You're making me crazy too, Savannah. Damn it, I've been ready for you since the first time you sat at the bar. I've watched you come into Arrow for over a year and I wanted nothing more than to talk to you, get to know you. Now that I have, I want more. I want to know you inside and out. I want to know the Savannah that no one else knows, not even you."

She stilled, her body heating as his words registered through her foggy, yet rapidly sobering brain. On shaky legs, she quickly cleared the space that had formed between them when she started her rambling and wrapped her arms around his neck. She had to stand on her tip toes to lessen the difference in their height so she could reach the place she so desperately wanted. Without a second of hesitation, she pressed her lips against his. His initial surprise left his lips hard and unyielding, but in no time they softened and molded against hers. He wrapped his arms around her, pulling her closer against him until every part of their bodies touched.

The moment was nearly perfect. In fact, the kiss was exactly as amazing as she dreamed it would be, but she wanted more. She parted her lips and flicked her tongue out to lick at his supple bottom lip. He groaned, a sound that vibrated through both of their bodies, but he didn't part his lips. She moved her hands up from behind his neck to tangle in his hair and pressed her body tighter against his, but he still didn't take the kiss further. Finally, he pulled away from her and took a step back causing her to lose her balance a little.

"I'm sorry, Savannah," he whispered as he steadied her. "I can't do this."

"What do you mean you can't do this?" she asked as she stepped back disengaging her arm from his hand. Her stomach sank at his words and the look on his face. He didn't want her. Despite what he had just said, he didn't really want her. At least not like this, not intimately. She felt tears fill her eyes, but she fought them off. He would not see her cry, not after he'd already seen her drunk and stupid and now humiliated.

"You don't want me, is that it?"

"God, no, that's not it. I want you more than I should, but I won't do this now. I can't. You're far too drunk for us to have a serious conversation, let alone do anything else. I want our first time together to be special, not some sloppy drunk moment that you might not remember. I want to make love to you Savannah and I want you to remember every blissful second of it."

And just like that, her anger melted away. For a bartender he definitely had a way with words, but it didn't change the fact that she was mortified by what happened. He pushed her away, turned her down and no amount of romantic words could make her feel less stupid in that moment. She turned to leave, but realized as she tried to walk toward the door he had his hand on her elbow again.

"Just let me go Gabriel. Please," she pleaded without looking at him.

"Fine," he conceded. "I'll let you go for now, but I want you to come into Arrow tomorrow night for dinner. We obviously need to have a talk because from what I've gathered I have some explaining to do to you. Not everything is as it seems Savannah and I really want to clear that up with you."

Before she could respond, he kissed her on the forehead and let go of her elbow. She couldn't look at him, so she walked toward her door, the jangle of her keys filling the night with noise as she pulled them from her purse. Without looking back, she knew that Gabriel stood on the sidewalk watching her, making sure that she got inside safely. Just one more thing to add to the list of reasons that he was an amazing man and even though she was embarrassed, she knew that stopping them from doing anything was going to be added to that list as well. She just wasn't sure how long it would take her to get over the humiliation.

All she knew was that she sure as hell wasn't having dinner at Arrow the next night and possibly not on the night of her next date either. She needed a little space from Gabriel so that she didn't end up drunk and humiliated again.

Once was enough for her lifetime.

Chapter 4

Gabriel wasn't surprised when Savannah stood him up for dinner on Sunday night. Hurt, yes, surprised no. He also wasn't surprised when she ignored his texts and calls until she ignored them on Monday too. He figured that on Sunday she was recovering from her night of heavy drinking, but when Monday came around and he still hadn't heard from her, he knew that it was personal and that hurt even more. Even though she'd been drunk Saturday night, he felt like there was a breakthrough of sorts, that maybe they were finally on the same page, or at least reading the same book. Now he wasn't so sure.

The only bright side he could see was that it was Tuesday night and she was scheduled for a date. Hopefully they'd be able to talk when she came in early and he'd finally be able to clear the air between them. She obviously had some strange misconceptions about him and what he did at Arrow. And those misconceptions seemed to be holding her back, that and the fact that she had at one point thought he was a player. The thought made him laugh, even though he knew where she had gotten the idea from. He couldn't dispute the fact that a lot of the bartenders he knew, both men and women, were players. It was relatively easy to take what was offered, but that wasn't something Gabriel had ever been interested in. Not once, since he'd taken over Arrow, had he done anything with a customer, he'd never even been tempted. At least not until Savannah started sitting at his bar. She made him break one of his rules and if he was honest, he'd let her make him break a hundred more if he could just be with her.

The day dragged on at an unbelievably slow pace. Every time he'd look at the clock it felt like an hour had passed, but it had only been ten minutes. He tried to busy himself with side tasks and other random things, but since he couldn't leave the bar, his options were limited. More and more Gabriel was beginning to think that it was time to hire another bartender. Most nights it was almost too busy for him to handle everything alone. If he had a second bartender, he could actually take a night off here and there. Or maybe catch up on the miles of paperwork in his office without having to spend 15 hours of his day at the restaurant. First, he figured he'd offer the position to Ray and see if he wanted to make the move from the dining room to the bar. The other man knew what he was doing and had covered nicely for Gabriel on Saturday night when he had to take Savannah home.

When five o'clock rolled around, Gabriel started to feel nervous like he usually did when he knew he was going to see her, but the nerves were almost ten times worse than normal. What if she came in and told him she never wanted to see him again? What if she didn't come in at all? The possibilities were endless and frustrating. Of course he couldn't think of anything other than the worst case scenarios. Those situations kept getting worse as the minutes ticked down to six and Savannah still hadn't shown up. Gabriel felt his heart sink as he started to think that she really wasn't coming.

At six on the dot, Gabriel heard Sylvia greet Savannah and watched as the blond escorted her to her usual table. When she sat with her back to him, Gabriel wanted to walk over to her table and shake her. Then he remembered how she had told him that looking at him during her dates was too difficult, so he let it go, hoping that was the reason she wasn't facing him. He no longer wanted to think about the bad possibilities. She was there, it didn't matter that she hadn't come in early she had at least come in. That meant he could grab her before she left so they could have the talk he desperately needed to have with her.

Her date lasted an hour and a half, which felt like the longest ninety minutes of his life. Of course as her date was winding down, life behind the bar got a little hectic. He nearly missed her completely and was barely able to catch her on the street before she got in her car. At first when he called her name, she ignored him, but when he grabbed her elbow she finally turned to face him.

"Hey, I've been trying to get a hold of you. I really need to talk to you," he told her as he put his hand under her chin so he could lift her eyes up to meet his. She tried not to make eye contact with him, looking anywhere but into his eyes. "Savannah, talk to me."

"I can't...I don't...damn it," she stammered.

"Look, I know you think I rejected you Saturday night, but I didn't. I want to be with you so bad, saying no was one of the hardest things I've ever had to do. I just didn't want you to regret things in the morning. When we finally get together I want you to be 100% into it and I don't want you to have any regrets."

Savannah sighed, but still didn't lock her eyes with his. He wanted to know what was going through her head. He wanted her to talk to him, to finally tell him, while sober, how she felt and what she wanted. There was no way he was going to let her leave without hearing what he had to say.

"I really need to talk to you so can we please just go back inside? We'll go into my office where it'll be just the two of us and we can get everything out in the open. I have a few things that I think you should know; that I need you to know. Hell, you don't even have to say anything if you don't want to. Just please come back inside with me," he pleaded trying once again in vain to make eye contact with her.

She still didn't speak to him, but with a nod of her head and a sweep of her arm, she started toward the entrance to Arrow. He grabbed her hand so that he could lead her to his office and was surprised when she didn't try to pull it away. Their hands fit together like they were made for each other, which he had no doubt they were. He had felt a pull toward her since the very first time he watched her walk into Arrow, but he hadn't been in the right frame of mind to take any steps toward discovering what that pull meant. Now, it was the only thing he thought about...she was the only thing he thought about.

Once inside the front door, Gabriel told Sylvia where he was going and to have Ray cover the bar while he was gone. The blonde gave him a sympathetic look and then headed off to relay his message. Not wanting to waste any more time, Gabriel led Savannah passed the bar and through the kitchen doors. Thankfully the restaurant wasn't too busy, so the kitchen wasn't a frantic mess and they didn't have to dodge the chefs or any of the other staff members. As soon as they were past the prep counters and the ovens, he took a sharp left to walk down a narrow hallway where the employee break room and his office were located. As soon as they were at their destination, he guided Savannah inside then closed the door behind them.

Arrow's office was tiny, which was usually fine since he rarely used it, but now as he maneuvered the single chair in the room from behind his desk to the front of it, he hated how small it was. He motioned for Savannah to sit in the chair before he cleared off a spot on top of his desk for him to sit on. Normally if he had to meet with someone he did it in the break room because it was bigger, but he didn't want to take the chance of someone walking in on their conversation, so the office would have to do. For some reason the air felt stuffy and hot. His palms started to sweat and it was then he realized how nervous he was about being in such a confined space with Savannah.

"Ummm, do you want anything to drink, water or wine or something?" he asked, his throat suddenly dry.

Savannah shook her head so he figured he should go without as well. There was an uncomfortable silence that filled the room, but he wasn't sure where to start. He hated bringing Saturday back up, but it was really the beginning of what he knew. All that mattered was that if he didn't start talking, she was going to walk out of his office and probably out of his life. That was the last thing he wanted.

"So, Saturday night you said some things," he started and felt bad when he noticed the blush that crept up her cheeks. "Things about me just being a bartender and not being stable. How you're looking for commitment and you didn't think that since I was "Mr. Fun Time Bartender" I could give you that. Do you remember saying those things?"

The blush on Savannah's cheeks darkened, but she nodded her head. Her eyes were focused intently on her hands in her lap. If he wasn't so frustrated by her lack of connection, Gabriel might have thought she looked adorable, but instead looking at her made him want to shake her. He wanted to snap her out of whatever head space she was in at the moment. What he was going to tell her was important and he needed her to understand, so he grabbed a framed photo that was sitting on his cluttered desk and handed it to her.

"That is my brother Jonathan. He was two years younger than me and because he was the baby of the family he got away with breaking tradition and venturing out into the world on his own. He always loved to cook and when he was 18 he went off to culinary school. When he was 26, he came back to Seattle and opened Arrow. My father still wasn't happy that he didn't follow in our footsteps and become a lawyer, but he wanted to make mom happy so he supported my brother's endeavor," Gabriel paused,

taking a deep breath hoping that he could fight back the emotions that were threatening to overtake him.

"For three years Jonathan ran Arrow, watching as it became one of the best new restaurants in Seattle. Things were going really well for everyone at the time. His restaurant was a success; I was about to become the youngest senior partner at my father's law firm. We were both engaged, getting ready to start families of our own and then one night, Jonathan and Lacey were driving home to West Seattle from a party at our parents' house on Mercer Island. A drunk was driving the wrong way, Jonathan tried to swerve out of the drunk's way, but got hit by him anyway, sending them into the cement barrier."

Savannah's gasp brought Gabriel out of the horror of the memory for a moment. She was staring at the picture of the two brother's smiling, their arms draped over each other's shoulders. It had been taken the night of the party. They were celebrating their parent's 30th wedding anniversary and although their dad was a hard ass, they were still family. Gabriel and Jonathan were best friends and their mother had been affectionate and amazing, up until that night.

"Jonathan died instantly. Lacey was in a coma for a month before she passed away. When they read Jonathan's will, he had left me Arrow and his house out here in West Seattle. Despite my father's best efforts to keep me in the family business, I quit working at the firm and rented out my townhouse near Green Lake so I could come keep my brother's dream alive," Gabriel hesitated for a moment, unsure if he should tell her the rest of the story. "About a year after that, only a month before our wedding, I caught my fiancée in bed with one of my best friends, but when I called off the wedding, I took the heat. Her father was too good of a man to break it to him that his daughter was so horrible. She was all he had after his wife died eight years earlier, so I let him think everything was my fault. I was going through a really rough time, so it was easy for everyone to believe. Of course, that didn't go over well with my dad, since he thought Valerie was the perfect kind of trophy wife for me and he had hoped that she would lead me back to the firm where I could make the family proud. He hasn't talked to me since the day I told him we broke up."

"Oh Gabriel," Savannah whispered as she gripped the frame so tight her knuckles turned white. Gabriel watched as a tear fell onto the glass. His heart seized in his chest as he realized that she was crying for him even though she wasn't speaking to him for some reason. Dropping to his knees in the tight space between his desk and her chair, he tried again to lift her chin so he could look into her eyes. This time she didn't fight him, rather her tear filled eyes met his and he was lost. All he wanted to do was lean in and place a kiss on her lips, to wrap his arms around her and pull her into his lap; instead he brought both hands up to cup her face, his thumbs swiping across her cheeks to catch the tears that fell.

"Shhh, there's no need to cry Savannah. I miss my brother and I worry about my mom, but I've never been happier. And you coming into my life is a big part of why I'm so happy. Please just give me a chance to show you that I can be exactly what you're looking for. Please let me prove to you that I'm the man you need."

"God. I want to let you show me those things so badly. I'm sorry for judging you; for having the wrong idea of who you are. It doesn't matter if you're just a bartender or something else. I don't care about anything else except seeing where this can take us. I don't want to fight these feelings anymore."

Gabriel couldn't hold back any longer. He put his arms around her and pulled her into his lap like he wanted to before. When she was steady, he wrapped his left arm around her waist and ran his other hand through her hair. Their eyes never strayed from each other as he leaned forward, his mouth suddenly so close to hers he could feel her breath against his lips. Everything about the moment felt right, felt perfect. Just like the other night in front of her house, their bodies fit together and he knew their mouths would too. Without a second thought, he pressed his lips against hers lightly at first, but when she shifted her body so she was even closer to him and wrapped her arms around his neck, he deepened the kiss.

Her lips were softer and more enticing than he remembered. There was no doubt in his mind that he could kiss this woman forever and never tire of it. Parting his lips slightly, he swept his tongue across the seam of her lips, which she immediately opened, her own tongue greedily meeting his in a seductive dance. The kiss deepened, becoming more and more frantic as their denied passion was finally released. Without breaking the kiss, he pulled her closer to his body, wrapping his left arm tighter around her before moving his right arm beneath her knees. Climbing to his feet, he turned until the desk was behind her and then set her down on the edge where he had been sitting.

Breathlessly they broke apart, their eyes meeting again as Gabriel moved between Savannah's legs. With a smile, she wrapped her legs around his waist and pulled him into her until he could feel her heart beating against his chest. He liked knowing that even though he felt like his heart was going to break out of his chest, her heart was beating just as hard as his was. She was just as affected by him as he was by her. As he reignited the kiss, he felt her legs tighten around him, her hands skimming along his forearms. Her touch sent chills down his spine. All he wanted to do was spread her out on top of his desk and devour her. His cock hardened at the thought of her naked and aching for his touch, but it was all too soon.

Fuck, I sound like a chick, he thought while he tried to control his raging hormones. The last thing he wanted to do was tell her no again, but he also didn't want to move too quickly. What he wanted with Savannah was more than just sex, was more than just physical. He wanted it all and he couldn't let his base desires get in the way of what could be the best thing that ever happened to him. But then again, if she wasn't going to stop things, then maybe she wasn't worried that taking things further would do any damage to their fledgling relationship.

As if she could read his mind, Savannah broke the kiss, her legs loosening around him as her thumbs traced random patterns onto his already decorated arms. Her chest rose and fell rapidly as she tried to catch her breath. Gabriel tried not to stare at the hint of cleavage that her sweater showed off. Her lips were kiss swollen and when she ran her tongue along her bottom lip before pulling it between her teeth he had to fight the urge to kiss her again. Instead he moved his hands from her lower back onto her thighs, resting his forehead against hers.

"God, I want you so badly," she said softly. She slowly brought her right hand up until it was resting against his whisker roughened cheek, her eyes closing as her skin made contact with his.

"I know the feeling."

"We just can't do this here. Not now. You were right on Saturday and a quickie on your desk isn't really how I want our first time to go either. And I don't want to fuck this up. While I know that this is going to have to happen before we both explode, I think we have to wait. Get to know each other better. Maybe hang out like we talked about."

"I'd really like to do that. I hate that you had this misconception of me that was keeping you from seeing me…even if I think you were being slightly judgmental," he said with a smile and then gave out a yelp as she pinched his arm. "I told you I want to know you, the real you. And I want you to know the real me."

"I've got seven dates left. We can't technically date until those are over, but if you're not busy in the morning maybe we can go for a run and get coffee? Just two people hanging out, getting to know each other…"

"That sounds perfect. Just two friends getting coffee, nothing more, nothing less…at least for a few more weeks," Gabriel said as he watched the most beautiful smile light up Savannah's face. Finally, he was getting his chance to be with her. It wasn't exactly what he wanted, but a few weeks with her as a friend was better than not having her in his life at all. He just had to make sure that he did whatever it took to keep her once her blind dates were over.

****

The next five weeks were the longest of Gabriel's life. While he spent a lot of time with Savannah, it wasn't the kind of quality time he craved. He was dying to take her out on a real date and get the chance to kiss her again. Since they weren't able to actually date, neither wanted the temptation of a physical relationship. Since the night in his office, they had done nothing but hug goodnight a few times. It sucked and they both hated not touching, but he didn't want to ruin anything and neither did she. The more time he spent with Savannah, the more he wanted her not just in his bed, but in his life, permanently.

So instead of dating, they simply hung out; never just the two of them unless they were running. Nearly every night, she came into Arrow for dinner. If it was a date night, she came in early so she they could chat. Non-date nights she sat at the bar for hours, having dinner and drinks, while chatting with Gabriel when he could. In the morning, he would head into Delectable Delights and have coffee with her before she got too busy. Her sister Brooklyn was often there or one of the other staff members. Savannah rarely got to actually sit down and drink her coffee, but it didn't matter to Gabriel as long as he got to see her.

The only good thing that came out of the long waiting game was that Gabriel was able to work out a way to give himself time away from Arrow. Ray jumped at the chance to be promoted to behind the bar and Sylvia and Meghan were more than willing to take on the extra work with the promise of their own promotions once he got things in order. Knowing that he didn't have to worry about Arrow was a huge weight off of his shoulders; one that he hadn't been rid of since the day Jonathan's will was read.

Although, now that he was free, he didn't really know what to do with himself. He had promised that he wouldn't go into the restaurant as it was officially his first day off in three years. It was also his first official date with Savannah, which made the fact that he had nothing to do even worse. He spent the majority of the day a nervous wreck; afraid that what he had planned for their date wouldn't be enough. Gabriel had over a month to plan the perfect date, but he wasn't at all satisfied that he had actually done it. Of course, he knew he was his own worst critic. It didn't even matter that he had heard over and over from Savannah's best friend and sister that he had done a great job, he still wasn't 100% certain Savannah was going to enjoy what he had planned.

Gabriel tried to clear his mind by taking a run along the beach before his date. The fresh air helped a little, but he still couldn't shake the nerves. He had waited so long for Savannah and now that he was finally going to take her out on an actual date, he was more nervous than he had ever been in his entire life. Arguing major cases in front of judges and juries had never been as nerve-racking as what he was facing. Dealing with his father after Jonathan's death had never made him feel this way. In every instance, he had something to lose, but nothing was as important to him as Savannah.

There was no doubt in Gabriel's mind that he was falling for her…hard. Every day he found something new that he loved about her and they hadn't even really had a chance to be alone together. He constantly wondered what Savannah would think about a certain topic and he couldn't picture his life without her in it, even though her involvement had been so limited. On the rare occasion that they couldn't see each other, his day was ruined, which made him no fun to be around.

The nerves were nearly at full blown panic attack level by the time he pulled up in front of Savannah's house; his palms were damp, his heart beating faster than normal. He was early, which was normally a good thing, but he was a half an hour early, not just ten or fifteen minutes. For a moment, he thought about driving around the block a few times, but decided that would make him look worse, so he parked his truck and walked up to Savannah's door. Taking a deep breath to try and calm the nerves, he knocked softly. As he waited, he cursed himself for being so early. Now he worried that she was going to feel rushed and that the date was going to start off on the wrong foot. Before he could think about it too much, the door opened and he nearly stopped breathing all together.

Whether she was dressed up or covered in flour, Savannah was always the most beautiful woman he had ever seen. Standing in front of him now, she looked even more amazing than normal. For once, she was dressed up just for him and not one of the guys she had been fixed up with. Gabriel slowly took her in, memorizing every detail of how she looked in that moment. She wore her long

blonde hair loose and wavy over her shoulders, exactly the way he

liked it. He clenched his hands at his sides, fighting the desire to

reach out and run his fingers through the soft curls. Her make-up

was light, but perfectly accentuated her bright blue eyes and plush,

full lips. Again Gabriel fought against his urges, this time to pull her

close to him so that he could kiss her berry pink lips.

Gabriel hadn't told Savannah what they were doing, but had

instead told her to dress like she had for her previous dates. He was

pleasantly surprised to see that she had opted for a dress, since she

had worn mostly pant suits during the last half of her dating spree.

She had also told him once that she felt like a phony when she wore

a dress because she was more of a jeans and t-shirt type of girl. She

wore a cable knit black sweater dress that went to the middle of her

thighs, seeming to accentuate her shapely legs. It had long sleeves

and a high neckline that met her collarbone. The dress looked warm

enough for her to be outside and free enough for her to move around

the dance floor. On her feet, Savannah wore a simple pair of black

heels that he hoped she'd be able to walk in. Although, he'd gladly volunteer to carry her around or massage her feet if the shoes were as uncomfortable as they looked.

"Hi," Savannah finally said breaking Gabriel out of his drawn out perusal of his date. His eyes traveled back up her body to meet hers. She was smiling widely and he loved the way that it shown in her eyes. All of the nerves he had been feeling seemed to melt away as he smiled back at her.

"Hi. I'm sorry I'm so early," he told her.

She laughed, shaking her head. "I've been ready for the last half hour. I've just been pacing my living room, trying to make the nerves go away."

Gabriel felt his smile widen as he realized that she was just as nervous as he was. Although they had spent hours getting to know each other at Arrow and Delectable Delights, it had never been just the two of them and it had never been as intimate as it was going to be tonight. He watched as a blush crept across Savannah's cheeks.

"I've been so nervous all day, I paced, I went running, and then it took me nearly an hour to pick out which suit I was going to wear. Most of my suits look exactly the same, so there really isn't a good reason why that would take so long."

"Wow, we make a great pair don't we? I was so embarrassed about being nervous, even before I admitted it to you. I just couldn't understand why, after all the time we've spent together I had a herd of butterflies in my stomach. I've never been so comfortable with someone in my life, yet my palms are sweaty and my heart is beating so hard I'm surprised you can't hear it."

"I probably could, if mine wasn't beating so hard."

"I don't even know what to say to that," she admitted. "Ummmm...do you want to come in? I just need to grab my purse and then I'm ready to go."

Gabriel followed her into the house, admiring the sexy back of her dress as she walked in front of him. It was cut a lot lower than he had been expecting, just barely covering the bottom of her spine. He fought the urge to place his hand on the expanse of exposed skin and instead focused on the house around him. He smiled as he took in every detail while he descended into her sunken living room. The space was decidedly Savannah, functional with a ton of personality. There were pictures and paintings covering the walls and flat surfaces that represented everything that was important to her. The furniture looked comfortable and modern, yet showed pieces of

Savannah's sass in the color of the throw pillows and the lamp sitting on a table next to the recliner.

"You look great, by the way," Savannah said as she picked a small black purse up off of the coffee table. "I've never seen you so dressed up. It looks good on you, but I kind of miss the tattoos."

Gabriel smiled again as he turned to look at her. "Don't worry; I'm sure I'll roll my sleeves up eventually. I kind of hate having my arms covered. And I'm sorry I didn't say this sooner, but you look amazing."

He took a step closer to her and then another until they were nearly touching. Savannah's eyes met his as she closed the tiny gap between them, her hands lightly brushing against the lapels of his suit jacket. All he wanted to do was lean down and brush his lips against hers, but he worried that if he started to kiss her, he wouldn't be able to stop. He ran his right hand through her hair, his thumb brushing along her temple and then over her cheek to her chin. Savannah's eyes fluttered as he touched her, but her bright blue orbs never left his until the moment he started to lower his mouth toward hers.

Their lips brushed together softly, making his heart beat faster. Gabriel cupped her face in his hands, tilting it just enough so that their lips molded together. He tried not to take the kiss any further, but Savannah had other ideas. Her arms snaked up to wrap around his neck as she opened her mouth, her tongue gliding out to lick at the seam of his mouth. His lips parted with an appreciative groan, his tongue finding hers. This kiss was what his dreams had been made of since the night in his office where they had decided to see what could develop between them. Her lips were just as soft as he had remembered and she tasted like chocolate and wine, a deadly combination.

Before it went too far, he pulled back a little so that their mouths were no longer touching, but close enough to torture them both. He rested his forehead against hers, a sigh escaping his lips.

"I've been dreaming about kissing you for far too long," Savannah said, her voice breathy and full of promise.

"Me too. God…and as much as I want to just stay here and kiss you until the sun comes up tomorrow, I've got something pretty great planned for tonight. Something that I hope will show you how much I care about you."

Savannah smiled as she stood on her tiptoes to place a chaste kiss against his lips. "I'm sure I will absolutely love whatever you have planned. Should we go? I don't know if I can be held responsible for anything that might happen if we don't leave now."

Twenty minutes later, Gabriel led Savannah from his truck to the Argosy cruise terminal. They had reservations for the dinner cruise, which was something that Savannah said she always wanted to do. It was a fleeting comment during one of their pre-date conversations, but he had known right away that it would be where he would take her on their first date.

"How did you know I've always wanted to go on the dinner cruise?" Savannah asked after they checked in.

"You told me about a month ago. We were talking about things around Seattle that we've never done, but have wanted to. This was one of your things."

"Wait, you remembered that?"

Gabriel smiled, wrapping his arm around her waist. "I remember everything that you say."

He could tell by the look on her face that Savannah was surprised. She didn't say anything else while they waited in line to board the ship. They were led to a table for two near one of the large windows. When he made the reservations, he had made a lot of requests and offered to pay to make sure those requests were met. There was nothing he wouldn't have done to make sure that this experience was all she hoped for and more. The last thing he wanted to do was share a table with another couple; he wanted Savannah all to himself. He also wanted to make sure that they had the best view possible. While they both lived in the area their entire lives, neither of them had ever seen Seattle this way.

The dinner and the scenery were amazing, but it was the dancing that Gabriel looked forward to. Holding Savannah close to him, showing her once again that he listened to the things she said, even in passing. She had never truly slow danced with someone before; not as an adult anyway. As soon as he heard that, he knew that was another thing he needed to make happen. The lessons he took prior to his ill-fated wedding had paid off. He loved seeing the look on Savannah's face when he twirled her around, then dipped her dramatically. They spent nearly an hour on the dance floor, laughing and dancing, relishing in the fact that they were finally able to be together.

"I can't believe you did this for me," Savannah said as they disembarked the cruise ship. Her smile lit up her face in a way he had never seen before. She had the most beautiful smile in the world and he loved that it was just for him…because of him. As they walked, he held her hand, stopping every once in a while to twirl her in the middle of the crowded sidewalk. Each time she giggled and gave him that smile and each time he fell even more for her.

"There isn't anything I wouldn't do for you Savannah."

They walked further down the Seattle waterfront, occasionally, stopping to look in windows or check out merchandise. The waterfront was packed with other couples and groups which wasn't that surprising for a Saturday night in June. The weather was great, although colder than it had been in West Seattle since they were closer to the water. Savannah had brought a thin jacket, but Gabriel could tell it wasn't doing the trick. Stopping before they reached their final destination, he took off his suit jacket and draped it over her shoulders.

"Thank you. I didn't think I was going to get cold," Savannah said while putting her arms into the too long sleeves.

Gabriel hated that the jacket nearly covered her entire dress, but he couldn't help but love seeing her in his clothing.

"I should have told you what we were doing so you could have been prepared. I'm sorry," Gabriel said as he found her hand beneath the sleeve.

"I've loved what you've planned tonight. I can't believe you remembered those things. Being a little cold is well worth being with you."

They resumed walking toward their next stop, which was something she'd mentioned during a brief conversation with her sister Brooklyn. Gabriel had been sitting at Delectable Delights watching them work when Brooklyn had mentioned the giant Ferris wheel on the waterfront. It hadn't been open for a year yet, but they both wanted to try it out because it sounded so romantic. The view from the top was supposed to be amazing at night, but both sisters lamented that the experience wouldn't be as special since they didn't have significant others in their lives. Gabriel had immediately put the conversation in his date vault while also deciding to make sure that Brooklyn got to enjoy the view someday too.

As they approached Fisherman's Restaurant, Savannah gave Gabriel a questioning look. He still hadn't told her where they were going, so her confusion at stopping at another restaurant after they'd just eaten dinner was understandable. Instead of explaining, he smiled at her and led her to the stand where they had to check in. Savannah squeezed his hand as she gave a little squeal. When he announced that they were checking in for the VIP package she squealed again.

After the champagne toast, their escort led them to the front of the line so they could board their private glass bottom gondola. Of course, the privacy had been extra, but Gabriel didn't care. He knew this was what she wanted and he also knew he didn't want to share this experience with anyone but her, especially not strangers.

"I don't remember ever telling you about wanting to go up in The Great Wheel."

"A man has to have his secrets, Savannah."

Savannah scoffed, "Did Brooklyn tell you?"

Gabriel shook his head before reaching down to wrap his hand around hers. The wheel continued to move slightly so that each gondola could be emptied and then filled with new passengers.

Savannah radiated with excitement, nearly bouncing in her seat every time the wheel moved. The higher they got, the more they could see, but Gabriel didn't care about the view outside of the tiny room. He couldn't stop looking at her, while she looked around in wonder. There was no doubt in his mind that she was the most beautiful woman in the world and her beauty definitely wasn't just superficial. She was by far, the nicest, most caring person he had ever met as well. It was obvious the first time he saw her, that she was something special and now he finally had her all to himself.

"This is incredible Gabriel."

Never taking his eyes off of her, Gabriel agreed. She was incredible; more so than he ever realized. They'd only technically known each other for a few months, but he knew all that he needed to. Savannah St. James was the one for him. In her, he found all of the things he never realized he wanted and even some things he never really thought would fit in his life. A future filled with love, happiness, and children; a family that cared about each other no matter what happened. He had never felt the way he felt with her, not about himself and not about another person. Savannah made him proud of who he was, but also made him want to be an even better version of himself.

There was nothing he wanted more in the world than to make her happy. He just had to hope that she felt the same way. Gabriel knew that it wasn't the right time to have a conversation about feelings. It was their first real date after all; he didn't want to scare her by moving too fast. He'd already done that once before and now that he was finally getting his shot with her, he didn't want to risk it.

"Are you even paying attention or are you just staring at me?" Savannah asked breaking him from his thoughts about their future together.

"Sorry. I just can't seem to take my eyes off of you," Gabriel admitted as he brushed hair away from her face. "Nothing out there could be more stunning than the view in here."

"Oh you're good. No wonder you used to win all of your cases."

Savannah smiled up at him, her hand letting go of his so she could adjust her position on the bench seat. Slowly, she brought one hand to his stubble roughened cheek. Gabriel fought the urge to close his eyes as she traced a finger along his jaw to his mouth. He loved whenever she touched him, which before that night had been few and far between. Her skin was soft and he knew her lips were even softer. He couldn't wait for them to touch his again. Thankfully, from the look in her eye, he wouldn't have to wait long.

"This has been the best date I've ever been on, first or otherwise. Thank you for making me feel so special," Savannah said before leaning over and pressing her lips against his.

Gabriel wrapped his arms around her, pulling her as close to his body as she could get without being in his lap, which was where he really wanted her. The kiss was innocent at first and though Gabriel desperately wanted to take the kiss further, he gave control over to Savannah. Aside from the drunken night in front of her house, he had always been the one to initiate things, now it was her turn. There was a moment of hesitation before Savannah's lips parted, her tongue darting out to deepen the kiss. Her hands tangled in his hair, while she tilted her head ever so slightly. Their mouths fit together perfectly and he knew that their bodies would too eventually. At the thought of her body up against his, he let out a groan.

"How many times does this thing go around?" Savannah asked, her lips still pressed against his, her hands in his hair. "I don't want to wait any longer. I want to take you home."

The twenty-minute drive back to her house felt like it took three hours. He had been waiting for this moment to happen between them since the day they met. The near misses were enough to give him something to imagine and boy had he imagined…in the shower, in his bed, in his office, but he knew that what he had imagined was going to be nothing compared to the real thing.

The tension between them kept the conversation from the pier to Savannah's house light. There wasn't much they could say that would keep either of them from thinking about what they were going to do once they got back to her place. As he drove, he pictured all of the ways he planned to take her. He was so distracted that they were lucky they made it home without getting pulled over or into an accident.

Once inside her house, they still didn't speak much as Savannah led Gabriel up the stairs to her bedroom. It wasn't the first time he'd been in her house, but this time was different. He wasn't getting a tour of her home; he was heading into her bedroom so that he could bury himself between her thighs. He'd never wanted anything more in his life than the moment he was about to have with the most beautiful woman he'd ever met.

"I feel like I've been waiting my entire life for this," Gabriel whispered into her ear as he shut the door behind them.

Spinning around, Savannah threw herself against him, nearly knocking him over in the process. Her arms twined around his neck as she pulled him down to place her lips against his. Kissing her was like a dream that he never wanted to wake up from. Her soft lips parted as she sucked his bottom lip between her teeth. She nibbled on it and then soothed the sensitive skin with her tongue. Gabriel loved the way Savannah took control during the kiss, it proved that she was just as excited by this moment as he was, but he had plans for her and it didn't involve kissing against her bedroom door.

Breaking the kiss, Gabriel stepped back from her, letting his eyes once again travel from her face, to her long, luscious legs and then slowly back up while his hands stroked her arms. The way her dress was cut, he knew that Savannah wasn't wearing a bra and he had a feeling she wasn't wearing any panties either. He knew the minute that he slipped that dress off of her shoulders she was going to be bare to him. Part of him wanted to push the dress to the floor and devour her, the other part wanted to uncover her silky skin inch by inch, kissing and caressing it as the dress slid to the floor.

"Fuck," he murmured against her lips, his hands trailing over the expanse of naked skin from her neck to the top of her ass. His hands slid lower, cupping her ass so he could pull her tighter against him. She moaned into his mouth as she rubbed against him, their tongues tangling in a seductive dance that only succeeded in making him harder.

"We need to be naked," Savannah said before moving her hands to the front of his shirt.

She quickly made work of the buttons, pushing the shirt off of his shoulders before moving on to the button of his slacks. Reluctantly, he removed his hands from her body long enough to let his shirt fall to the floor. Before he could go back to helping Savannah remove her clothing, she was shrugging out of her dress. He watched, transfixed, as she was bared to him. In his wildest dreams, he couldn't imagine the perfection that stood before him. Her full pert breasts, with their hardened nipples were practically begging to be licked, sucked, and nibbled and from where he stood he could see the signs of her arousal on her inner thighs.

"God, you are so beautiful Savannah."

Her hands traced along his abs as she smiled up at him. "You're not too bad yourself."

Gabriel brought his mouth back down to hers so he could feast on her as he helped her step out of her shoes and the dress that was pooled around her ankles. Once she was free from any entanglements, he walked her back toward the bed. He was getting impatient with each moment that passed. While he loved touching her and kissing her, he dreamed of being between her thighs, first feasting on her core, using his tongue and fingers to coax her over the edge, then burying his cock deep inside of her until she was shattering around him, screaming his name.

Breaking the kiss, he helped her sit on the bed. Savannah bit down on her lower lip, looking up at him as she scooted into the middle of the bed. Her eyes hooded, her skin flushed with desire while she watched him kick off his shoes and remove the rest of his clothing. As soon as his dick was free, she licked her lips, her eyes widening as she tried to grab him. He pulled back a little, just enough to be out of her reach, laughing when she made a noise that told him she wasn't happy.

"You can touch that all you want later. Right now...I've got somewhere I desperately need to be."

Savannah whimpered as he crawled up onto the bed. Propping herself up on her elbows, she watched while he positioned himself between her open thighs. He pushed them further apart, taking a deep breath to inhale her heady scent. Her thighs were already coated, her folds slick with her arousal. He slid a finger from her clit down to her entrance and then back up again, slowly teasing her and himself. Without a second thought, he traced along the same path with the tip of his tongue, smiling against her when Savannah let out a yelp, her hips bucking slightly.

"You taste so fucking good," Gabriel said, his hands moving up to hold her hips in place as he worked his tongue around her clit and then down into her entrance. He worked feverishly, sucking, nipping, and licking until she writhed beneath him. Her head fell back against the bed as he pressed a finger deep inside her. Moving his mouth up to suck on her swollen nub, he pressed a second finger in and then a third. Crooking his fingers slightly he felt around until he knew he'd found the magic spot. Savannah thrust her hips against his hand a moan escaping her as he worked his fingers in and out of her, all while making sure her clit wasn't neglected.

"Oh…oh…I'm going to…" Savannah started, her body giving away what she was trying to say before she could finish. Her body clenched around his fingers as she cried out his name, once, twice. He lapped at her folds, not wanting to miss any of the juices that flowed from her. She tasted so sweet, so amazing that he never wanted to stop, but as she came down from her high, he knew that if he didn't get inside of her soon, his dick was going to explode.

"Bedside table on the right side," Savannah said suddenly. Listening to her instructions, he crawled over her, placing a quick kiss on her lips before leaning over to the right side of the bed. The drawer in question was filled with an assortment of toys, lubes and condoms, all things he couldn't wait to explore and use with her, but for now, he just needed one of them. Pulling off one of the foil packets, he closed the drawer and then moved back until he was on his knees, between Savannah's legs. His cock stood at attention, rock hard and waiting to be put to use. Savannah, once again propped up on her elbows, looked down at him, her tongue darting out to wet her lips.

Ripping open the package with his teeth, he rolled the condom onto his cock in what he thought had to be record time. Gabriel lowered himself over her, crushing his mouth against hers in a kiss that showed just how badly he wanted her. She sucked his tongue into her mouth, her hands roaming over his back and down to his as. She guided him to her opening until the head of his dick just barely pressed into her.

"Are you ready?"

"Fuck, I've been ready for months," Savannah said as she gripped his ass tighter, pulling him against her while her hips lifted slightly off the bed.

Her eagerness had him slipping into her, a moan escaping them both as he filled her. Slowly, he pulled out, almost completely, before sinking back into her warmth. Her legs wrapped around his waist as he crushed his mouth against hers, their lips parting immediately so their tongues could tangle and tease. He continued pulling out of her, only to plunge back in until he was completely surrounded by her, filling her up, but he still didn't feel deep enough.

Reaching underneath her, he shifted her hips off of the bed, changing the angle just enough for him to slide home completely. And home was exactly what it felt like. Gabriel stilled for a moment, reveling in the way it felt to finally be inside of her. Her slick heat gripped him as she tightened her muscles around him.

"You better start moving again soon," Savannah threatened through clenched teeth.

Before he could answer, she thrust her tongue back into his mouth, her hips rotating up against his. He wasn't quite ready to move again, he knew if he did that this wouldn't last much longer, but he knew Savannah would be pissed if he didn't. She felt too good to stay put and they always had time for another round or two or three. He never wanted to leave her bed, her arms, her life. This is where he was meant to be.

With that in mind, he pulled out again and then surged back into her; back and forth, in and out. With each thrust of his cock, he got closer to the edge. Savannah panted beneath him, no longer able to keep up with the kisses. Her walls pulsed around him as her body tensed. She was close, so very close to breaking apart beneath him. His balls tightened as he picked up the pace, knowing that there were only a few short moments before they were both going to come. Reaching down between them, he massaged her clit.

"Oh Gabriel...oh god."

"I can't hold back Sav...oh shit..."

Gabriel's thrusts became more frantic as her walls clamped down around him. Before he knew it, he was emptying himself inside of the thin sheath of latex that separated them. Savannah writhed beneath him, his name once again falling from her lips. Their eyes met as they started to come down from the high of their orgasms and for the first time in his life Gabriel finally understood what people meant when they said sex was better when feelings were involved. Now that he had been inside her, had gotten as close to Savannah as two people could get, Gabriel knew that there was no going back; he had fallen for her, fallen fast and hard and it was the most incredible thing he'd ever felt. Now all he had to do was make sure that he didn't scare her before she was ready to admit she'd fallen for him too. A task that he knew would be no easy feat.

Chapter 5

"Look at you. You're freaking glowing."

"Shut up, Brook. I'm not glowing. You're being weird."

Savannah couldn't even look at her younger sister as they stocked the pastry case next to the register. Delectable Delights had been open for an hour, but they had both been there since a little after five in the morning. From the moment they walked through the door, Brooklyn had been pestering her about her date with Gabriel. She wanted details and had been trying to get them since Sunday morning, but Savannah had been ignoring her phone calls and text messages. Now that they were face to face, she knew that trying to get out of talking about her date was futile. Her sister was a St. James after all and stubbornness ran through their veins.

"I've never seen you like this Sav. You're happy…ridiculously happy and I'm pretty sure a lot of that comes from you finally getting laid."

"Jeezus, Brooklyn," Savannah growled as she grabbed her sister's hand. Without a glance toward the bakery's seating area or the young woman manning the register, Savannah pulled her sister through the swinging door that led into the kitchen. She knew that if she didn't talk to Brooklyn about her date, her sister would make a scene and that was the last thing she wanted or needed. With her luck, it would get back to Gabriel and she definitely didn't want him to hear that she was "glowing" after their night together.

"Spill Savvy. I want details. I'm living vicariously through you right now. Plus, you owe me, since really I'm the one that got you and Gabriel together."

"What? How do you figure that?" Savannah asked while she tried to busy herself in the kitchen. Three trays of cupcakes were cooling on a rack in the corner. They were still too warm to frost and all of the other baking was done for the day unless a big order came in. With nothing else to do, she grabbed dishes that needed to be washed, putting some of them into the left side of the industrial sized sink to soak. The rest she decided to hand wash…slowly. With the water running, she hoped that Brooklyn would drop the subject, but she knew that wasn't likely.

"If I hadn't pushed you to do the dating thing with Kerrigan, you never would have sat at the bar in Arrow, which means you never would have talked to Gabriel. I knew I'd help find you love, if I had known I could've just bought you a few drinks at the bar, it would have saved me some money."

Savannah laughed, throwing a dish towel at her sister, who had decided to sit on one of the few empty counters in the backroom. It had been great getting to work with Brooklyn over the last few months. Before Brooklyn had come to work with her, they hadn't had a lot of time to spend together between Savannah's work and Brooklyn's marriage. After Brooklyn's marriage imploded she retreated into herself trying to figure out what happened and it was difficult for Savannah to see her that way. Plus, with her busy schedule, there had only been time for Survivor nights with all the chaos that surrounded them both. Savannah was no longer trying to do everything by herself, that coupled with the fact that they were each finally happy with their lives, made spending time together easier. Now if only Savannah could help her sister find love again, everything would be perfect.

"It doesn't matter though. Seeing you in love and so freaking happy, every penny I spent was well worth it. This is what I've been wanting for you and I am so glad you've finally found it."

"I don't..."

"Don't even say it. I know you love him Savannah. I can tell."

"It's too soon Brooklyn. We just went on our first date."

Brooklyn sighed, "You've been half in love with him since the first time the two of you first started talking. The night he told you about Jonathan, you fell all the way. It doesn't matter that you technically just had your first date, you've been seeing each other for months and your feelings have been there the entire time. Don't fight it, don't ignore them, just feel and once you get it through your head, don't hesitate to let Gabriel know."

"Are you crazy? I can't tell him how I feel yet. Even if it's not too soon to be feeling this way, it's definitely too soon to tell him. Feelings freak guys out. I don't want to scare him away when we've only just begun."

"If it makes things easier on you, I can guarantee he feels the same way," a new voice interjected.

Savannah whirled around, shocked to find Declan Reese standing behind her with a loaded hand truck in front of him. Her cheeks grew warm as she turned away from the man that she only recently learned was a friend of Gabriel's. She had no idea that both Delectable Delights and Arrow used the same wine vendor, let alone that the co-owner of the wine distribution company was Gabriel's childhood best friend. There was no telling how long he had been listening to their conversation, but it didn't matter since he obviously heard the most embarrassing part.

This was not how Savannah wanted things to play out. She didn't want to think about her feelings for Gabriel yet. Although Brooklyn had been right, they'd been getting to know each other for months, they only really truly started dating. She couldn't admit her feelings yet. The entire situation scared the crap out of her and now that Declan knew the truth it was only a matter of time before Gabriel found out. The fallout was inevitable. Because her sister couldn't leave things alone, the relationship she was starting would be over before it truly began.

"How could you possibly know that?" Brooklyn demanded, her tone going from sweet to antagonistic immediately. "Guys don't talk about this kind of stuff. I'm sure Gabriel hasn't admitted his feelings to you."

"That's where you're wrong Princess," Declan said, his voice nearly as hostile as Brooklyn's.

Savannah looked over at her sister, surprised by the sudden change in her attitude. Quietly, she watched as Brooklyn and Declan seemed to forget that she was there. They traded barbs and argued about her relationship with Gabriel like an old married couple. When Declan stopped stacking cases of wine on the metal shelving unit against the wall and moved so close to her sister they were nearly touching, Savannah realized what was really going on between her sister and her boyfriend's best friend. They liked each other, like really liked each other, but obviously neither wanted to admit it. Instead they reverted back to elementary school.

"Guys don't talk about feelings to each other. They talk about sex and how hot a chick is, but not about feelings."

"You couldn't possibly know what we talk about. It'd obviously surprise you if you did. We aren't just a bunch of horn balls that only talk about tits and ass, although we do talk about

those things too. Is it wrong to admire a woman with our friends? I

know you ladies do it to us when you get together. Don't try to deny

it."

"You're such a jerk."

Savannah wouldn't have been surprised if Declan reached

out to pull Brooklyn's hair or if Brooklyn started chasing him around

like they were on the playground. The images playing through her

head made her laugh, but she didn't want to disturb the dance

happening in front of her. Unfortunately, no matter how hard she

tried she couldn't hold in her laughter, the snort that escaped her

ended up reminding them that she was still in the room. They both

looked at her, embarrassment evident on their faces.

This development gave Savannah hope for Brooklyn's future.

Declan was a great guy and absolutely gorgeous with his almost too

long black hair, constant five o'clock shadow and piercing green

eyes. He was at least 4 inches taller than her super model height

sister and was in very good shape as far as Savannah could tell

through the delivery uniform he wore. The olive green button-up

shirt with the Reese Wine Distributors logo over his left pec and the black slacks he wore fit his athletic build like a second skin. If Savannah hadn't been 100% into Gabriel she might have been inclined to drool over his best friend the way her sister was.

"I'm sorry I stuck my nose into your business Savannah," Declan said, his voice returning to the sweet, deep sound that she was used to. "Gabriel has talked about you non-stop for longer then you've technically known each other. I didn't know it was you he was talking about until the night he finally learned your name. I never told him I delivered to you until he recommended I see how you felt about your current wine vendor."

"Thanks for your input Declan, but I still don't think I'll be declaring my feelings any time soon."

Savannah hated that the attention was back on her and her feelings. Their bickering was far more entertaining and less stressful for her, but Brooklyn was being unusually quiet and so was Declan. Now that he had said his peace, they both stood on opposite sides of the large metal table that sat in the middle of the kitchen. Occasionally, they would look at each other, but for the most part they stared at her like their intense looks could get her to change her mind.

"Well ladies, it's been great, but I have more deliveries to do today," Declan said as he handed his clipboard to Savannah. "Don't worry; I won't mention this conversation to Gabriel. Your secret is safe with me, I promise."

"Like we can trust him," Brooklyn muttered barely loud enough for anyone to hear.

Savannah gave Declan an apologetic look before signing the invoice and handing him back the clipboard. There was definitely something going on between Declan and her sister. Whatever it was, she couldn't let her sister continue to be a jerk to one of her vendors, even if he obviously antagonized her. Brooklyn would have to be the bigger person even if it killed her. Either that or she was going to have to admit that their grade school antics meant that she was interested in Declan and then do something about it, that was the only way she'd allow Brooklyn to continue to treat him the way she was.

"What the hell was that Brook?" Savannah asked as soon as she heard Declan's truck start up in the alley behind the shop. How she didn't hear him pull up early, she didn't know. It was probably the fact that thoughts of Gabriel seemed to easily distract her.

Whatever it had been, she would have to be more careful. It could have been Gabriel standing behind her listening to her talk about how she was in love with him. That would have been ten times worse than his best friend hearing all about it.

"That guy just rubs me wrong, okay."

"More like you want him to rub you down," Savannah said. "You are totally into him, Brooklyn. The way you two were acting with each other, I felt like I was watching two kids in elementary school. I was waiting for him to pull your hair."

"I am not into Declan Reese!"

Savannah snorted at her sister's protest. "You are. And he likes you too. I can tell."

Brooklyn wasn't happy with her sister throwing her words back at her, but her reaction made Savannah smile more.

"How about we forget all about Declan and get back to you and Gabriel? You love him and you finally got laid. Saturday night was a big deal for you."

With a groan, Savannah tried to busy herself in the kitchen again, hoping that her sister would leave her alone. She should have known there was no way Brooklyn would stop asking about her night. The girl was like a dog with a bone and no amount of distractions or teasing would keep her from eventually getting the information that she wanted. If Savannah pushed about Declan, Brooklyn would push even harder for details about Gabriel. And if Savannah continued to tease her sister about Declan, then all hell would break loose and Brooklyn wouldn't hesitate to make sure she embarrassed her big sister.

"Can we not talk about this here? Declan walking in while we were talking about my feelings was bad enough; I would die if anyone else heard us talking about my date. Dinner and drinks after work? My treat and we don't even have to go to Arrow."

Savannah hoped her sister took her up on her offer. Although she didn't want to admit it, she did want to talk about Gabriel, her feelings and the amazing night that he had planned for their first date. She wanted to gush about everything and have Brooklyn tell her that she wasn't crazy for feeling the way she did. If Brooklyn agreed, she might even invite her best friend Finley so she could get a cynical person's perspective on the situation.

While Brooklyn was all sunshine and rainbows where love was concerned, Finley was doom and gloom. Savannah always thought it was weird the way it worked out considering Brooklyn had gone through a bad marriage and a nasty divorce. Finley on the other hand, had never had a serious relationship that lasted more than a year. And even the few that hit near the year mark were never all that serious, more like friends with benefits than a real relationship.

Although they had been friends since college, Savannah still had no idea what made her best friend tick, at least not in most cases. Finley was one of the best people that she'd ever met, yet she didn't want people to know that. She was a badass, always acting like a tough bitch so that people would leave her alone. Most of the people that Savannah had introduced her to over the last decade and a half always wondered what Savannah saw in Finley that made her keep her around. They didn't see the great friend that Finely was. All they saw was the heavily tattooed and pierced girl prone to flipping people off and breaking up bar fights.

"Fine, we can do dinner," Brooklyn agreed, her voice breaking Savannah out of her thoughts about Finley. "And before you ask, go ahead and invite Fin, but I'm inviting Kerrigan. All the work she did to find you a man and you found one before your first date even started, she deserves to hear all about this too."

Savannah rolled her eyes, but agreed to let Kerrigan come to dinner too. It was going to be a girl's night out, which she hadn't had in a long time. She was definitely looking forward to hanging out and having drinks with the girls, but she knew that if Gabriel had the night off, she would have never suggested it. One date and she was already ready to drop her friends for a guy. He'd completely knocked her world off its axis and now she couldn't get enough of him. They didn't even have to talk or have ridiculously amazing sex for her to want to be with him. Just being near him was enough, although it was ten times better when he had her wrapped in his arms like he had most of Sunday.

It didn't matter what any of the girls said at dinner, Savannah knew she was a goner. Gabriel Archer had done a number on her from the very first moment she saw him. She lusted after him until she got to know him better and then she fell in love with the incredible man that he was. There really was no way she could deny that her sister was right. She was in love with Gabriel and if she wasn't careful, she'd be shouting it from the rooftops before the day was over.

****

Two weeks later, Savannah was no closer to telling Gabriel how she felt than she had been the night she spent with the girls. They all tried to convince her that she should get it out in the open, even Finley. No matter how hard they tried to persuade her it was the best thing to do, she wasn't going to budge. She planned on waiting until he told her how he felt before she admitted her feelings to him. Either way it didn't really matter. She no longer worried that what Declan told her wasn't true. After everything Gabriel had done for her since their first date, she could no longer deny he had feelings for her too. It was pretty obvious, but she wasn't convinced yet that his feelings were as deep as hers. Did he care for her? Yes. Did he love her? Probably not.

They spent nearly every night and every morning together, either at his house or hers. It felt like they'd been together for years instead of weeks. In her entire life, Savannah had never felt more comfortable with another person, not even her sister or her parents. There was no longer any doubt in her mind that Gabriel was the "one". He was that elusive creature everyone talked about, but she never thought she'd find. Or really cared to find, if she was honest.

Checking the clock on the kitchen wall, Savannah sighed in frustration. It was only a little after four in the afternoon and she still had over an hour until Gabriel was supposed to be at her house. She was anxious to see him, even though they had woken up together that morning. There wasn't anything she could do to keep her mind busy while she killed time until he arrived. The house was already clean, the kitchen already set up for the cooking lesson that she had offered him. She had been shocked to learn that although he owned a restaurant, he had no idea how to cook. Even the basics were beyond his skill level in the kitchen.

"You can't cook?" she asked again, bewildered by the concept of a restaurant owner who couldn't boil water.

"I never had reason to learn. Growing up we had help, then when I got older I was too busy with school and the practice to take time to learn something I was never going to have the time to do. Cooking was always Jonathan's passion, not mine. But now, I wish I knew how to at least do the simple things. It would be nice to make dinner for you for a change and to be able to take care of myself

146

when you're working late. I eat out, both at the restaurant and other local places, every night and often for lunch too. And I pretty much eat cereal or toast for breakfast, unless I go somewhere."

"But you've owned Arrow for years now."

"And in that time I learned how to run a business and make drinks. I didn't really have time to learn the cooking part too. Maybe you can teach me sometime?"

"Just name the time and place and I'll be there. We'll at least make a cook out of you...then maybe we can move on to making you a chef."

Savannah picked something really simple for Gabriel to make. It didn't take a lot of skill to make spaghetti with meatballs, garlic bread and salad. She was even going to have him make dessert, an easy cherry pie with store bought crust. There wasn't a whole lot about what they were making that he could mess up, despite his request that they have a back-up dinner on standby. The sauce was in a jar, the pasta in a box and the garlic bread just needed to be stuck in the oven in its foil package. For the salad, he had to chop and mix up the ingredients, which was a fairly easy task. The most difficult part of the meal was probably the meatballs, since he had to actually form and season the meatballs before cooking them.

She gave one last look around the kitchen, noting that everything was ready, before she turned up the iPod that was sitting on the docking station. One of her favorite songs was playing so she started to dance around the kitchen, giggling at how silly she probably looked. She couldn't remember a time when she was so carefree and happy; when she got to spend a Saturday at home, fretting over her date and dancing around the kitchen instead of what was happening at work. The stress of opening a new location was still there, but it no longer ruled her life. Her love for Gabriel did.

By the time Gabriel finally knocked on her door, she was hot, a little bit sweaty and out of breath from dancing around her kitchen. She had completely lost track of time as she enjoyed herself. Letting loose and forgetting about everything was a luxury to Savannah and it felt good to let go completely. Without looking to make sure it was Gabriel at her door, she threw it open, a huge smile plastered on her face.

Every time she saw him, he took her breath away. He smiled down at her, reading her obvious enthusiasm. His smile lit up his green eyes and brought out the dimples that she loved so much. His hair was perfectly styled in that disheveled mess that made her want to run her hands through it. He wore dark blue jeans and a dark grey short-sleeved t-shirt that hugged his body like a second skin. The delicate lines of his tattoos stood out against his tanned skin, begging to be traced with her tongue like she had the night before.

"God, I've missed you," Gabriel said gathering her into his arms. "I know I just saw you this morning, but I…"

"I know. I missed you too," Savannah admitted while wrapping her arms around his neck. She pushed up onto her tip toes so that she could meet his mouth with hers. The kiss was sweet, filled with the hours that they were away from each other, the desire that they had for each other. Every kiss sent her further down the rabbit's hole. She could easily get lost in Gabriel and the way he touched her, kissed her. Every moment had meaning; every touch felt like Gabriel was trying to memorize her body and it was always amazing.

"Come on, before you distract me, we should get to this cooking lesson," Gabriel said. He let her go and picked up a grocery bag that he had set down on the porch.

She watched him walk toward her kitchen, admiring the view as her lips still tingled from his kiss. Gabriel was one of the best looking men Savannah had ever been around, which was always evident by the attention he garnered. Wherever they went, women went out of their way to get his attention, but he never gave it to them. The only exception was when they got a little pushy and he wanted to make sure they realized he wasn't interested because he had a girlfriend. He never checked out the scantily clad women that filled Finley's club or that leaned over the bar when he was working at Arrow. He always made her feel like she was the only woman in the room, sometimes even in the world.

"Are you coming? Or are you just going to stand there checking out my ass all night?"

Sticking her tongue out at him, she followed him into the kitchen, watching as he unpacked his grocery bag. Since she had promised to pick up all of the dinner ingredients, she wasn't sure what he could have had in the bag. He pulled out two bottles of wine, her favorite and set them on the center island. He then handed her a bouquet of carnations that had been in the bag. The flowers were also her favorite and the bouquet he got her was a beautiful

150

variation of pinks, reds and white. The fact that he remembered the little things that most people didn't was one of the many reasons she had fallen in love with him.

While he opened one of the bottles of wine, she found a vase to put the flowers in. They smelled amazing and looked great in the middle of the dining table where she set them. She turned back around to face Gabriel, contemplating kissing him to show her thanks, but decided they would never get to the cooking if she started showing her appreciation now. Instead, she accepted the glass of wine he held out to her and walked back over to the island where everything was set up for their lesson.

"I promise this will be easy and it translates to other things besides spaghetti, so once you learn this, you should be able to cook other meals."

"Alright, just tell me what to do, teacher, I'm ready to learn."

Savannah quickly pulled out the cold ingredients for the meatballs that her mother had taught her to make, setting them next to the large bowl that he would need to mix the ingredients in. Since he wanted to do everything himself, she pulled up one of the stools she kept at the island for informal dining. She set it up next to him so she could give him instructions and help if he needed it. As soon as she was situated she started going through the directions, having him empty the jars of sauce into the large pot on the stove first so that it could start to heat up while he put together the meatballs. His movements in her kitchen were like his movements behind the bar. He was organized and confident even though he didn't really know what he was doing. There were only a few moments he even seemed a little unsure of himself.

After the meatballs were formed and browned in a pan of oil, things progressed rather smoothly. He put the cooked meatballs into the pot with the sauce setting it on low heat so that the mixture could marry. They couldn't start the rest of the warm ingredients until the sauce had simmered for at least a half an hour. Once that was done, they'd throw the bread in the oven and the noodles in the water to boil.

Gabriel joked with her, while he chopped up tomatoes and cucumbers for their salad. They continued to drink through the wine that he brought, finishing one bottle and then opening the other. Once again, Savannah felt completely at ease, she felt special knowing that this was something he'd never done with anyone else.

And she had to admit to herself that although sometimes it made her sad knowing that he had been engaged to someone before he met her, she knew that a lot of what they did together was new to him, especially the way they felt about each other. Just thinking about that filled her body with a now familiar warmth.

Savannah wasn't sure why knowing that he had feelings for her turned her on so much. In fact, she had been in a near state of arousal since she officially met Gabriel. Between his ridiculous sexiness and his affection toward her, she couldn't seem to get herself in check. It didn't matter that he was definitely taking care of her needs multiple times a night and sometimes during the day. She constantly felt like she was one look away from an orgasm. Now sitting in her kitchen watching his forearms flex while he moved the knife through the vegetables, she had to fight the urge to move her hand between her legs. Instead she took a large gulp of her wine and calculated the time they had until dinner was ready. Setting her glass down on the counter, she hopped off of the stool and started throwing the vegetables into the big bowl they were using for the salad.

"Hey, that's my job," Gabriel said as he tried to stop her from helping.

"By my calculations we have about twenty minutes before we need to start the rest of dinner."

"I guess so, why?" Gabriel asked a mischievous smile playing across his face.

"Because I need some relief and I really don't want to take care of it on my own. Will you help?"

"I can't really leave the food unattended Sav. Can't it wait?"

Savannah laughed, knowing that he was just messing with her. She could tell by the look on his face that he wanted it as much as she did. Taking a step backward, she started unbuttoning the thin red blouse she was wearing. The cool air hitting her flushed skin felt amazing once she slipped the garment off her shoulders. She let it fall to the floor, followed soon after by her denim shorts.

"The dining table is sturdy and I can't wait…can you?" Savannah asked as she reached behind her back to unhook her bra. It fell to the floor with the rest of her clothes leaving her standing in front of him in just her skimpy panties. Gabriel let out a low growl as he quickly cleared the distance between them. He pulled her roughly into his arms, his mouth meeting hers in a demanding kiss. Her sensitive nipples hardened against the softness of his t-shirt, but she needed to feel his skin against hers. She pulled back just enough to remove his shirt and then moved back in to press open mouth kisses against his chest.

As soon as her tongue found one of his nipples, she sucked it into her mouth, nipping it gently with her teeth. Her hands moved down to his jeans, flicking the button open easily before lowering the zipper. Gabriel pulled her tighter against him, a moan escaping him as she gripped his cock through his boxer briefs. Without any warning, he put his hands under her butt, lifting her off of the ground and carrying her to the dining room table.

Setting her down, he kissed her hard. Her hands roamed over his body, her legs still wrapped tightly around his waist. She rubbed against his erection while he palmed a breast in each hand, his thumbs flicking over her nipples. Leaning forward a little, she pushed his jeans and underwear down to pool around his ankles on the floor. Gabriel removed the last piece of clothing she was wearing and then moved back between her legs; his hard, thick length rubbing against her swollen clit. Slowly, he ran a finger along her wet folds, spreading her arousal over her sex.

"God, you're so wet Sav…so fucking wet," Gabriel murmured against her lips before kissing her again.

She pushed her hips up against him, moaning as his cock teased her entrance. Her body ached to be filled by him and time was not on their side. Even if it had been, her patience was surprisingly thin. To hell with foreplay, she needed him to fuck her. They could do the romantic, drawn out lovemaking later, but for now she needed it quick and hard and soon or she was going to explode.

"Fuck me Gabriel, please just fuck me," she moaned as he rubbed against her clit again.

"I don't suppose you have any condoms stashed in the kitchen?" he asked before his mouth latched onto one of her nipples and drew the hardened peak between his teeth.

"No, but it'll be fine. I'm on the pill and we're both clean. Plus, isn't going bareback on the kitchen table the reason we got tested in the first place?" she teased.

Gabriel let out a low growl before pulling her hips tighter against him, his cock once again rubbing against her clit. Her breath caught in her throat, as he dipped a finger between her folds. With a satisfied smirk on his face, Gabriel lifted Savannah's ass off the table slightly so his cock was poised at her entrance. Pushing forward, he entered her quickly, a moan escaping both of them. He stilled, allowing them both time to relish the new sensation of him inside of her without anything between them. Nothing compared to the feel of him bare inside of her, skin against skin, moist heat against rock hard steel. She loved the way Gabriel filled her like he was the missing piece to her puzzle. It sounded stupid and completely clichéd, but no one had ever felt so perfect inside of her body.

Wrapping her legs back around his waist, Savannah met Gabriel thrust for thrust, her hips rotating up off the table. It was obvious that it wasn't going to take either of them long to get off and really they didn't have the time. She just needed to come and she knew he did too. They were insatiable, addicted to the way they made each other feel. It was heady and all-consuming and downright hot. And it was made ten times better with nothing between them.

Gabriel continued to move inside her, his cock hitting just the right place to put her on edge. Her eyes fluttered shut. She was so close, the slow build of her impending orgasm sending tingles through her body. Reaching between them, Gabriel used his thumb to massage Savannah's swollen bundle of nerves and that was all she needed to send her over, stars shattering behind her eyelids. Her legs tightened around Gabriel's waist, her core clenching around him.

"Oh god," she moaned her back arching off the table.

Gabriel continued to pound into her, harder, faster until he finally stiffened. Opening her eyes, she watched as his body tensed. She loved the look he made when he came. It was purely sexual and animalistic and it was all for her. He pumped into her a few more times as his body relaxed. Her skin tingled, her body languid. It was a good thing walking wasn't in her near future since she was pretty sure her legs wouldn't work if she tried. Instead, she relished the feel of Gabriel on top of her, inside of her, both of them coming down from the high of an incredible orgasm. This was what dreams were made of.

The beeping of the oven timer brought Savannah out of her sexual haze long enough to stop her from trying to get Gabriel to go another round. He pulled out of her slowly and rushed over to the sink to grab two towels out of the drawer to the right. He ran one under the tap and then returned to where she still lay on the table.

She had propped herself up on her elbows so she could watch him, enjoying the view of his naked body moving around her kitchen.

"Looks like we have perfect timing," he said with a grin as he proceeded to clean them both up. "For the record, I'm a fan of quickie kitchen sex without a condom, but we're going to have to remember how much of a mess it makes. This table definitely needs to be disinfected before dinner's done."

Savannah laughed, pulling him back between her legs, her arms wrapping around his neck. She didn't care how much disinfectant they had to use, what she wanted now was to christen every inch of her kitchen and dining room before the weekend was over. There was plenty of counter space that she wanted to feel against her bare ass and an island that was the perfect height for her to be bent over it, her bare chest pressed against the cold granite. She smiled at the thought of checking one spot off of the list while the bread was in the oven. It probably wouldn't take much to get Gabriel to agree to her plan, but if not, there was always time before dessert.

Chapter 6

"Why are we here again?" Gabriel yelled over the deafening dance music assaulting his ears and making his head throb.

"You tell me. This is definitely not my scene, although I'm not going to complain about the view," Declan said before taking another long pull of his beer.

Gabriel sighed as he leaned back against the plush booth. He scanned the crowd on the dance floor below them looking for something to keep his mind off of how much he didn't want to be there. The last place he wanted to be after a long, irritating day at the restaurant was a loud club filled to capacity with frat boys and barely dressed girls looking for a quick lay. Unfortunately, he had promised Savannah that they would go to Finley's club, Heat, over a month ago and he couldn't back out just because he'd had a shitty day at work. This night was a big deal for Savannah since she thought it was important that their friends got along. He didn't really care either way. Their friends had no bearing on their relationship. If his friends didn't like Savannah or any of her friends, then Gabriel wouldn't hang out with them at the same time. He would make it work because Savannah was important to him and he wasn't going to lose her because his friends were jerks.

The dance floor was packed with writhing bodies, most of them women, which explained Declan's comment about the view. Smack dab in the middle of the floor was Savannah, her sister Brooklyn, the matchmaker Kerrigan and of course Finley. The four of them were dancing together, oblivious to the bodies around them. From his vantage point, Gabriel could see that a lot of the male eyes around the dance floor were on them, but no one had taken the chance to approach the girls, which was perfectly fine with him. He didn't want to deal with some handsy, asshole trying to dance with his girlfriend. He was not in the right mood to deal with that, but Gabriel knew it was only a matter of time before it happened. The guys around the dance floor were practically drooling on themselves.

Four women dancing with each other was a sight to be seen, but when he finally noticed what the girls were wearing, he understood the real draw.

"What the fuck?" he said through clenched teeth. He could feel Declan looking at him and then looking back out to the floor. When Declan tensed next to him, Gabriel knew he wasn't the only one reacting to what he was seeing.

"Jeezus."

They were all wearing more clothing than most of the females in the club, but that really wasn't saying much. The one dressed the raciest was definitely Brooklyn. Savannah's little sister was wearing a tight pair of black leather shorts that barely covered her ass. Her long legs made to look even longer with a pair of black stiletto heels. On top she wore a sheer white tank top with a black bra underneath. Gabriel completely understood why his friend couldn't take his eyes off of the statuesque blonde now that he noticed her.

Savannah on the other hand wore a low cut burgundy mini dress covered in black lace. She also wore leg accentuating sky high heels on her feet, which he more than appreciated, but knew that at the end of the night, she was going to hate herself for wearing. The back of her dress was nearly non-existent and reminded him of the dress she wore on their first date. He wanted to kiss and lick up her exposed spine. With thoughts like that, he couldn't help but get hard watching her dance. Her short skirt slid up and down her thighs as she moved. He could imagine his hands sliding up and down with it, disappearing underneath the fabric to discover she had nothing on underneath.

"We should go down there," Declan said.

Gabriel just shook his head. He didn't want to dance; didn't want to be stuck in the middle of a swarm of sweaty bodies unless he absolutely had to. So far, there wasn't a need for him to be down there and he hoped it stayed that way. The headache he had when he left the restaurant throbbed in time with the dance remix of some Lady Gaga song that he knew Savannah loved.

Taking a swig off the bottle of water he'd grabbed before sitting down, he scanned the VIP area behind him looking for his friends Oliver and Braeden. The last time he saw them, they had been talking to Meghan and Sylvia at the bar. Gabriel had no doubt that his friends were trying to take his employees home for a night of fun. Little did they know they wouldn't have to try too hard to get them to agree. Numerous times in the past, Meghan and Sylvia had mentioned their interest in his friends. Gabriel usually brushed off their onslaught of questions, but the girls had no shame when it came to guys. He knew it was only a matter of time before they made the first move.

"Are you sure man; we're the only people still up here."

Gabriel turned back around to check out the floor beneath them and noticed his missing friends immediately. They stood out amongst the scantily clad women since they were the only men on that part of the dance floor. They seemed to quickly find their groove, dancing closely with Meghan and Sylvia. He looked over at Savannah, watching as she pulled her hair off of her neck. Sweat covered her skin, as she turned so that her back was pressed against Finley's front. Her eyes met his and she smiled the big bright smile that he liked to think was reserved just for him. Blowing him a kiss, she crooked her finger, beckoning for him to join her all while never losing her rhythm.

Groaning, he shook his head, his pants growing tighter as he watched her dance seductively. Her eyes kept meeting his, making it apparent that the show was for him. He couldn't take his eyes off of her, his hands fisted on his thighs. What would it hurt if he just went down there and gave in? A dance or two and he could sit back down to nurse his headache.

"Suit yourself Gabe. I can't stay up here while she looks like that," Declan said while setting his beer down on the table and getting up off of the couch. Gabriel had barely registered his friends retreat by the time Declan made it down to the dance floor. He had to have broken some kind of record getting down there so he could dance with Brooklyn. No matter how many times Declan told him he wasn't attracted to his girlfriend's sister, Gabriel knew the truth and he was honestly glad to see Declan showing interest in someone after all the years of self-imposed dating exile.

Leaning forward Gabriel watched the writhing bodies on the dance floor, his eyes barely ever leaving his girlfriend. She seemed surprised to see Declan joining her sister, which then turned to something that he could only guess was disappointment that he . hadn't joined her. The look passed quickly as she started to enjoy the music again. He really needed to get over his crap and join her. His bad mood was nothing compared to how hot she looked dancing with their friends and Gabriel knew the view would be even better pressed against her.

Taking another sip of water, he thought about going down to dance with his girlfriend and their friends. Dancing really wasn't his favorite past time on a good day, but with Savannah he was willing to do anything she wanted. He was so fully wrapped around her finger that he was surprised he hadn't jumped up the first time she crooked her finger at him. With one last sip of water and a sigh, Gabriel stood so he could lean against the railing. Savannah smiled up at him, her eyes sparkling in the overhead lights. He held up his finger for her and mouthed one minute before breaking eye contact with her.

After making a pit stop in the VIP bathroom, he headed down the back stairway so he could make his way to the dance floor. He was eager to get his hands on her, to press himself against her. His cock stirred at the thought of her soft body against his and he noticed that his head wasn't pounding any more. Apparently, all he needed to heal what ailed him was thoughts of Savannah.

Pushing his way through the crowd he groaned each time an elbow came in contact with his ribs or someone stepped on his foot.

He needed to see Savannah, get close to her. She was the only thing that would make venturing into the sea of people worthwhile. Girls that barely looked old enough to have graduated high school, let alone be out after midnight in a club, tried to grind against him as he passed, which only irritated him more. The distance from the edge of the dance floor to where Savannah danced hadn't seemed as far when he was upstairs, but now he felt like he was in a never ending throng of people. Finally, he spotted Brooklyn and Declan who were next to Finley and Kerrigan and he knew he was almost home.

Pushing past his friends, he stopped short, the sight in front of him made his skin crawl, his fists clenched at his sides. Savannah was dancing as seductively as she had before, but her eyes were closed as she ground back against some guy. His hands were on her hips, his lips near her ear. Anger burned inside Gabriel as he watched the scene in front of him. He couldn't believe what he was seeing. In the short period of time he had taken his eyes off of her, some douche had moved in and she had let him. And worse than that, she looked like she was enjoying it.

"Are you fucking kidding me?" he yelled over the music. Those around him stopped dancing, including his friends.

Savannah's eyes opened, shock registered on her face. She turned quickly, looking at the guy behind her and then back to Gabriel.

"You couldn't wait until I got down here?"

"I..."

"Hey man, get your own chick. I'm dancing with this one," the meathead behind Savannah said, obviously unaware of the situation that was unfolding.

"Hey man," Gabriel mocked. "You better get your hands off of my girlfriend before I break one of them."

"She didn't seem to mind where my hands were a minute ago."

"I didn't know...I thought it was you, Gabriel," Savannah protested, her hand pushing against Gabriel's chest.

Gabriel seethed, his hands clenched and unclenched at his side as he fought the urge to punch the asshole that had touched her. How could she possibly think that the man behind her had been him? Didn't she know what he felt like by now? He would never mistake another woman for Savannah. No one smelled the same, felt the same. No one could ever match up to her.

"Gabriel, don't do anything stupid. I don't want to have to kick you out." Finley's warning broke through the anger enough that Gabriel became more aware of his surroundings. It wasn't just his friends that had stopped dancing, but now half of the floor was staring at them, probably all hoping to see a fight. The guy that had been dancing with Savannah wasn't backing down and Gabriel didn't want to either. Savannah stood between them, her hands still on his chest, her eyes pleading with him to let it go. He knew he should, he knew that leaving it alone was the best bet, but then the guy put his hand back on Savannah and smirked at Gabriel, taunting him.

"You son of a bitch," Gabriel growled as he stepped forward ignoring the cries of Savannah and his friends. Someone grabbed his arm from behind, stopping his forward progress. Anger coursed through him like fire and every moment that the guy was in his line of site, the flames stoked higher. It didn't matter that Savannah moved away from his touch or smacked the guy herself. He was still standing there trying to get Gabriel to make a move.

"You, get the hell out of my club," Finley yelled. "Savannah, get Gabriel off this floor. I don't need this shit out here, so either take him back to my office or take him home."

Savannah grabbed his hand, trying to pull him away from the scene. The grip on his arm tightened as he tried to break away to go after the guy. Behind him, he heard a familiar voice, but didn't really register what they were saying. He was still pissed, his blood boiled. He couldn't seem to shake the anger that was coursing through him. Gabriel wasn't just mad at the guy, he was mad at Savannah and ultimately he was mad at himself. If he had just gone down to the dance floor when Declan or the guys went, he would have saved them all from the drama, but he was too caught up in his bad mood to make the move.

"Dude, don't do it. Just go with Savannah."

The voice finally broke through the anger, reminding Gabriel where he was and what he was doing. Declan stood next to him, his hand still tightly wrapped around his bicep. Oliver and Braeden stood around them looking ready to do whatever they needed to get Gabriel under control. It was then that he realized just where he had been letting his anger take him. He hadn't been down that deep, dark

170

hole in years, but it was something that he was intimately familiar with thanks to Jonathan's death and his ex-fiancée's deception.

Looking over at Savannah, he stilled. The look on her face was no longer pleading, no longer worried. Instead she looked angry; angrier than he ever thought she could get and he felt horrible about it. This was supposed to be a night of fun. This was supposed to be a time for their friends to bond, for everyone to get to know each other. This wasn't supposed to end in an angry display of possession and jealousy. He hated that he had let it all get so out of control.

"I'm sorry."

"Don't...not here. I can't listen to this crap right now Gabriel. That caveman behavior doesn't work with me. Come on."

Gabriel followed behind Savannah as she weaved her way through the few dancers that were oblivious to the drama unfolding near them. The evening was a mess and there was no one but him to blame. He was going to have to do some serious groveling when they reached their destination. There was no doubt that Savannah was beyond pissed at him, he just hoped they weren't past the point of no return. He had to make sure she was able to forgive him for being such a jackass.

She led him past the bathrooms, down a dark, narrow hallway. For a moment, he thought she had decided to send him home rather than take him to Finley's office, but instead of taking him through the large double doors beneath the glowing green exit sign, she turned down another hallway. The music was barely noticeable, which gave Gabriel some peace. He could finally hear himself think and it was there in the quiet that he realized his headache was back in full force, if it had ever truly gone away. Now that the adrenaline and the hard-on had faded, he was back to feeling as miserable and irritated as he had when he first arrived at Heat.

"I can't believe you did that out there," Savannah screamed at him as she turned, her index finger jabbing into his chest as she spoke. "I'm so embarrassed. That was completely humiliating, Gabriel."

"You let some guy touch you and you looked to be enjoying it. How do you think that makes me feel?"

"I thought it was you, asshole. Do you honestly think I'd let someone else touch me on purpose?"

Gabriel sighed, "I'd know it wasn't you, Sav. I'd know because no one else smells or feels like you. I'd know if some random chick was touching me instead of you because it wouldn't feel like home."

Savannah's mouth opened and then shut again. Her eyes met his and he felt something in his chest tighten. The anger was still very much evident on her face, but her eyes were much softer than they had been before. Her sigh filled the silent hallway, heavy with everything she wanted to say, but wasn't.

"Sav…"

"I'm so mad at you for how you overreacted out there, but damn it. I can't stay mad at you after what you just said. Sometimes though, I hate the way you make me feel. I'm so freaking confused and scared and ridiculously happy. I wanted tonight to be perfect. I want our friends to get along, but maybe coming here was a bad idea. Maybe you were right."

She ran a hand through her damp hair and sighed again. "Damn it. We should have just had a barbeque or a game night or something. You never would have acted like a Neanderthal if we would have just stayed home."

"I don't know babe; I can get pretty competitive when it comes to board games. I might have had a caveman moment…especially if my guys were involved in the game."

Savannah laughed, although Gabriel could tell she didn't really want to.

"I'm sorry that I was such an ass out there. I saw red the minute I saw his hands on your hips. That dress you're wearing had already killed my resolve and then to see someone else touching you, while your eyes were closed and you seemed so into it. I just…I lost it. I'm sorry."

"I know."

"I haven't been that angry since Jonathan died, Savannah, and this time it seemed so much worse. I haven't cared about anything or anyone as much as I care about you. Never think that you're the only one afraid or confused or ridiculously happy in this relationship because I'm right there with you. Just know that no matter what happens, I wouldn't change a thing."

"Neither would I," Savannah said, her voice barely a whisper. She took a step forward, closing the distance between them.

The anger they'd been feeling had subsided, replaced instead by sexual heat. He was still turned on from watching her dance and he could tell she was turned on as well. This was their first fight. It would be wrong to not take advantage of the make-up sex opportunity. It didn't matter to him that they were in Finley's club or that they were in the middle of some back hallway that led to who knows where. It didn't even matter to him that anyone could come by at any minute. He just knew that he needed to be buried deep inside of his girlfriend and soon.

Quickly, he pushed her back against the wall and captured her mouth with his. The kiss was rough, filled with everything he had felt since he saw her dancing with her friends. Moaning into his mouth, she ran her hands up his chest before tangling them in his hair. With one hand wrapped in her sweat dampened hair, he nudged her legs apart with one of his, the motion pushing her dress up her shapely thighs. His cock throbbed as he pressed it against her thigh, his other hand snaking over her other thigh and under the lace of her dress. When his hand came in contact with her bare center he let out a low moan.

"I knew you weren't wearing anything underneath this dress," he muttered against her lips.

"Panty lines," was all she was able to say before he ravished her mouth again.

He buried two fingers into her slick channel, scissoring them a little to open her up. His thumb pressed against her clit as he worked her with his fingers. With his other hand, he grabbed her wrists, pinning them against the wall above her head. With her trapped against the wall, he worked his fingers faster, loving the way she started to squirm as she got closer and closer to the edge. Within minutes she shattered around his fingers, his mouth catching her screams of pleasure.

With a smile, he removed his fingers and brought them to his lips. He sucked her juices from his fingers while she watched and then leaned in, kissing her long and hard, making sure she could taste herself on his tongue. Still keeping her hands pinned against the wall, he pushed her legs father apart so he could fit himself between her thighs after pushing his jeans and boxer briefs off of his hips.

"Please..." she begged as he brought her right leg up to wrap around his waist. Placing his free arm around her back for stability, he slipped inside of her, burying himself as deep as he could with the first thrust. He stilled, reveling in how she felt around him. He still hadn't gotten used to not having a latex barrier between them. It felt incredible, better than anything he'd ever experienced before. He had never been intimate with someone without a condom before, not even his ex-fiancée. He loved that this was another first he got to experience with Savannah.

"Oh god," he moaned as he started to pick up the pace of his thrusts, knowing that it was only a matter of time before someone came down the hall.

Savannah met his thrusts as best she could in her position. With her hips bucking against his, he pounded into her harder, felling his release nearing as her walls started to contract around him. He knew he wasn't going to last much longer, so he let go of her wrists and moved his hand between them to rub against her clit. Moaning loudly, she wrapped her other leg around his waist allowing him to thrust deeper and harder a few more times before they both came apart.

"Holy crap," she murmured a few minutes later. He still held her against the wall, but his legs were threatening to give out. He could feel her heart beating rapidly against his chest and she was still breathing heavily, he wasn't sure how she could even speak as his brain was only slowly forming coherent thoughts.

Sex with Savannah was always amazing, but there was something to be said about post fight sex. Not to mention sex in a near public place. His dick twitched just thinking about it. If they didn't leave soon, he wouldn't hesitate to take her again in Finley's club. He was definitely ready for round two.

"Yeah…although I hate fighting with you, I think I've become a fan of make-up sex. It is as great as everyone says it is."

"And up against the wall sex…definitely a new favorite for me."

Surprisingly, the position and the make-up sex were both firsts for Gabriel. Even given the volatile nature of their relationship, he never had either with Valerie. He was thankful now that there seemed to be a lot of things they never did during their time together.

"We should probably get back," Savannah said, breaking him from thoughts about his ex. "They're all probably wondering where we are, although probably not wondering what we've been doing."

"Which is probably a good thing since it's gonna be pretty obvious you've just been fucked. You've got that glow and your hair is a bit messed up, but I love it," Gabriel told her before he helped her lower her legs to the ground.

"And there's my caveman," Savannah said, straightening out her dress so it covered her assets once again. "Did you want to pull me back into the club by my hair?"

Gabriel laughed. "No, but I might want to tug on it a little bit when we go for round two later. Would that be okay?"

Instead of answering, Savannah just shook her head and laughed. Grabbing his hand, she pulled him back down the hallway toward the pounding music and their friends. Surprisingly, he no longer had a headache and this time he was pretty sure he wasn't going to have any problems joining his girlfriend on the dance floor.

****

"Are you sure you want to do this?" Savannah asked the uneasiness evident in her voice.

Gabriel smiled as he squeezed her hand trying to reassure her that he wasn't planning on backing out. They had been sitting in his truck in front of her parent's house for nearly ten minutes. Her family knew they were there, but Savannah was reluctant to get out of the car. From the minute he had picked her up, she tried to give him an out, telling him that she understood if he thought it was too soon to meet her parents. They had gone over everything that morning in bed, but she still wasn't convinced that this was the best idea. As he had driven to her parent's house, he could feel her tension grow the closer they got to their destination. The fact that she was so nervous about him meeting her parents surprised him. Especially after everything he told her earlier that day and every day since she'd invited him to the family barbeque. Her family sounded like everything he always wished his family had been.

"You have to stop worrying that meeting your parents is going to send me running, Sav. I'm not going anywhere," he told her again.

This was a step that Gabriel had wanted to take because he knew how important her family was to her. He met her sister and her best friend and they seemed to like him, but he knew that parents were usually harder to convince. He was worried that they would have the same preconceived notions about him that Savannah had regarding his tattoos and his job. Savannah told them a little about his history, but knowing and seeing were too different things.

Gabriel was determined that he had to win over those that meant the most to Savannah. There was no doubt in his mind that this was the woman he was going to marry someday and he wouldn't have a chance in hell at doing that if her family didn't approve. Once he convinced them that he was the one for their daughter, he'd have to convince Savannah. Sometimes he wasn't sure which was going to be more difficult, the family or the daughter. Savannah was ridiculously stubborn and sometimes obviously blind to how he felt about her. It didn't matter how long it took though, he would spend every day for the rest of his life, if he had to, convincing her that she was all he needed.

"I know, but I can't help it. They can be a handful, especially when it comes to my relationship status. I told you how Mom and Brook tricked me into the whole dating service thing. And you should have heard them whenever I'd report back about my dates.

They told me I wasn't trying hard enough and that I was sabotaging things on purpose."

"But she didn't know about me. If only you'd told her that you'd already found the one, you just couldn't date him, she probably would have given you a break," Gabriel laughed which earned him a light smack to the arm and a huge smile from Savannah.

"Gabriel, I've never brought a man home to meet my family. Brook is the only one who's ever met anyone that I've ever dated and that was only because she happened to be in the right place...or wrong depending on how you look at it. Really, I've never liked anyone enough to care what my family thought about them. I've never been more scared that someone is going to meet my family and run screaming because they're crazy."

Gabriel laughed. "I'm not averse to a little crazy you know. I have a feeling that everything is going to work out great. But no matter what you say and no matter how long we sit here, I'm going to meet your family tonight, babe, so we might as well just head in and get it over with."

Savannah sighed dramatically and then looked at him with her terror filled blue eyes. Within seconds the terror seemed to change to resolve; she knew she couldn't stall the inevitable any longer. She smiled up at him, grabbing her purse off of the floor next to her legs. With a deep breath, she pushed her shoulders back and opened the door so she could climb out. Gabriel laughed at the show she was putting on, like she was resolved to head into her execution instead of a nice dinner with her family. He followed her out of his truck and then met her on the other side so they could walk in together. Wrapping his arm around her waist, he gave her a quick squeeze before they started toward her parents' front door. This was definitely going to be an interesting evening.

Before they could even get part way up the sidewalk, the front door swung open, a woman who was maybe in her mid-fifties filed out onto the porch followed closely by a man about her age. Brooklyn and Finley stood behind them, both looking like they were up to no good. Savannah probably thought they were going to be on her side, but he had a feeling that Savannah's sister and best friend were only going to add to the craziness instead of leveling things out.

"Oh honey, he's even more gorgeous than you described," the older woman blurted out as she pulled Savannah into a hug. Before anyone could respond, she pushed Savannah away and pulled Gabriel into a tight embrace.

"Mom..." Savannah groaned.

"Oh come on Savannah, look at him," her sister said as she eyed him up and down.

Gabriel couldn't help but laugh which got him another smack on the arm from Savannah. Her mom seemed to think it was great that he was laughing at the situation. She grabbed his arm, a smile on her face while she introduced him to her husband. As she ushered him into the house, he looked over his shoulder to see Savannah still standing on the sidewalk, shock written all over her face. As soon as their eyes met, she scowled at him, which only caused him to laugh some more.

"Thank you for inviting me to your home today, Mrs. St. James. I've been looking forward to meeting you, although I almost feel like I know you all from everything that Savannah has told me."

"It's Rebecca dear. I'm so glad you could make it. I've been trying to get my daughter to bring you over since the moment I

184

found out about you. For a while I was wondering if she made you up to get us off her back."

"Mom!"

"It's true Savvy. I started to think Gabriel wasn't real. If it wasn't for your sister insisting he actually existed, I would have never believed you were dating someone until I met him, especially since he sounded too good to be true."

Gabriel watched as his favorite blush crept up Savannah's cheeks. It made him wonder what exactly she had said about him to her family. Maybe later he'd turn it into a game to see if he could coax it out of her, unless her mom decided to spill the beans first. Rebecca smiled at her daughter, either unaware or not caring that she had just embarrassed her eldest child. Gabriel figured it was more likely the latter. Rebecca St. James didn't seem oblivious; in fact, if Gabriel had to guess he'd say that everything she did was calculated. He wouldn't be surprised if the photo albums containing naked baby pictures of Savannah were already sitting on the coffee table ready to be shown to him after dinner.

"Now I'm curious to hear what your daughter's been saying about me. Hopefully, she hasn't been building me up too much. I'm

185

really not that great. Did she tell you how she didn't want to date me because she thought I was just a bartender?"

"Savannah!"

"Gabriel, really?" Savannah let out another sigh before walking past them into the kitchen. Gabriel laughed, knowing he was getting himself into trouble, but he really couldn't help himself. He kind of liked seeing her rattled. It didn't happen very often; Savannah was almost always in complete control; calm, cool and collected. But all of that went out the window as soon as they started to get ready to head to her parent's house. Gabriel really didn't understand why she was so nervous, but then he also wasn't close to his family. Odds were Savannah would never meet his parents, even though he was absolutely sure his mother would love her.

"Uh oh, looks like Savannah's about to lose it," Michael St. James announced with a snicker. "We should probably stop picking on her though. Poor Gabriel here probably hasn't seen that side of her yet. We wouldn't want to scare him away. Plus, if we let him continue to push her buttons, he definitely won't be getting laid tonight."

"Michael!" "Dad!"

186

Brooklyn and her mother yelled at the same time which only made Michael laugh. Gabriel had barely gotten to know these people, but he knew he liked them already. It was easy to see where Savannah got her humor and attitude from. This was what a family was supposed to be like; supportive, fun and humbling all wrapped up in a ton of love. The affection that the St. James family had for each other was plainly written on their faces and evident in the way they poked at each other trying to get a reaction.

Rebecca led him into the kitchen where Savannah stood unloading the salad ingredients they brought. Her cheeks were flushed and he could tell that her jaw was clenched tight. Gabriel really hoped she wasn't angry with him; that she knew everything he had done and said since he walked up to her parent's front door was in fun. Walking up behind her, he wrapped his arms around her waist and kissed her cheek. Her body started to relax a little, but he could tell that she was still a little tense.

"I'm sorry," he whispered into her ear.

"It's supposed to be us against them."

"But I want them to like me," he told her as he grabbed the salad dressing out of the bag. Since the bag was empty, he put his hands on Savannah's hips and spun her around so she faced him. She was sulking, refusing to meet his eyes. With his thumb, he pushed her chin up, forcing her to lift her head so he could look into her eyes. She looked anywhere but at his face, which only made him smile.

"Babe…impressing your family is important to me, but not if it means upsetting you. For the rest of the night it's us versus them and we are totally going to win."

With a laugh, Savannah wrapped her arms around Gabriel's neck. It was moments like this that Gabriel cherished. Even though he knew that her family and best friend were in the room, he didn't even notice them. In that moment, only he and Savannah existed. He leaned down, brushing his lips against hers in a chaste kiss. Her arms tightened around him as their lips met a second time and it was all he could do not to take things further. Thankfully, the clearing of a throat behind him helped keep him in check.

Breaking the kiss, he rested his forehead against Savannah's and waited to make sure she was okay. The beautiful blush that he loved so much covered her cheeks even though she didn't seem the least bit embarrassed by their public display of affection. She smiled up at him before removing her arms from around his neck so she could turn to face her family. Gabriel stole one more glance at Savannah before looking at her parents. Michael seemed to be fighting back a smile; the women on the other hand weren't trying to fight anything. Rebecca and Brooklyn had matching grins on their faces; even Finley had a knowing smile on her face, which from what he knew about the woman was something of a rarity.

"If you guys are done with the make-out session in my kitchen, I could use a hand with the grill," Michael said while trying to keep from laughing.

The women, once again, didn't bother holding in their laughter. Even Savannah started to laugh, to which Gabriel shook his head. He leaned down and kissed her on the cheek before following her father into the backyard. Laughter filtered out of the kitchen for a long time after he left, which reinforced in Gabriel that this was exactly what a family was supposed to be like. They enjoyed each other's company, ribbed each other good naturedly and seemed to support each other unconditionally. None of those things had ever been a part of his family and it made him sad to know that his brother might have never known what it was all about. He just hoped that Jonathan had been able to feel something like this with Lacey's family before he died.

"You know, I think in these situations I'm supposed to interrogate you and ask you what your intentions are for my baby girl, but after seeing that exchange in the kitchen, I have no doubt that you love my daughter."

"Savannah means more to me than anyone in the world."

"I've been worried about her. I know she's happy with the way her life's been going. She loves her work, but I've been worried that she's lonely and I never wanted that for her. I think her sister's divorce scared her more than she'd ever admit. For a while there I thought she planned on going through the rest of her life alone, which would have been fine with me if I thought that was what she truly wanted."

"Your daughter is fiercely independent sir. And stubborn. I think she wanted to prove to herself and others that she didn't need to have someone in her life to accomplish her dreams. Now that she's sure of that, she's open to being in a relationship. Honestly, I have to say I'm glad she waited or we never would have happened. Any earlier and I wouldn't have been in the right frame of mind...I wouldn't have been the right man for Savannah. Before Jonathan's death I was just going through the motions, living my life the way my father wanted me to. After my brother died, I was angry and wasn't really the best person to be around. It took years for me to get here. Now that I'm here, this is the only place I want to be. I want to spend the rest of my life with your daughter."

Gabriel watched Savannah's dad as he moved the steaks around on the grill. The older man didn't say anything for a long time which made him a little nervous. Instead of dwelling on the silence, Gabriel took in his surroundings. The St. James backyard was large and spacious with multiple levels. Off the deck was a grassy area that would have been a perfect play area for kids. He could almost imagine a young Savannah playing there with Brooklyn. On the left side of the yard were raised flowerbeds filled with a bunch of flowers he didn't recognize.

The far end of the yard was where Mrs. St. James' garden was. Savannah had told him about her mother's desire to grow every vegetable she could in the Washington weather. Some years she had a great turnout, other years it was a bust, but for as long as either of the St. James girls could remember, their mother had a garden in their backyard. Savannah often joked that it was how their parents stayed married for so long. Her mother would take out her frustrations on the weeds in the garden instead of on her father.

"Savannah has been an entirely different version of herself since you came into her life. She's practically glowing and just being around her, I can feel the change. She's happier than I've ever seen her and even though I know she's stressed out about the new opening, it's not at the same level that it's been in the past. You mellow her out, which is amazing to see and I have to thank you for that. But I also have to tell you, that if you ever hurt her, I'll have to kill you," Michael finally said his eyes showing the truth in his statement.

"I would expect nothing less sir. In fact, if I ever hurt her, you might have to get in line behind me, Finley and your other daughter. I appreciate what you're saying though and believe me when I say that I never want to hurt Savannah. I never want to be the reason that she is sad or angry or heartbroken. I will do everything in my power to make sure that doesn't happen."

Again silence overtook them as they finished cooking up the meat and peppers. Before anything else could pass between them the

192

women filed out onto the deck, their arms filled with bowls of food and bottles of wine; their laughter breaking the peace that the men had found. Michael plated the steaks and handed them to Gabriel before putting the vegetables he'd grilled onto a plate as well. Gabriel watched as his girlfriend's father, set the plate on the table and then leaned down to lovingly kiss his wife. He had never seen his parents show affection to each other, let alone when there were guests at the table. Once again he was struck with the recognition that this was what a real family was like and Gabriel had to admit that he loved being a part of something so warm and inviting.

Sitting down next to Savannah, he watched as she interacted with her family. Her face was lit up with excitement and happiness from being surrounded by the people she loved. This was what Gabriel wanted in his life. He wanted a family to share things with and he wanted to create a family like this one. He wanted to grow old with Savannah and have children with her so that someday, they could sit in their backyard meeting their children's significant other. Never in his wildest dreams did he think this was what he would ever hope for in life, but he also never knew what he was missing.

Someday, he would be the one kissing his wife while everyone looked on and he couldn't wait.

Chapter 7

After meeting her family, Gabriel became an even more
permanent fixture in Savannah's life. She had been scared that he
would run, not wanting to deal with the craziness that was the St.
James family, but he fit right in, like he was meant to be a part of the
clan. He didn't care if they teased him, but when they teased her, he
jumped to her defense and then harassed them right back. She loved
seeing him bond with the people she adored most.

Since that nerve-racking Saturday night, Gabriel had joined
her for more than a dozen meals with her parents and had gone out
or stayed in a bunch of times with Brooklyn and Finley. Whenever
they weren't with their loved ones or at work, they were together.
She had never felt more comfortable with another human being in

her life, especially not this quickly. In less than half a year, Gabriel had become an important piece of her life. He was her heart and she was terrified that something bad was going to happen. She loved him, but she couldn't tell him. It didn't matter that she knew deep down he felt the same way. Saying the words out loud was petrifying, mainly because Savannah had never said them to anyone outside of her family and Finley.

For the last week she realized how much she loved Gabriel. Even though they had been sharing the same bed, their schedules had kept them from actually spending time together. She would have to leave before Gabriel woke up and he would come home after she fell asleep. Occasionally, they'd wake each other up in the middle of the night for some fun, but it wasn't the same. Their relationship was about more than just the mind blowing sex. She wanted to spend time with him, talk to him about his day and tell him about hers. Not being able to spend quality time with him made her heart hurt.

For the first time in over a week, Savannah had been able to work her butt off to clear her schedule. With Brooklyn volunteering to work late, Savannah could surprise Gabriel at Arrow. Of course, he wouldn't be able to leave with her, but they could have dinner together and she could hang out with him until he could leave. He was working on hiring more staff so he didn't have to spend so many hours at the restaurant, but the process was slow going. Gabriel trusted Ray, Sylvia and Meghan, but he had to hire people to replace them before he could promote them, which had proved to be easier said than done.

"Are you sure you're okay to stay?" Savannah asked her sister again.

"Stay tonight and open tomorrow. I'm absolutely positive. You and your man need a good night together. Plus, what else would I do with my time? I'd much rather be productive here, than sit on the couch and watch another episode of Property Brothers at home."

Savannah laughed. "I owe you big time for this. I know I see him every day, but waking up to a sleeping boyfriend is not the same as actually hanging out with said boyfriend. Hopefully he can cut out a little early so we can have some quality time at home."

With one more thank you and a hug, Savannah left Brooklyn in the office at Delectable Delights and headed down the street to Arrow. She had grabbed a box of cupcakes before she left to give to the staff. Of course Sam still wasn't her biggest fan because of her pastries, but he was coming around. She even caught him eating one of her cupcakes the last time she dropped some by. It probably helped that she almost always ordered dessert when she was at the restaurant, whether she ate dinner or not.

Walking into Arrow, she waved at the new hostess and headed toward the bar where she figured Gabriel would be. She was surprised when she saw Ray there instead of her boyfriend. She scanned the rest of the restaurant to see if he was in the dining room before deciding that he was probably in his office. With the cupcake box in hand she started toward the kitchen to find her boyfriend.

"Hey Savannah, he's not here," Ray called out to her from behind the bar. Turning back around, she walked over to him a smile on her face to mask her confusion.

"He said he was going to be here working late. Did he step out for a bit or something?"

Ray nodded. "I'm pretty sure he doesn't plan on coming back. He's out with Donna for the evening."

Savannah felt her heart stop for a moment as Ray's words sunk in. Her boyfriend was out with someone named Donna…for the evening. He wasn't actually working like he said. Before she could ask any more questions, Ray was called away by a customer, but really Savannah had heard all she wanted to. Gabriel had lied to her. That was all that mattered.

Feeling tears fill her eyes, Savannah set the box of cupcakes down on the bar before hurrying out of the building. She did not need any of them to see her cry. No one needed to know the hurt she was feeling at Gabriel's betrayal. He knew how much she hated liars. They had gone over the deal breakers they each had before making their relationship official and dishonesty was number one on her list, followed closely by cheating. And here he was probably breaking both of them.

She felt like she'd been kicked in the stomach as she silently walked home. The tears kept threatening to fall, but she would not cry; especially not out on the street. The hurt would go away soon, replaced by the anger she could feel boiling in the pit of her stomach. Now she was glad she hadn't told him she loved him. It was obvious he didn't feel the same way and that she was wrong when she thought he did. He played her for a fool and she willingly walked right into it. Those were the thoughts that fueled her walk home.

Before she realized it she was in her kitchen trying to find a way to drown her sorrows and irritation.

Opening a bottle of wine, she wanted to feel numb. She didn't want to feel the pain or the anger. All she wanted to do was to forget she had stopped by Arrow; forget that Ray had shattered her world with one stupid name. Between glasses she tried to convince herself that she was wrong. That there was a simple explanation to the lie that Gabriel told her. Then the name Donna would flit through her head and she'd picture some Amazonian beauty with dark hair rubbing all over her boyfriend and her stomach would do flips, threatening to expel the alcohol that she inhaled.

At some point she must have passed out because the next thing she knew her front door was opening. Glancing at the clock, she realized a few hours had passed since she had first walked in the door. Instantly, the anger and pain filled her again and she didn't want to see him. She didn't want to hear his excuses; didn't want to know why he did this to her. Quickly, she poured another glass of wine, finishing the bottle she originally opened. She downed what little had been left and then stood to find another bottle to open.

Wobbling a little bit on her sleepy legs, Savannah grabbed the first bottle that looked good and opened it. As she poured another glass of wine, Gabriel finally made his way into the kitchen. He immediately pulled her into his arms, hugging her tightly against him. Her stomach lurched when he kissed the top of her head. She could tell he was happy and it just made her angrier. Pushing away from him, she walked back to her glass and filled it, downing it swiftly before filling it again.

She could feel his eyes on her; watching her, but she didn't want to look at him. Was their lipstick on his collar? Did he smell like her? She hadn't noticed when he was hugging her, but then again she hadn't been thinking about it. All she'd thought about was getting away from him before she threw up. Now her stomach was threatening to rebel because she couldn't stop picturing him with someone else.

"Babe, what's wrong with you?" Gabriel asked stepping toward her.

Savannah stepped back, one hand clenching the wine glass, the other pushing her chair in front of her to put something else between them. She took another long drink of her wine, wishing that she had been drinking out of the bottle instead. Gabriel was still watching her and she knew he was confused, but she was afraid to speak to him. She really didn't want him to know how bad he had broken her with his betrayal.

"How long has it been going on?" she asked her voice barely above a whisper.

"How long has what been going on? What are you talking about Sav?"

For the first time since he had entered the room, she looked at him. Concern was written all over his face until he looked into her eyes and saw the anger. Then that concern was replaced by confusion.

"How long have you been cheating on me Gabriel?"

Gabriel sighed, "Savannah are you drunk? What the hell is going on?"

"I stopped by Arrow tonight to surprise you. I got my work done and Brooklyn volunteered to work for me tonight and in the morning so that we could actually spend some quality time together. Imagine my shock when Ray told me you were out with Donna tonight and likely wouldn't be back."

"So you automatically assumed that I was cheating on you? You think so little of me do you? I can't believe that you could think I would hurt you like that, especially after what Valerie did to me...especially knowing how I feel about you."

"If you're not cheating on me, then who the hell is Donna?" Savannah yelled, her anger finally taking control.

"She's my real estate agent...a nice little 70-year-old lady who's been showing me some great commercial properties downtown. Sometimes her husband of over fifty years comes with us since they own the company together," Gabriel said with a sigh. "You inspired me Savannah, so I've been trying to find a place to open a new Arrow. I want to expand Jonathan's dream so Donna's been helping me find a way to do that. I've been working on it for a couple of weeks now, but I haven't really wanted to say anything because I wanted it to be a surprise. I just can't believe that you would think I could ever do anything to hurt you...especially something like that."

"What else was I supposed to think?"

"Have some faith in me Savannah...in us. I mean, can't you see how I feel about you? Don't you know that I would do anything for you? I haven't said anything before tonight because I didn't want to scare you off, but I don't understand how you can't tell that I am ridiculously in love with you. I'm so in love with you that I can't see straight. I think about you all the time. In fact, I think about you so often that I've actually called Meghan Savannah a few times at work. The girls think it's hilarious, especially since she looks nothing like you. Ray likes to make fun of me for it and I can't really blame him. I'm a lovesick fool because of you."

"Ww…ait…what?" Savannah stuttered, her shoulders slumping a little as she tried to process what she just heard.

"I love you Savannah. So much that it scares the crap out of me, but it also makes me feel more alive than I've ever felt before. I know that you are absolutely it for me. I would never jeopardize losing you by cheating on you."

"Gabriel…"

"Look, don't worry if you aren't ready to say it back. I know you will be and I can wait, but it's obvious that you needed to know so you'd never have another night of doubting me like this. I'm in this for the long haul. I'm not going anywhere unless you force me and even then I won't give you up without a fight."

The tears she'd been fighting hard against earlier, finally spilled down her cheeks as she looked over at Gabriel for the first time since she'd started yelling at him. She could see the sincerity in his eyes. He loved her and she knew it, but she'd talked herself out of it. What the hell was wrong with her? Deep down she knew he would never cheat on her, yet she allowed herself to think every horrible thing that he could have possibly done to hurt her. The whole time he was thinking about her and his brother. He was being secretive because he wanted to show her how she'd inspired him and she had turned it all to shit with her insecurities and craziness.

"God Gabriel, I'm so sorry. I don't know what the hell I was thinking, but I'm so sorry I ever doubted you. I love you too, but was too afraid to say anything because I was scared you didn't feel the same way. I'm such an idiot and I hate that it took such a screwed up moment for us to finally tell each other how we felt."

"Babe, I would have told you months ago if I thought you wouldn't run on me," Gabriel said as he rounded the kitchen table.

Savannah could tell that he was tired of the distance between them and honestly she couldn't blame him. She wanted his hands on her body, his mouth on hers. She wanted to show him how much she loved him and trusted him, even though her words and actions thus far had shown him otherwise. They needed to wipe this argument from their minds and remember the good that had come from it.

Gabriel pulled her into his arms and she gasped as his mouth met hers in a hungry kiss. His hands tangled in her hair, as her tongue traced the seam of his lips. He opened immediately, his tongue darting out to massage hers. Their pace was frenzied as they undressed each other, leaving clothes scattered down the hallway and up the stairs. They'd had make-up sex before, but Savannah could tell this was different. They weren't just making up after her stupid assumptions; they were officially going to make love. The thought sent chills down Savannah's spine, goose bumps pebbled on her arms.

Once in her room, hands roamed over bare skin, fingers traced valleys and plains while her lips made their way from his mouth, to his ear, down his neck. Only an hour ago, Savannah thought she'd never get this chance again; never want this chance again, how quickly things could change. She wanted to worship his body, show him how much she loved him, trusted him, even if her earlier words said otherwise. His bronzed skin was hot to the touch, his muscles quivered as she kissed her way over his pecs before dropping to her knees in front of him.

"Savannah, you don't…"

"I want to. Please. I want this," Savannah said.

In front of her was a perfect specimen of man, from head to toe, he was amazing. His cock jutted out from between masculine thighs, thick, rock hard and ready for her. Reaching out, she wrapped her hand around him, reveling in the feel of rigid steel encased in silky soft skin. With a firm grip, she stroked him from root to tip, until a delicious drop of moisture formed at the tip. Her tongue darted out to capture the drop of salty fluid before she looked up at him. Catching his eye, seeing the look of passion on his face, nearly did her in. She could feel the moisture pooling between her legs. Having control over his arousal was something that Savannah couldn't get enough of. She loved knowing that what she was doing…what she was about to do, was driving him crazy.

With one hand still gripping the base of his cock, she wrapped her lips around him, sucking him into her mouth as deep as she could, her cheeks hollowing in the process. Her free hand reached between his legs so she could massage his balls as she took him deeper, her tongue running along the underside. Every so often, she'd nearly let him fall from her mouth so she could take special care to suck and lick at the sensitive tip of his cock. Savannah knew exactly what she needed to do to make Gabriel lose his mind, the right amount of pressure, the right amount of suction to get him off. Gabriel's hips jerked, his hands tangling in her hair. She knew he wanted to take over, set the pace, but he wouldn't. While the act was about him, overall the moment was about them and she knew he didn't want to start the night coming in the back of her throat.

"Shit...Sav..."

She felt his balls tighten and knew she had to stop or things wouldn't go much further, at least not for awhile. Part of her wanted to let him come, to make up for the way she treated him earlier. She could wait to make love to him, he would take care of her in the meantime while he recovered from the orgasm, but she could tell that wasn't what he wanted. With one last hard suck, she pushed back, releasing his glistening cock from her mouth. Reaching between her own legs, she slipped a finger through her folds, knowing that he was watching every move she made. She looked up, her eyes meeting his.

"I think I'm ready," she purred.

Reaching down, he scooped her into his arms, her squeal of surprise making him laugh. When he deposited her onto the bed, she looked up at him, loving the way he looked at her. He wasn't just looking at her like he wanted to devour her. There was love there too; she had no doubt now that she had been seeing it there for a long time. Even if they'd both been too afraid to admit it, the feelings had been between them for awhile. She waited until he crawled onto the bed next to her, before making her move. Rolling him onto his back, she straddled him.

"I love you Gabriel Archer. I just wanted to tell you that again before I take you for a ride. I hope you don't mind, I'm kind of digging the being in control thing."

Savannah placed her hands on his chest, her fingers tracing along his pecs, down to his hardened nipples. Leaning forward, her ass in the air, she took one of his nipples into her mouth, sucking on the nub until he arched his back. Reaching behind her, she gripped his cock, positioning it ever so slightly so that it was in the right spot. Slowly, she sat back, lowering herself until his tip brushed against her entrance. She lowered herself a little further until just the head of his cock was inside of her and then a little lower until his eyes fluttered shut.

Gabriel gripped her hips, stopping her from pushing off of him like she had planned. Instead, he pulled her down until he was fully seated inside of her. A moan fell from her lips, the deliciously full feeling making her forget that she had planned on teasing him a little. She rotated her pelvis slightly before lifting up and then quickly lowering herself back down. From there she continued a frenzied rhythm, riding him hard and fast, her hands pressed against his chest for leverage. His hands moved from her hips to her breasts so that he could cup the heavy mounds.

He teased her nipples as she teased his. So many sensations were taking her closer to the edge, overwhelming her with the need to come, but she fought it off. She wanted them to come together, to go over together. Continuing the fast and furious tempo, she tried to ignore the tingling that was starting in her toes until she felt his cock jerk inside of her. That was her cue that she only had a few minutes, if she was lucky, before he would be emptying himself inside of her. Leaning over until their chests touched, she allowed him to take control of the thrusts so she could rub her pelvis against his, the pressure against her clit giving her the last little push she needed.

Gripping her hips harder, he thrust into her once, twice, before she felt the heat of his seed filling her. She cried out his name, her body squeezing his, milking him for every last drop he had to offer. She continued to move against him for another few minutes until the quaking inside of her body subsided. Sitting up, she felt their mixed fluids leak down her thighs, which for some reason always turned her on.

"I know that look on your face," Gabriel said from beneath her.

She smiled down at him, trying her best to look innocent. "What look?"

"The 'you better be ready for round two soon' look. You're already raring to go."

"Hey, it's not my fault that you've turned me into an insatiable sex fiend. I can't help myself whenever you're around."

Savannah laughed as he rolled them over; his semi-erect cock still buried inside her. Pinning her hands above her head, he crushed his mouth against hers. She bucked against him, her back arching off the bed, her breasts pressing against his chest. With her hands still trapped in one of his, he gripped her right hip with his other hand, holding her down so she couldn't move.

"Oh I know what I've created and I love it. I love you," Gabriel admitted. "And now, for round two, we're going to do things my way. I'm going to make love to you Savannah and it's going to be long, slow and perfect. I hope you're ready for a really long night because I don't plan on letting you go until I've had my fill."

Without another word, Gabriel lowered his head until he could suck one of her nipples into his hot mouth. His teeth scraped deliciously over her sensitive skin. If these were the kinds of things he planned on doing to her all night long, she definitely wasn't going to protest. She felt his cock hardening inside of her and she knew there was going to be no break before she was taken to the brink again and she didn't mind. This was what she had always wanted, a beautiful, caring man to make love to her. Now that she had him, she wasn't going to let him go.

****

The next morning, Savannah felt better than she could ever remember feeling. She was waking up in the arms of the man she loved who amazingly loved her back. There was a moment the night before when she thought she'd ruined everything, but Gabriel loved her and she knew now that he wasn't going to willingly give up on her even when she was being stupid. He was going to fight for her, for them, and that was the greatest gift that anyone had ever given her.

Rolling over so she was curled up against Gabriel's side, Savannah watched him as he started to stir. The arm wrapped around her waist, tightened, pulling her even closer against him. She wasn't sure how he did it, but no matter what, if they were in bed together, Gabriel was touching her. Either their legs were tangled together or his arms were around her. It made her feel safe, secure and most importantly loved; all things that she had never felt with anyone other than her immediate family.

"Hey babe," Gabriel said, his voice rough with sleep. His eyes slowly focused on her and she could see how much telling each other how they felt had opened him up to her. He was no longer guarded or wary and that made it easier for her to drop her guard too.

The last thing she wanted was to get hurt or to hurt Gabriel in the process, but she knew at some point she'd have to let go and trust in what they had.

"Hey sleepyhead."

"How long have you been awake?"

Savannah laughed as she placed a soft kiss on his bare chest, her fingers tracing over the colorful lines of the Celtic tattoo that flowed from his arm over his right pec. It was one of the many beautiful pieces of artwork that he had on his body. She loved to trace each of them with her fingers or her tongue.

"Only a couple of minutes. I was enjoying watching you sleep though. You looked so peaceful."

Goose bumps formed along her skin as Gabriel lightly ran his hand down her spine. "I want to take you somewhere today, to meet someone. You still have the day off right?"

"I am completely, 100% free for the day. Who do you want me to meet?"

"I want you to meet the most important person in my family, if that's okay."

Savannah smiled; Gabriel hadn't really mentioned anyone in his family aside from Jonathan and she was eager to get to know anyone who meant something to him. She knew that he didn't have a great relationship with his mother or father, so she had no idea who the mystery person could be, but whoever it was, it meant a lot to her that he wanted her to meet them.

An hour later, after a quick and very dirty shower, a bowl of cereal for breakfast and a quick stop at the grocery store for two mixed flower bouquets, Savannah sat in Gabriel's truck watching the scenery pass by as they headed eastbound on I-90. The sweet scent of the lilies, carnations and other flowers filled the cab, making Savannah's nose itch a little. She still had no idea where they were going or who she was meeting, but she was happy. Neither of them talked during the drive, allowing the radio to fill the silence. At first, she had watched Gabriel to see if she could get a read on where he was taking her, but his features gave nothing away. He was obviously thinking about something, lost in his head once again.. In the end, she gave up trying to figure him out and instead focused on the lake as they drove over it.

Before she realized it, they were slowing down and Gabriel was pulling off the main road into an area surrounded by a large wrought iron gate. The gate was pulled open allowing for traffic to come and go, but there was no signage that Savannah could see. It took a moment of driving for her to realize where they were. The headstones placed throughout the grass on either side of the road were all she needed to see to know who she was meeting. The realization made her heart break a little. Even in death, Gabriel's brother was the most important member of his family. She hated that it was like that for him, but was still overjoyed that he brought her to meet Jonathan.

"I hope this is okay. I know it's a little weird, but honestly, I come here a lot to speak to him; especially when I need guidance," Gabriel said as he pulled the truck into a parking spot and turned off the engine. He still looked straight ahead instead of at her. Removing her seatbelt, she turned so she could look at him.

"This isn't weird at all Gabriel. I can't begin to imagine how you feel, but I can say if it was Brooklyn buried over there, I'd probably be here every day telling her about my life...about you. I can't wait to meet your brother. I just wish I could've actually known him the way you do."

Gabriel looked over at her, unshed tears shining in his eyes as he reached for her hand. "Thank you for being so wonderful and for understanding me better than anyone else ever has. I love you so much; I hope you never forget that."

Savannah's chest ached as he brought her hand to his lips and kissed it softly. She could see the love he had for her in his eyes, could feel it in his touch. It seemed like everything changed in their relationship the night before when they admitted how deep their feelings ran. Things were more intense, more real, more amazing. Savannah had never felt like this before and in moments like this, she almost felt like she could drown in the emotions that filled the cab of his truck.

"We'll stop by Lacey's grave first, so I can leave some flowers there. I'm still so angry at my father for not allowing them to be buried next to each other. But I shouldn't have been surprised since he never thought Lacey was good enough for Johnny. He's such a selfish, uncaring bastard. I even told him that he could bury her in the plot he bought for me, but he refused. Pretty morbid that he already has plots purchased for the four of us isn't it? And ridiculous that he didn't think even further ahead and realize that Jonathan and I would probably prefer to be buried with the women we love and not the asshole that treated us so poorly."

She didn't know what to say to Gabriel's outburst. It was the most he had ever really said about his father, other than that they didn't talk. She could feel the anger seeping out of him. Richard Archer sounded like a piece of work; it was no wonder Gabriel hadn't spoken to him since Jonathan's death. Savannah was almost glad she wouldn't have to deal with the man if this is what he did to his own children.

"I'm sorry; this was supposed to be a nice moment. Come on, let's forget about my dad and go pay our respects."

They stopped at Lacey's grave first where Gabriel left one of the bouquets. There were already a few bouquets and single flowers resting there. It was obvious that people still visited Lacey often. The way Gabriel talked about her it was easy to see that she had been an amazing woman who was loved by many. How his father couldn't see that was beyond Savannah. It just proved again what a horrible human being he was. As they walked to their second destination,

Gabriel reached for her hand while admitting that he brought fresh flowers to both of them every other week. It was clear to Savannah that he missed his brother and Lacey more than he could ever express. It was also clear that he held on to some guilt and he hated that he almost let their father push them apart before Jonathan's accident.

"I should have been there for him. I should have spent more time with him instead of wasting time working or with Valerie or my dad."

Savannah didn't know what to say as they approached the ridiculously large Archer headstone. It spanned across an expanse of land that she guessed could hold 4 coffins given what Gabriel had said earlier. At the moment, only Jonathan's information was carved into the stone under the Archer name. Gabriel dropped her hand, so she stopped walking and let him go forward on his own. She had the sudden urge to step back, to walk away so she could give him privacy, but instead she stayed where she was and watched Gabriel approach the giant headstone. Kneeling down on the perfectly mowed grass, he propped the new flowers against the stone before picking up the dying bouquet that had fallen to the ground.

"Hey Johnny. I figured it was finally time to introduce you to Savannah. I know you were probably thinking she didn't exist, but she is definitely real. I never thought I'd find the type of love that you had with Lacey, but I was wrong. She is by far the best thing that has ever happened to me. She's my everything and ultimately, I have you to thank for bringing us together."

Gabriel looked back at her in that moment and her chest started to ache again. He held out his hand, beckoning her to join him. She walked forward, kneeling beside him in the grass, tears threatening to spill down her cheeks. The entire situation was new to her; being in love, dealing with the death of a loved one. She wasn't familiar with any of the emotions swirling through her and it nearly overwhelmed her. Taking a deep breath, she put her hand in Gabriel's, her eyes meeting his before he turned back to the headstone.

Before she realized what was happening, he had introduced her to Jonathan and then excused himself so they could talk. He stood and walked a little way down the walkway so that she was alone at the grave. She didn't know what to say or do; she almost felt silly sitting there talking to nothing, but this was important to Gabriel so she knew she had to say something.

"Hi," she said, her voice cracking slightly. "I'm new at this so please don't hold that against me. I love your brother more than I ever thought possible. I wish that I could have met you, but I know that your death is what brought Gabriel and I together. Sometimes, like right now, I hate that I am happy because of your loss. I promise I will do whatever I can to make your brother happy and to make your death worth something."

For another couple of minutes, Savannah told Jonathan about herself and her family and Delectable Delights. She still felt awkward talking to the cold slab of stone, but could tell why it made Gabriel feel better. There was something cathartic about getting things out even if there was really no one there to listen to what you were saying. By the time Gabriel rejoined her; she had practically given Jonathan her life story and told him all about her uncertainty about the new shop. She felt lighter, even though she also felt sad.

The promise she made Jonathan worried her. She hoped she could prove to be worthy of Gabriel. To be enough of a family for him, now that he had no one else. It was a tall order to fill, but she was going to do everything she could to make sure that she filled it.

He said she was his everything and she wanted to make sure he

didn't regret it. She just wasn't exactly sure how.

Chapter 8

"Hey, it's your turn to deal, stop texting your girlfriend and concentrate on the game man."

Gabriel looked up from his phone and flipped off his friend Braeden who sat on the other side of the table from him. "If you must know, I was actually texting with Ray since he's in charge of the restaurant tonight. I just wanted to make sure there weren't any fires that needed to be put out."

"Sure you were buddy," Braeden responded laughing at his friend. "Look at this place; it's pretty obvious that your girl has you whipped."

Looking around, Gabriel saw the small feminine touches that had invaded his home since he and Savannah started dating. Each time she stayed over something new would show up, not to replace what he already had, but to add to his décor; a blanket or throw pillow here, a framed picture there. He loved looking around and seeing Savannah in his house, but he knew that his friends would give him crap about it. Since the poker games rotated through each of their houses, this was the first time they had been at his place since Savannah had been spending more time there.

"I don't mind being whipped," Gabriel admitted. "I love that woman and come on…at least she's not replacing my stuff with hers; she's incorporating them all together. I don't have doilies and shit all over the house, like Paul did when Maryann moved in."

"Man, did you have to go there?" Paul asked his face turning a shade of red slightly darker than his hair.

"Oh yeah. That was some ridiculous shit man. I love that it was all a test though. To this day, I maintain that Maryann is one of the coolest chicks ever," Oliver piped up reminding them all why Paul's now wife had redecorated his entire apartment when they first moved in together.

"I thought Paul was going to lose his shit when we all walked in to that lacey, pink mess, but he just looked at her like she was the most amazing thing ever. Even after we all started laughing and giving him crap, he told her that she could do whatever she wanted to his place, since it was now their home. I wanted to gag, but he passed the test and I guess in the long run that was all that mattered," Gabriel said. "Now I completely understand why he let her do it. Love definitely blinds you to the little things. All that matters is her. Savannah could turn this place into a palace fit for a princess and that would be okay with me as long as she was with me."

"I, for one, am happy for you Gabe. It's about damn time you found the right woman and settled down."

Gabriel looked over at his best friend, surprised to hear Declan talk about settling down. He was the last person he expected to be happy for him given his past. He was weary of women, constantly worried about their motives and he had a right to be to an extent. Gabriel just hoped that Declan would eventually realize that not all women were the same and that there was someone great out there for him too. Perhaps a statuesque brunette that happened to be related to his girlfriend would finally be the one to break him out of his renouncement of relationships and women in general.

"Hey, I'm happy for him," Braeden said as he looked over at Declan. "Hell, I'd be even happier for him if he re-introduced me to Savannah's hot ass little sister. I'd love to take her for a ride."

Gabriel groaned, knowing exactly what Braeden was trying to do and by the look on Declan's face his plan was working. His jaw was tense; his face turning an angry shade of red, but Declan didn't say a word. Gabriel knew it was because his friend was trying to get Braeden to move on. If he didn't react, their friend would move on to something else, but Braeden didn't seem to want to stop. He continued to comment on Brooklyn and how gorgeous she was, all while trying not to laugh at Declan's clenched fists and scowling face.

"Dude, calm down, you look like you're about to explode. I'm just messing with you. I'm still a devoted follower of bros before hoes. I would never encroach on your woman, no matter how hot she is," Braeden finally relented.

"Hey, can we not call my girlfriend's sister a hoe please?"

"She's not my woman," Declan insisted. "She's so frustrating. I can't even be around her on deliveries without arguing with her. There's no way…"

226

"You can try to deny it all you want, but you're into each other. It's obvious to everyone but the two of you," Gabriel said earning a dirty look from Declan.

"I've only seen you around each other once and I could tell. Maybe it's not a love connection like Savannah and Gabriel, but there is definitely something between you. Could be you just need to fuck her out of your system and then go your separate ways, but I'm betting there's more to it than that," Braeden said with a laugh.

"Again man, can we refrain from talking like that about Brook? Hopefully, she's going to be my sister-in-law some day and I'd rather not have to kick your ass for being a dick about her."

"Sorry Gabriel, but you know I'm right."

Declan sighed, "look Brooklyn's hot and all, but she's a pain in my ass."

"Maybe a pain in the ass is exactly what you need. The few women you've dated since high school have either been pushovers or users. Brooklyn is neither of those. She'll definitely keep you on your toes and she's too damn independent to use anyone if she can help it."

"Yeah well I can't really deal with that kind of crap when I have Erin to worry about," Declan said, running an angry hand through his messy black hair.

"You also can't keep using Erin as an excuse not to be happy. She's old enough for you to talk to her about what you want in life. She'll be heading off to college soon and then what will you do with yourself?"

Slamming his hand down on the table, it was obvious that Declan had enough of their crap. "What the fuck you guys? I thought we were here to play poker and give Gabriel shit about his love life. Can we just get back to that? I'm not going after Brooklyn. End of story."

Gabriel shook his head, trying not to laugh at his friend's outburst. "Whatever you say man, hand me the cards."

"Fuck you guys," Declan mumbled as he passed the cards to Gabriel.

That was all it took to break Gabriel's hold on his laughter. The rest of the men broke down as soon as he did, which only pissed Declan off even more. As he shuffled the cards, he looked around at his friends and realized that it wasn't only Savannah that had made him happier than he had been in years. He was finally feeling like himself again and getting to hang out with guys he had known since high school definitely helped that feeling. He was grateful that he had them in his life again. He was lucky they wanted anything to do with him after the way he treated them when he was with Valerie and then after Jonathan died. Sometimes he wondered if he deserved their friendship, but he definitely wasn't going to question it. He learned the hard way that life wasn't worth living if you didn't have people to share it with. He would never make that mistake again.

"So Braeden, when are you going to find a good woman and settle down? Don't you think it's about time to give up the playboy way? You too, Oliver? Aren't you both a little old for that?"

Gabriel ducked when one of Savannah's throw pillows was hurled at him. Unfortunately, he didn't see the Cheeto coming from his left until it smacked into his face. The room filled with laughter as he wiped cheese dust off of his face before picking up the Cheeto and throwing it into his mouth.

"Thanks for sharing Oliver, I was a little hungry, although you missed my mouth there buddy."

Oliver flipped him off, a scowl on his face that he couldn't hold for long. "Screw you Gabe. Just because you and Paul have found your ball and chain doesn't mean the rest of us want to or are even meant to. Plus, we aren't old. Look at Hugh Hefner, we've got a ton of playboy years left in us."

"Yeah well A) Hugh was married once and B) he's Hugh freaking Hefner, he's rich and connected, of course he can be a playboy until he dies. Maybe if you get married and divorced and then start a nudey mag, then you could become the next Hef and be a playboy until you die, otherwise I don't think it's going to work that way for you."

"Thanks for raining on my parade," Oliver said before throwing another Cheeto at Gabriel. This time Gabriel was fast enough to catch the Cheeto in his mouth.

"In all seriousness though, I want what Paul has, what you have, but until I find the one, I'm going to have fun with the many. Is there something wrong with that?" Oliver asked.

"No man, there's nothing wrong with that," Gabriel admitted as he started to shuffle the cards again. He couldn't fault his friend for not wanting to be alone; for wanting to find pleasure where he

230

could. He just hoped that Oliver found what he was looking for soon and that he didn't let Braeden and Declan hold him back. If either of those two ever fell in love, Gabriel would have to assume that the world was ending since neither of them wanted the family life that he and the others wanted.

Gabriel smiled as the thought of starting a family filled his head. After Jonathan died, he figured he would never find happiness that he would spend the rest of his life alone and then she walked in and he was a goner. Now a future with Savannah, their kids running around the backyard, was all he could think about and he loved it. He couldn't help, but hope that his friends would all someday find the happiness that he had found. He didn't care if that made him sound like a girl or a fool, love was what mattered and he knew now that everyone deserved to find it.

"Enough of this sappy shit, are we going to play cards or what?"

****

Gabriel couldn't believe how much his life had changed in the six months since Savannah walked through the door of his restaurant and sat at his bar. It didn't matter to him that they had only officially been a couple for three of those months; his world was rocked the minute she looked up at him. He'd made some major decisions during that time and today he was solidifying the biggest one yet. Looking over at the picture of Savannah on his desk, he smiled. The feeling he got when he thought of her or saw her proved that no matter what anyone else said, he was making the right decision.

It didn't matter to him that people would say he was moving too fast. He knew, beyond a shadow of a doubt, that he was meant to spend the rest of his life with Savannah St. James. Weeks ago he had picked out a ring for her; today he was going to make sure that the ring passed her best friend Finley's approval before he finally gave the jeweler his money. He couldn't wait to officially make Savannah his and as soon as Finley saw the ring, he didn't have to. He just wished she'd hurry up.

Anxiously, he looked around at the other additions to his office. All of them were pictures of Savannah. Some with him, some with their friends, but always with her beautiful face smiling at the camera or at him. He was supposed to be concentrating on the stack of paperwork on his desk, but between the butterflies and being easily distracted by his girlfriend, he was having a difficult time comprehending what was in front of him. Reluctantly, but with great motivation from Savannah, Gabriel had finally hired more help at the restaurant and had relinquished a lot of the day to day work to focus on continuing Jonathan's dream of expanding Arrow. He had always wanted a bunch of locations and probably would have had two others open by now if the accident had never happened. On top of the business expansion, Jonathan would have been married to Lacey with at least two kids running around by now too. His brother was always the one with ambition and Gabriel was always the one that felt obligated to take the hit so Jonathan could do whatever he wanted.

Now that Gabriel was out from under his dad's thumb, he was bound and determined to do things right. Making Jonathan's dream a reality was one of the things he wanted...no needed to do and that included both the expansion of Arrow and the perfect family. He just hoped that Savannah was on the same page.

That was really where he hoped Finley was going to come in. He not only wanted her opinion on the ring, but he also wanted to gage what Savannah's reaction would be. Savannah was still sometimes skittish; sometimes worried that they were moving too fast or that things were too intense and serious. For a woman who had been looking for a stable, committed relationship, she sure was wary of what he was offering her and it was making him a little restless. There was nothing in the world that he wanted more than to be her everything; she just needed to let him.

He tried again to concentrate on the list of locations that his real estate agent had given him. There were still a ton of places to look at, but he wasn't sure what the best option was. Although Savannah was in the middle of her own expansion, it was probably time that he asked for her opinion on the matter. She had more experience running a successful business than he did. Plus, if they were going to have a future together, he wanted her to be involved in the growth of Arrow, to feel like she had a say in what happened to the restaurant.

Thankfully his contemplation was interrupted by a knock on the door. Without waiting for him to answer, Finley walked into his office. Her jet black hair was streaked with a deep red and pulled up into a messy ponytail. Paired with the black tank top, dark blue jeans and the combat boots she wore, it was obvious to Gabriel that she had come from the club. The smudge of dirt on her forehead told him she had likely been accepting deliveries before coming to meet him.

Just as he figured she would, she crossed her arms against her chest as soon as she was in the room. The placement of her arms pushed up her more than ample breasts, but he barely noticed because of the look on her face. She was smirking at him, the overheard light glinting off the two hoops pierced through the left side of her bottom lip. She looked skeptical and he really couldn't blame her. His plan was crazy and impulsive and he had to admit, scary as hell. All thoughts of teasing her about the dirt smudge vanished as he waited for her to lecture him.

"Are you sure about this? Do you know what you're doing?" Finley asked, the smirk never leaving her face.

"No....Yes...Maybe?" he answered before standing up and walking around to meet her at the still open door. "It feels right. Everything about her...about us, feels right. God, I just hope that this

235

doesn't scare the shit out of her. I don't want her to try and run away from me."

"You guys haven't been together that long."

"And I'm not planning on proposing tomorrow unless the moment is there. I want to though, don't get me wrong. I want to propose tomorrow and marry her the next day so I know that she is mine," Gabriel admitted. "I've been engaged before Fin and it never felt like this, not even when the relationship was new. Savannah is it for me and no amount of time will change that."

Finley smiled up at him, "That's all I needed to hear. You've got my support; now let's go see if your taste in jewelry is as impeccable as your taste in women."

Gabriel followed Finley out through the kitchen and into the dining room where he left instructions with Sylvia and Meghan. They had been amazingly helpful with transitioning from him being there every minute of every day to him taking time off here and there. He was hoping to give them the recognition they deserved by promoting them both to management positions, but wasn't quite sure how to work it out. It would be nice to know that he could not come in for an entire week if he didn't want to or if he had plans with Savannah. He knew in all likelihood the girls and the rest of the staff could definitely handle him not being there. They had done it right after Jonathan's death when Gabriel still wasn't sure what to do with the restaurant. Now though, he wasn't sure he could let go enough. Being a control freak was something he inherited from his father and something he hoped he could get over someday.

They walked the few blocks to the jewelry store in silence. She was busy text messaging the manger of her nightclub and he was too busy thinking about the possibilities for his future. Everything seemed to be coming together for him both personally and professionally. The only thing that he wished was that his brother was still alive. The only problem with that was if Jonathan was alive, Gabriel would likely still be miserable working as a lawyer and probably miserably married to Valerie. It made Gabriel sad to think that if Jonathan was around, then the happiness that he was so wrapped up in wouldn't exist. He'd just be the Gabriel that let his dad dictate what he did with his life even though he hated everything about it.

"Oh Mr. Archer, it's so good to see you again," Mr. Flannery said as he and Finley walked through the door of Flannery and Sons. The jewelry store had been a West Seattle staple since before the old man had even been a thought in his parent's heads. Now, even though he was well into his 70s, he spent most of his time at the store and had helped Gabriel pick out the perfect ring when he'd come in weeks earlier. He'd also been patient with him when he came in nearly every day since to look at it.

"Is this the lucky lady?"

"No, Mr. Flannery, this is Finley, the lucky lady's best friend. I wanted her to see it just to make sure I picked out something that Savannah would love. If Finley approves, then I'll go ahead and take the ring today."

Finley looked around the shop as Mr. Flannery went to pull the ring out of the vault. Gabriel paced in front of the case, his nerves nearly getting the better of him. He was on the verge of a life-changing moment; one that he couldn't predict the outcome of. If he was honest with himself that had pretty much been the case during his entire relationship with Savannah, even before they actually started dating. From day one, he wasn't sure exactly what he would get from her and part of him liked that she kept him on his toes. But then he wasn't always fond of the rolling feeling he got in the pit of his stomach when he tried to figure out what she was thinking about their future together. There was no doubt in his mind that he wanted her to be his future, but did she want him? His palms began to sweat as he thought about Savannah and the uncertainty she made him feel.

"Alright, Mr. Archer, here she is," Mr. Flannery said interrupting Gabriel's thoughts. Finley stopped walking around and headed back to the case where the older man was opening the black ring box that housed the perfect ring for Savannah. He heard Finley gasp before she reached out to grab the box out of the old man's hand. She held the ring up to her face so she could get a closer look at it.

"Oh Gabriel, its fucking perfect," she muttered before looking up suddenly at the jewelry store proprietor. "Shit...sorry. I didn't..."

"It's alright young lady, it is fucking perfect," Mr. Flannery said.

They all laughed as Finley continued to stare in awe at the ring. It was made of solid white gold with two elements on each side that twisted together to meet the 1.5 carat oval cut diamond in the center. One strand on either side was made of several tiny diamonds that sparkled in the overhead light. When he had come looking for a ring, Gabriel thought it would take him forever to find one that he thought fit Savannah and her personality. The minute Mr. Flannery pulled out the tray and he saw the ring that Finley was now oohing over, he knew it was the one. Everything about the ring screamed Savannah. It was classic, yet not overdone. He knew she wouldn't appreciate a huge diamond that would get in her way and cause problems, but he also knew that she loved beautiful things. The center diamond of the ring was a little flashy, but not over the top.

He let Finley continue to examine the ring while he pulled out his wallet so he could pay Mr. Flannery. He handed the older man his credit card and waited while he rang him up and then handed him the slip to sign. There was no going back now, but that didn't matter. The nerves were absolutely non-existent now. Whether Savannah balked or not, she was his future. She would wear his ring someday, even if he had to wait months, even years. There was no doubt in his mind that he would make it happen.

Once the transaction was finished and he finally wrestled the ring away from Finley, he tucked the box into his pocket where it would stay until he could put it into the safe at Arrow. He couldn't take it home in case Savannah found it too soon and the safe was really the only secure place he could think of to put it. He just needed to make sure that he hid it from Sylvia and Meghan and even Ray. Those three wouldn't be able to keep his secret and Savannah would know about the ring before he even had a chance to propose.

Lost in thoughts about Savannah, Gabriel parted ways with Finley outside the jewelry store. She had to head back to the club to get ready for the night and he had to get back to Arrow to prepare for the dinner rush. He hoped that Savannah would be able to come visit him at work that night, but she was getting busier and busier as the countdown to the new opening began. Even with her sister helping out, things were becoming even more chaotic than usual. He couldn't help the smile that spread across his face as he thought of Savannah wrapped up in that chaos. No matter how hard she tried, she always ended up with flour or some other ingredient on her clothes, skin or hair. It was one of the many things that he loved about her.

So wrapped up in picturing how Savannah probably looked at that moment, Gabriel didn't notice the person that was standing outside of Arrow. If he had, he might have turned around to avoid her, but by the time he reached her it was too late to make an escape. She said his name softly, her voice cracking half way through. Something was wrong, he knew just by looking at her. There was no way, she would have ever been caught dead looking the way she did, eyes puffy and red from crying, her nearly perfect face devoid of all make-up, her designer clothes mismatched and hanging off of her body. Although he never wanted to lay eyes on her again and had told her so when he broke it off with her, now that he was looking at her, he knew something wasn't right and all he wanted to do was pull her into his arms. Instead, he stood there too stunned to speak until finally all he could do was say her name.

"Valerie."

Chapter 9

Savannah knew she should be working. The pile of things she needed to do was only getting bigger, but she couldn't focus on anything other than Gabriel. Things between them had been nothing less than intense since they'd gotten together. She was undoubtedly in love with him and he was in love with her, but sometimes she felt like they were moving too fast. Deep down she knew that it was because she was scared about getting hurt. The way she felt about him, he could easily destroy her if he ended things and she hated knowing that. She hated that her happiness, her well-being was dependent on someone else.

But that was what being in a relationship was all about and it was what she had been searching for when she decided she wanted

243

to find someone to share her life with. She knew the risks, the consequences. She had no idea why she was now suddenly scared of how things were going to work out. From the start, she knew that there was a chance that she'd end up brokenhearted like her sister, but there was also a chance that she'd spend the rest of her life with her soulmate like her parents.

Her brain had been working overtime lately, dwelling on all of the possible bad outcomes of her relationship with Gabriel. She knew where her issues were coming from and why she was only thinking about the bad things. It was because of Valerie and her sudden reappearance in Gabriel's life, when she walked back into his life two weeks earlier with the news of her father's death. Since then, Savannah felt like a third wheel, but only on the rare times she actually got to spend time with Gabriel. On every other day, she almost felt like she was single again. Sure she'd occasionally get a phone call or a text to check in with her, but for the most part she'd barely heard from or seen Gabriel since Valerie showed up.

Savannah understood that they were grieving. Hank Meadows was more of a father to Gabriel, than his own dad had ever been. Even after he and Valerie called it off, Gabriel tried to keep in touch with Hank, but since Gabriel had taken all the blame for the break up, Hank wasn't always receptive. Eventually, they lost contact and now he was gone. Gabriel admitted to her, more than once, that he felt guilty about letting their relationship dwindle. Since Hank's death, Gabriel had shut her out, never letting her in on how he was feeling. It was obvious the same wasn't true with Valerie. They were sharing something that he should have been sharing with Savannah and it hurt that he wasn't.

All she could do was hope that it would pass and that he would come back to her. The nightmares that had him returning to Valerie would go away and her insecurities would be erased. She just had to remember that Gabriel loved her. He told her so whenever they talked or texted and he had told her sister, her parents and her best friend numerous times. There wasn't any doubt that he loved her and wasn't likely to stop, but was it enough to keep him with her? Did he love her more than Valerie? The two of them were friends first, before they were together for six years. At one point they were going to get married. There was a lot of history between them. Savannah and Gabriel had only been together for a few months and while he said he never felt for Valerie the way he felt for her, what did that really mean?

"You need to stop thinking and start talking," Brooklyn said. She sat in one of the chairs in front of Savannah's desk a scowl marring her pretty face. Savannah sighed knowing that if she didn't fess up her sister wouldn't leave things alone. Brooklyn knew something was wrong just by looking at her. They had always been able to read each other, which was how Savannah knew things weren't right between Brook and her ex-husband long before Brooklyn was ready to admit it.

"There's really nothing to say. I'm just feeling sorry for myself."

"He loves you, you know that."

Savannah sighed again, "That's not the point. I miss him Brook. He's my boyfriend, we're supposed to support each other through difficult times and he barely even sees me. I haven't spoken to him in two days; all I've gotten are text messages letting me know he's hanging out with "Val". He didn't even want me to go to the funeral with him. And then after the funeral he spent all night drinking with her. I found them passed out on his couch the morning after when I went over to make him breakfast. Her head was in his lap, his arm draped over her. I keep seeing that picture in my head."

"You don't think..."

"God no...at least I don't think so. Gabriel's not the cheating kind. Even if he's grieving, I don't think he'd do anything physical with her. But I'm not gonna lie. His going to her instead of me in regards to his emotional needs is threatening to break my heart Brook. I don't know if I can deal with this much longer."

Brooklyn leaned over, reaching across the desk to take her sister's hand. "You need to talk to him. Tell him that you want to be there for him and how you feel about Valerie."

"Is it horrible that I think she's using their shared grief as a way to get back into his life? She only looks that sad when Gabriel's next to her. There've been times where I've seen her on the phone and she looks like nothing has happened. Then when Gabriel is with her you'd think the world has ended and Gabriel is the only one who can soothe her broken heart. I don't trust her. And I know for a fact that this isn't the first time that she's come sniffing around Gabriel since he broke it off with her. I'm afraid this time she might get what she wants."

Savannah closed her eyes trying to fight back the tears that had filled them. The more she talked about it, the more she worried that she was losing Gabriel to his ex. She knew Brooklyn was right and that she needed to talk to him about it, but she was scared of what he might say. What if she confronted him and he told her that it was over? What if he told her that she was wrong about him and he had slept with Valerie? The thought made her sick to her stomach and the tears she had been fighting off squeezed past her eyelids.

"Go to him Savvy. No matter what, at least you'll know where you stand. You won't have to spend all day wondering what's going on and where his loyalties lie. And if things don't work out, I'll cut his balls off for you and I'm sure Finley will have her own imaginative way of making him pay for hurting you," Brooklyn said as she squeezed Savannah's hand.

Savannah wiped her eyes and checked the clock over her office door. It was just after four in the afternoon and she knew that Gabriel should be at Arrow. He had been planning on finally getting back to work after taking time off. Savannah just hoped he was actually there and that he was without his sidekick. The last thing she needed was to try and have the conversation with her around.

She needed as much of Gabriel's undivided attention as she could get.

Thankfully, she was working in her West Seattle office so she wasn't far from Arrow. She shut down her computer and grabbed her purse. When she turned toward the door, her sister was standing near the chair she had been sitting in. Quickly she flung herself into Brooklyn's arms and gave her a much deserved hug. Her sister always knew the right thing to say and had been nothing but a huge help over the last couple of months, both personally and professionally. Savannah wasn't sure that she'd have survived without Brooklyn and she was pretty sure that her sister felt the same way about her. They were more than sister's, they were best friends and Savannah knew she was lucky to have Brooklyn in her life.

Savannah let Brooklyn walk her out, reveling in the moments that they got to spend together no matter how small. She sucked up the strength that her sister was offering her and headed toward Arrow. It took her no time at all to reach the restaurant that had changed her life. Sylvia was behind the host stand when she walked through the door. She offered Savannah a hug and a smile and then told her that Gabriel was in his office. A scowl and a look toward the bar caused Savannah to follow her gaze. Sitting at the bar on Savannah's stool was Valerie. Gabriel had always made sure that the stool was free for her even after they had started dating. Her heart sank as she took in the beauty that seemed to be taking her place.

Valerie's thick black hair curled down her back and over her shoulders. She wore a skin tight white dress that seemed shorter than all of the barely there skirts that Savannah had seen her wear previously. On her feet were mile high red stilettos that Brooklyn always liked to call "fuck-me pumps". There was no doubt in Savannah's mind that was exactly the kind of thing Valerie had in mind. As if she knew she was being watched, Valerie turned toward the hostess stand, her eyes meeting Savannah's. Her eyes were ringed in dark black eyeliner making the grey blue color pop more than usual. Her lips a deep, dark red made her look like the man eater that she was. Valerie smiled at Savannah and raised her glass before turning back to watch Ray behind the bar. She didn't even wait for Savannah to react and that pissed her off. Valerie wasn't threatened by Savannah's presence and that spoke volumes to her.

With a forced smile, she thanked Sylvia and headed through the dining room, into the kitchen until she reached the hallway where

Gabriel's office was located. Her palms started to sweat, her heart racing. She felt like she was going to throw up, but she forced herself to continue forward. His office door was ajar and she could hear his voice coming through the opening. From what she could hear it sounded like he was on the phone with a supplier and when he said the name Declan, she knew who he was talking to. But the conversation was obviously all business even though Declan was Gabriel's best friend. It seemed she wasn't the only one that Gabriel was pushing away with his grief.

As the conversation died down, Savannah knocked lightly on the door before walking into the office. Gabriel barely looked up from his desk before holding up a finger to let her know that it would be a minute. It was the coldest greeting she had ever gotten from him and it hurt. Even at his busiest he had always smiled at her. If he was on the phone, he would motion for her to come to his side of the desk so he could kiss her. But all of that was apparently in the past. Today, he kept his head down, continued his conversation and   . motioned for her to take a seat in a chair she'd never seen before.

His office was tinier than most and the chair barely fit between the desk and the open door with any room for someone's

251

legs. She quietly closed the door behind her and then adjusted the chair so it wasn't so close to the desk. It had been at least a week since she'd been in his office, but aside from the chair and a new frame that was on the wall to her right, the room looked the same. Curious, she moved past the chair to look at the new picture. She needed to make sure her eyes weren't playing tricks on her and they weren't. In the frame that was now hanging in a prominent place in Gabriel's office was a picture of Valerie and Gabriel and an older man that Savannah assumed was Hank Meadows. Valerie and Gabriel were staring into each other's eyes, holding hands, looking very much in love while Hank stood next to Gabriel, his hand patting Gabriel on the back, a huge smile on his face as he looked at the two of them. Her stomach was in knots as she got closer to the picture. In the background were balloons and party favors and when she looked at the entwined hands of her boyfriend and his ex, she saw the ring on Valerie's hand and instantly realized that the picture was likely from their engagement party.

Savannah felt like she'd been punched in the stomach. She couldn't catch her breath as she tried to walk back to the tacky chair that she figured had to have been purchased by Valerie. The model probably got tired of the uncomfortable break room chairs that Gabriel would usually bring into the office and wanted something that was comfortable since she rarely seemed to leave his side. She barely made it to the chair before her legs gave out on her. The room seemed to spin as she started hyperventilating. All she needed to do was calm down, but in that moment, where she felt like her world was ending, that was easier said than done. She just had to remember that the picture and the chair didn't mean anything. In fact, they both made Valerie's motives even more suspect.

With that thought in mind, Savannah tried to still her breathing, but when she finally looked at Gabriel's desk, her breath caught in her throat. The last time she had been in the room, there had been three pictures on his desk, one of him with his brother, one of her by herself and then one of them together. Now, all three pictures were face down on the desk, papers strewn over the top of them. Did Gabriel even notice? Or was he the one who had knocked them over in the first place? She was freaking out and had no idea how to stop herself. This was exactly what she'd been afraid of. He was going to break her heart and there was nothing she could do to stop him.

As she continued to try to compose herself, she heard Gabriel end his phone call. She looked up at him hoping that he would finally notice that she was there, but he just kept looking down at the desk writing feverishly on a notepad. Savannah waited, figuring that maybe he needed to just finish what he was doing before he could give her his attention. When he looked up at her and set his pen down, she felt relieved to be right.

"What are you doing here Savannah? I thought I told you I was busy tonight," he said, his voice rough and unfriendly.

"Too busy to stop for a second and have a conversation with your girlfriend or just too busy for me in general? I noticed Valerie was already sitting at the bar in my spot waiting for you."

"Valerie can sit wherever she wants. She knows it'll be a while before I'm able to get out there, if at all. I've got a lot to catch up on after missing the last two weeks. I don't really have time for anything else right now."

Savannah bit the inside of her lip, willing the tears that she knew were coming to fade away instead. She would not cry about this; not in front of him. But the way he was speaking to her made her want to break into a thousand pieces. There was something she

254

had to say and then she would leave. She would put everything into his hands, the ball in his court. It would be up to him where they would go from here, but there was one thing that she knew for certain. Never again would she let someone treat her the way he had been treating her the last two weeks. Grief or no, she was worth more than that.

"I know you're hurting right now Gabriel. I'm sure Hank's death brought up memories of Jonathan, but I'm your girlfriend, not Valerie. In case you've forgotten, she cheated on you for months with one of your best friends all while you were planning your wedding. When you're hurting, you're supposed to come to me, rely on me. I love you and I thought you loved me too. I want to be here for you, but you've shut me out and you have no idea how much that hurts me."

Gabriel made a noise that sounded like a snarl, but Savannah couldn't believe that was what she heard. But when he swiped his hand along the top of his desk, knocking papers and one of the frames to the floor, she realized that no matter what the sound actually was, it came from deep within him and it scared her. Trembling, she fell from the chair, kneeling down to pick up the frame and whatever else she could. As she set it down in front of her, she noticed that the glass in the frame was broken and had sliced through the picture inside. It wasn't lost on her that the picture was the one of the two of them and that the slice was nearly directly down the center of the picture.

"Don't talk to me about hurt Savannah. You've never lost someone the way I have. You don't know what I'm going through. Only Val knows what I'm going through."

"I don't trust her Gabriel. I don't trust her motives where you're concerned. It's not all about her dad with her; it's about getting you back. Look at that fucking picture. I'm sure there were better pictures of her dad that she could have put up for you, but instead she chooses one that is of the two of you so in love with each other you don't even notice the camera? Bullshit."

"Savannah," Gabriel sighed. "I'm not interested in Valerie that way. I just need someone who I can talk to about her dad and Jonathan. You didn't know either of them and you don't understand my guilt either. I can't...damn it. I can't talk to you about this right now. Or ever. Just let me deal with this my way and we'll be fine."

Savannah just stared at him unsure what to say. He was obviously brushing her off. He didn't care about her feelings or her reservations about Valerie. And not once did he give her any kind of assurance that he loved her. Just that they'd be fine once he was done grieving with Valerie. She was no longer just hurt, she was furious. Standing in front of his desk, she clenched her fists at her sides fighting the urge to punch something.

"So how long am I supposed to wait for you Gabriel? How long am I supposed to let my boyfriend get black out drunk with is ex-fiancée and not be hurt by it? I don't think you've betrayed my trust yet, but it's only a matter of time before she gets you in a compromising position and then will you be able to say no? What if being with her is what you need to dispel your guilt, your grief? I'm sure it'd be really easy for her to convince you of that while you're drunk out of your mind."

"I.."

"No. Don't say anything. I don't even want to hear you speak right now. I feel like my heart is being ripped out of my chest, yet I'm so mad I want to smash my fist through that fucking picture that she put up. I know you're hurting Gabriel, but you need to think long and hard about what we have. Is it worth losing us over your guilt and your grief? If it is, then so be it. But you need to have the decency to tell me. I'm not going to sit around and wait for you to be ready to be with me again. I have a life I want to live. I wanted to do that with you, but I can't be with someone who doesn't want to let me in. I may not know what it's like to lose people I love to death, but I'm sure learning and you're right…it hurts like hell. But the really fucked up thing…you're not dead."

Without another word, she marched out of his office, her head held high, shoulders back. She would not allow herself to cry, instead she forced herself to smile as she waved at the sous chef and line cooks that she knew. By the time she reached the dining room, she wished she had gone out the back door. Her shoulders shook with the sobs that wanted to escape from her chest. Eyes burning with unshed tears, she hurried through the restaurant with a wave over her shoulder at Sylvia and Meghan. Once outside, she broke. Tears streamed down her face as she walked as fast as she could to her house. She didn't want to lose too much of herself where almost everyone knew her. Unfortunately, by the time she was home, her cell phone was ringing off the hook. Turning the ringer off, she crawled into her bed and curled up and cried. She needed to be alone; she needed to lose herself to her own grief. Maybe later she could listen to Finley and Brooklyn plot Gabriel's demise and maybe later, she'd join them.

****

It had been a week since she'd stormed out of Gabriel's office. A week since she had her heart nearly severed in two. She hadn't spoken to him since that day, refusing his calls and avoiding his attempts to see her at home or her office. When she told him he needed to think things over, she meant it. His voicemails tried to assure her that he had thought about things and that he loved her. But none of that mattered, not when he was still hanging out with Valerie. Sylvia and Meghan had informed her of as much, plus he admitted it in one of his voicemails.

The last thing Savannah wanted to do was dictate who he could hang out with and who his friends were. She never wanted to be that kind of girlfriend, but it was obvious what Valerie was up to and she wasn't the only one that saw it. The girls at the restaurant hated Valerie and always did whatever they could to make sure that any time she spent at Arrow was interrupted by whatever they could think of. Sylvia had even shoved a bunch of maxi pads down one of the toilets in the women's restroom so that Gabriel would have to deal with that instead of hanging out with Valerie. While Meghan was constantly bumping into Valerie's stool whenever she had to go to the bar, which was way more often than necessary. If Savannah hadn't already adored the two girls, she would have after the stunts they pulled. They had her back and she appreciated that.

There were even more stories like that, which had been divulged one night while drinking too many bottles of wine at Savannah's house. Brooklyn and Finley had decided that they all needed a girl's night that had quickly turned into a Valerie bashing night once the wine started flowing. Surprisingly though they all backed Gabriel up. They told her not to give up on him that he was hurting more from her not talking to him than he had been from the rest of the crap he had been dealing with. It was evident in the way he snapped at everyone, including Valerie and the way he moped around Arrow. He even called Finley when Savannah wouldn't answer.

"I think he's thought about it enough Savvy. He wants to be with you. Yeah, he's still hanging out with that vulture, but only because you're not taking his calls. Go see him. Talk to him," Finley told her.

"He hasn't called me in three days. I think that's a sign. Don't you?" Savannah asked.

Finely took a sip of her wine and then smiled. "Sav…he's head over heels in love with you. Look, there are things I know that I can't tell you, but you have to trust me when I say that you're the one that he wants. Bad shit happens and people deal with it differently. His way was to cut you out so you wouldn't be tainted by it. He's ready to move on and he's ready to do that with you. Not calling for three days is probably just his way of giving you a taste of your own medicine."

"Yeah, the boss man has been at Arrow far more this week than in the last four months. And I know he's there tonight since that's the only way we could both get the night off," Sylvia pointed out. "You're both sad. I think you should put the both of you out of your misery and talk to him."

After another twenty minutes of singing Gabriel's praises, Savannah finally relented and agreed to go see him in the morning. She was ready to talk to him and if he was ready to move past his pain, then maybe things would work out between them. Tired of hurting, she hoped that the girls were right and there was really only one way to know if they were. She had to talk things out with him. They needed to figure out where they stood and what needed to happen to get them back to where they were before Valerie came back into the picture. She missed him like crazy and she could only hope that he missed her just as much, if not more.

"Now that we've got you feeling better could we please talk about Gabriel's hot friends for a minute?" Sylvia asked.

"Yes, can we?" Meghan agreed. "Savannah, what can you tell us about them? Are they single? Nice? Gay? Inquiring minds want to know."

For the first time since the girls had arrived at her house, a smile formed on Savannah's lips. If she was honest, it was the first time she had felt like smiling in weeks. Not even the stories of sabotage could make her break out of her heavy hearted mood. But seeing her friends get excited about talking about boys made her remember that there was life outside of Gabriel. She couldn't let her uncertainty about their relationship get her so down that she couldn't enjoy time with her friends. That wasn't the kind of person that she was and she had to remember that.

"Which friend are we talking about here? They're all really nice and very straight, although I'm pretty sure none of them are the monogamous type if that's what you're looking for."

Meghan smiled, "that makes my plan even easier and honestly, I don't care which one, all of them would be good with me, but I'll take whichever one I get. That Declan is pretty freaking hot though. Those eyes and those lips...damn. Then there's Braeden, total spank bank material, but I think that Oliver's more my speed. I just want to climb that tree and see how far he'll take me."

"Oh my god," Sylvia muttered as she sipped her wine. "That is for too much information for me. Don't you have a boyfriend anyway?"

"Nope. Dropped him like a bad habit after that night we went dancing. If I had known that the guys were as fun as Savannah is making them out to be, I would have dropped him before that. He was boring and horrible in the sack. I definitely need more than that.

263

What about you Brooklyn? When are you going to make your move on Declan? The way he's always looking at you, damn, if I wore panties I'm pretty sure they'd catch fire just from being in the proximity of that look."

Savannah snorted, unable to hold in the laughter that bubbled up at the look on her sister's face. Sylvia choked on her wine while Finley and Meghan erupted into laughter of their own. This was the kind of thing that Savannah had been missing while she'd been wallowing in her fear and misery. She needed more nights like this, although preferably ones that did not require cleaning wine out of her furniture, which she now needed to do because of Meghan's comment.

"All I know is Declan doesn't date or even hook up, at least as far as I can tell. Braeden is pretty much a manwhore and Oliver is too, but he's not nearly as bad as Braeden. I've at least seen Oliver with the same girl more than once. Braeden barely knows any of their names and he doesn't ever get their numbers," Savannah said as soon as she made sure that Sylvia was alright.

She noticed her sister wince when she mentioned Declan not dating, but her reaction was lost on everyone else in the room since they all seemed to be focused on Oliver and Braeden the easier marks of the group. Savannah knew that her sister was disappointed about the news, although she'd deny it if asked. It was obvious to pretty much everyone that Brooklyn liked Declan and it was nearly as obvious that Declan had a thing for her sister.

Unfortunately, they were both stubborn and determined to be alone no matter what. Brooklyn liked to say she was waiting until she was settled, but Savannah wasn't sure that she would start dating even when that finally happened. And Declan was a more complicated story. She knew he had a past that was painful, one that involved his daughter. It was that past that kept him from wanting to spend his life with someone else and it made Savannah sad to see. He was one of the nicest men she knew and an amazing father, it was too bad that he wasn't going to share that with someone else.

Savannah sat back, watching her friends gush about the men they wanted and the men that they had enjoyed in the past. All of them, except her sister, had more experience than Savannah although she was older than most of them. She spent so much time focusing on her career that she had cut out the things that most 20-somethings enjoyed doing the most. Now that she was comfortable in her career, she was committed to Gabriel and hoped that she would spend the rest of her life experiencing him. She didn't need or want a parade of men in her life, but she couldn't help but enjoy the stories her friends were sharing. Tonight, she'd live vicariously through them, in the morning she'd go win her man back.

The next morning, she stood outside of the house that Gabriel had inherited from Jonathan. It was a cute single story rambler with a huge front yard and a walkway that went from the sidewalk to the front step. Just like the day she confronted him in his office her palms were sweating and her heart was racing. She should have called first, should have let him know she was coming. Deep down, she was thinking that she should have made sure he was alone first, that Valerie wasn't here with him, but it was all too late, she was there and she was knocking on the door. When no one answered, she used the key he had given her to let herself in. There was a chance he was still sleeping or maybe out running, so she figured she would just wait. When she heard the shower running she realized he was home, but couldn't hear her at the door.

With her key in hand, she walked back to his bedroom trying to make as much noise as she could so she wouldn't startle him like he had done to her once in the very bathroom she was about to walk into. She smiled at the memory of him pulling back the shower curtain, her screaming and slipping on the wet surface of the bath tub, arms flailing and him catching her wet body in his muscular arms. For the first time in weeks she was excited to see Gabriel, to maybe hold him in her arms, to get back what they once had.

With the smile still plastered on her face, she walked into the master suite intending to head straight into the bathroom when she was stopped dead in her tracks by the naked woman sitting on her boyfriend's unmade bed. Bile rose into her throat as her legs buckled. Grabbing onto the doorframe she barely kept herself from falling to her knees. She tried to will herself to turn around and leave, but her nails were digging into the wood frame and she wasn't sure she could walk if she tried. Instead, she stared at Valerie, knowing that she would never forget the scene in front of her as long as she lived.

The gorgeous raven haired woman was sitting up against the pillows on the side of the bed that Savannah had always thought of as hers. In fact, sitting on the table next to Valerie was the book that Savannah had been reading the last time she stayed overnight. She had grabbed it out of the collection that Gabriel swore was Jonathan's, but that he seemed to know so well. She started to read it one night while he was watching TV, but had been interrupted by Gabriel initiating a night of passion that even now made Savannah blush. The book was still laid flat, opened to the page she'd been reading before everything started weeks before.

Valerie didn't bother to cover up; modesty was obviously not her thing. She paid enough money for her body that she always needed to flaunt it and now she seemed to want to rub her nudity in Savannah's face. It wasn't enough that she had stolen her man, but now the bitch was tainting every memory that Savannah had in that bed, in that house. Now all she could picture was Valerie in her place; Valerie having sex with Gabriel, Valerie down on her knees. Spots danced in front of Savannah's eyes, her breath catching in her throat as she fought back tears and the little bit of breakfast that she had eaten before driving over to Gabriel's house.

"Oh Savannah, it's so nice to see you, but I'm afraid you just missed Gabe. We had a late night and an early morning, so he really needed to get in the shower. I assume you're here to get your stuff?"

Valerie purred as she smoothed her mussed up hair over her right shoulder, the long tresses barely covering one of her fake breasts.

Savannah opened her mouth, but words wouldn't come. Her tongue felt thick, her throat dry. She couldn't believe this was happening, but then again she had predicted it would eventually. It was only a matter of time before he fell back in bed with Valerie, before they fell back into old habits. Her stomach lurched; she knew she was going to be sick, but she refused to do it in front of Valerie. Finding strength she didn't think she had, she turned and ran out of the room. She dropped the key on the table by the front door before she made her way outside. She wouldn't need the key anymore. There would be no reason for her to step foot in that house again.

Slamming the heavy wood door behind her, she stopped on Gabriel's front step. Turning to the left, she threw up in the bushes next to the house until she had nothing left to purge. As soon as she was done, she wiped her mouth on the back of her hand before carefully walking to her car. She hoped she could make it home before she completely broke down. Her house wasn't too far from Gabriel's, but she knew that the fallout from this was going to be bad. The worst had happened; her heart was more than broken. She felt like a piece of her had died and now she had to go home and deal with it. She would finally know how Gabriel had felt when he was dealing with his grief and she knew it wasn't going to be pretty.

Chapter 10

A slamming door shook Gabriel from his thoughts right as

the water turned cold. Once again he had been thinking about

Savannah and how much he missed her. He thought about her almost

all day every day since she'd stormed out of his office. He missed

her more than he ever thought possible and all he wanted was to see

her again, but she hadn't responded to his texts or phone calls since

that day. The slamming door gave him hope that she had finally

come to her senses. Besides himself, she was the only one with a key

to the house and he had been alone in the house when he'd gotten in

the shower, although, if Valerie had her way, she would have been

there with him. She tried her hardest to get him to bring her home with him the night before no matter how many times he told her he wasn't interested.

Valerie had been trying harder and harder to make him forget about Savannah since the fight. Their time together had gone from mourning their mutual loss to her constantly coming on to him. More than once he told her how much he loved Savannah and wanted to make things work with her. When she wouldn't get the hint, he told her that he couldn't see her anymore. That didn't stop her from coming to Arrow knowing that he wouldn't kick her out unless she provoked him. She knew he wouldn't cause a scene. So he let her sit there and spend her money while he tried to ignore her.

Most of the time she let it go, but the night before she had been relentless even stooping so low as to follow him outside when he left to go home. She tried to get into his truck, but he locked the door before she could open it. When that didn't work, she showed up at his house and wouldn't leave until he threatened to call the cops. She had officially lost her mind. Now he knew exactly what Savannah had been talking about. He hated that she'd been right and he hadn't listened to her.

Shaking his head, he turned off the cold water and pulled back the shower curtain so he could grab a towel. Part of him hoped that Savannah would walk in on him while he was drying off. It would break the ice and maybe he could convince her to have make-up sex before they actually made up. When he was finished drying off he wrapped the towel around his waist disappointed that she hadn't shown up.

"Sav, is that you?" he called out as he walked from the bathroom into his bedroom.

"Hey babe," a familiar voice said from his bed.

"Valerie. What are you doing here? How the hell did you get in?"

Gabriel turned to find his ex laying back on his bed, propped up on her elbows, her long legs kicking out from the side. The tight red tank top she wore barely contained her breasts and her black miniskirt hardly covered the part of her that he had once loved the most. He didn't have to look hard to know that she wasn't wearing anything under either tiny scrap of clothing.

"I came to apologize about last night Gabriel. I'd had too much to drink and came on too strong. I'm sorry."

273

"That doesn't answer my other question. How did you get into my house?"

Valerie sat up and held out her left hand. Sitting in it was a key that he instantly recognized thanks to the tiny heart he had drawn onto it with a red Sharpie. She had Savannah's key and it made him want to throw up. How had she gotten it? Where was Savannah? His heart sank when he realized what likely happened.

"I was about to knock on the door when she showed up. She handed me the key, told me to give it to you and then walked off."

And that was exactly what he was afraid of. Had she come to give him back his key and break up with him or had she seen Valerie and made the decision in the moment? Had Valerie once again ruined his life while he just stood by and let it happen? He was such an idiot. Maybe he didn't deserve Savannah. He should have fought for her after she walked out of his office. The best thing would have been to go after her and tell her that he loved her that she meant more to him than anything else in the world, but he was pissed and hurt and didn't understand where she was coming from until the next morning. Now he had to go after her and hope that it wasn't too late. He quickly threw on an old pair of jeans and a faded t-shirt that he pulled from his dresser not bothering to keep himself hidden from Valerie's over eager eyes. All that mattered was getting to Savannah.

"I wouldn't bother sweetie. As she was walking away, she told me that I could have you," Valerie said her tone happy and light even though he felt like his heart was being ripped out. "I think she's done with you. Maybe now you can give me a second chance. I promise things will be better this time. I'll be better."

Gabriel wasn't sure what to say. His heart was breaking yet again. It seemed he had lost yet another person he loved and he wasn't sure he could take anymore. It would be easy to fall back into Valerie. There was no way he could ever love her again, so there was no way she could hurt him. She could help him turn off the hurt. It was tempting and he honestly thought about it longer than he wanted to admit, but he knew he couldn't go through with it, not two minutes after hearing his girlfriend was breaking up with him. He wasn't that guy. Plus, he wanted to talk to Savannah. Hear the words come straight from her mouth. She had once told him that he needed to have the decency to tell her what he wanted and now he was going to demand the same thing from her, but first he had to head to the restaurant. There were things he needed to get out of the way and something he wanted to grab before he went to talk to her.

"Val…"

"Look, there's no need to make any decisions now. Just think about it. In the meantime, why don't we head to Arrow and drink? You look like you could use a few and I would love to be there for you as a friend," Valerie said and then stood up being surprisingly careful not to flash more skin than was already showing.

Her reaction surprised him and now he wondered if he hadn't been wrong about her. She had come on strong, but Valerie had always been one to go after whatever she wanted. The old Val would've thrown a fit when denied what she wanted or she would have continued to come on too strong. Her backing off now was new, different, definitely more mature. Maybe she had changed, but even if she had, he was still sure he'd never be able to fall in love with her again. Not after what she did to him. But relationships weren't always based on love; his parent's marriage was a prime example of that.

Without a word, he walked out of his bedroom and toward the front door. He needed to get out of the house and Valerie's plan to drink once they got to Arrow sounded like the best idea he'd ever heard. Grabbing the keys off the hook next to the door, he opened it and gestured for Valerie to walk out first. She really was completely underdressed for public consumption, but he didn't care. They were going to sit in his office and drink. By the time either of them was ready to leave, she'd be perfectly dressed for a night out at a club. He followed her out before closing the door and locking it. While turning the key, he took a deep breath, hoping the crisp morning air would help clear his head a little, but instead of the clean scent of Seattle he was assaulted by the distinct smell of vomit. Searching for the source of the smell, he finally found someone's stomach contents in the bushes next to his porch.

"What the fuck?"

He couldn't believe that someone, some person had thrown up in his bushes. There was no way that an animal had done that. His first thought was Valerie. She had been loaded the night before, maybe she was hung over and feeling shitty that morning. Or maybe it had been Savannah, but he couldn't figure out why she would have gotten sick? Either way, he had to clean it up, pissed that whoever did it, hadn't done that for him. Just one more thing to screw up his day, he definitely needed to drink a few to even things out.

After a quick hose down of the front of his house, he jumped in his truck and drove the mile from his house to Arrow. Valerie followed behind him in her cherry red convertible BMW. The top was down and he could see her black hair whipping around her head. Did he really want to spend more time with her? Maybe instead of wallowing he should get his shit together, go after Savannah and make her talk to him, but…nope, wallowing was exactly what he wanted to do. What he needed to do. He didn't care if that made him weak, his life was falling apart and he needed some time to deal with it the best way he knew how.

As soon as he reached Arrow, he checked in with the staff, and then told them not to bother him while he was in his office. He grabbed a bottle of whiskey from the overstock in the store room next to his office and a couple of shot glasses from the storage room across the hall. Before he could pop open the bottle of booze he noticed the frames on his desk. He had put them back up after Savannah stormed out of his office needing a reminder of what he was losing. Savannah and his brother stared back at him. He could almost feel their disappointment in him and in his decisions as he lowered each frame again. He then opened the bottle of whiskey and poured himself and Valerie a shot.

The liquid burned its way down his throat and into his stomach before she even had a chance to sit down in the ugly chair that she'd bought for his office. While she took the first shot he served her, he poured another for himself. The second shot was gone nearly as fast as the first. He definitely wasn't going to take this wallowing thing lightly. His heart hurt more than it had ever hurt before and he didn't know what to do about it. So instead of figuring that out he was going to drink until he either couldn't feel any more or until the answers magically came to him. Honestly he didn't care which thing happened first, all he knew was that he didn't want to hurt anymore.

"Gabe..."

"No talking Valerie. I'm not in the mood for talking or bullshit or anything other than drinking. If you want to stay in here with me, then just shut up."

Without a word, Valerie nodded and held out her shot glass. He filled her glass and then his before throwing back another shot.

279

The burn didn't last very long, but while it did it that was all he could feel which had been exactly what he was looking for. In silence, they continued to drink one mind numbing, feeling numbing shot after another. Gabriel had no idea how long they were at it; all he knew was that he wasn't as buzzed as he should have been given the amount of alcohol in his system. The bottle was nearly empty and he hadn't eaten anything since the night before. He should have been wasted with a foot near black out drunk, but he was barely feeling the fuzziness he usually felt when he'd had that much to drink.

Valerie on the other hand was loaded or at least almost there. With each shot, she got more and more blatant about wanting him. She didn't say a word because he'd told her to shut up, but she squirmed in her chair causing her clothing to shift in provocative ways. It would probably take only one small move of her hips for her skirt to lift just enough to show off her shaved pussy. She already had her legs spread so he could see whatever he wanted and he was having a difficult time not wanting to look. He knew she was turned on and raring to go; the room was so small he could smell her arousal and her nipples were tight buds beneath her thin tank top.

Valerie was the last thing he wanted, yet he was dangerously close to giving in to her seduction. The whiskey wasn't doing the trick. Maybe a trip between the thighs of a woman he barely liked would make the hurt go away. Self-loathing was a far better option than being broken hearted. And fucking Valerie on his desk would definitely wipe away the memory of when he made love to Savannah in the very same place. His mouth was dry, nothing that another shot of whiskey couldn't fix. As he took the shot, he watched Valerie shift slightly in her chair. It was like she could read his mind and she knew how close he was to giving in to her. He licked his lips removing the whiskey that had been on the rim of the glass as he continued to watch her.

With her eyes locked on him, Valerie leaned forward enough to drop her empty glass onto his desk before leaning back as far as she could in her chair. She spread her legs even further than they had been before which pushed her skirt up to her waist leaving her completely bare to his hungry gaze. He knew he shouldn't be looking at her, shouldn't indulge her, but he wanted to forget and she was offering him the perfect opportunity to do so. There was no way he could look away when Valerie trailed one hand down her stomach between her legs, her other hand snaking underneath her tank top to squeeze her breast. Her moan filled the small room and it was all he could do to keep himself from jumping over his desk. He didn't even like her, but a woman pleasuring herself in front of him was something that no man could ignore.

"Oh Gabriel, I wish these were your fingers…your cock," Valerie groaned as she worked her fingers in and out of her wet folds, her thumb pressed against her swollen clit.

He closed his eyes and listened to the sounds her body was making. More than anything he wished it was Savannah playing with herself across from him and with his eyes closed he could easily picture her sitting there. His dick throbbed against the tight confines of his jeans, begging for release. Reaching for his zipper he thought about how easy it would be to pretend he was fucking Savannah if he pushed Valerie down onto his desk and took her from behind. If he couldn't see her face, he could imagine anything he wanted to. He opened his eyes and started to stand as someone pounded on his office door.

"Fuck, I said I didn't want to be disturbed," he yelled surprised that the knocking did nothing to stop Valerie from continuing to finger herself. In fact, while his eyes were closed she had lifted up her tank top so her fake breasts with their hardened nipples were on display.

"I don't care what you want asshole, we need to talk," the knocker said as they threw open the door.

Valerie jumped in her chair, emitting a squeal of surprise as she tried to pull her clothes down while Finley busted into the room. The door swung open, hitting the back of Valerie's chair. Gabriel sat back down knowing that the shit was about to hit the fan. Finley glared at him from the other side of his desk and then looked down at Valerie who was sitting next to her. The tattooed woman nearly growled at the other woman before stalking over to Gabriel's side of the desk.

"I cannot fucking believe that you are in here with this…this…whore. How could you do this to Savannah? It fucking smells like sex in here. Did you bang her on your desk after you banged her at your house? Has this all been one fucking joke to you Gabriel?" Finley screamed.

"What the fuck, Fin. I don't know what you're talking about. I haven't banged Valerie at all. I barely want anything to do with her, but after Savannah basically broke up with me this morning, I don't really think what I do in my office is any of your concern."

"It was my fault Savannah came to your house this morning. I had finally talked her into going to see you and when she gets there she found this piece of trash there and you in the shower."

"Hey, it's not my fault that Valerie was at my house this morning, nor is it my fault that Savannah doesn't trust me. I would have thought by now she would have trusted that I wouldn't do anything with Valerie while I was with her...Fuck, Fin, I love Savannah with all my heart. I only want to be with her. I'm sorry she assumed the worst, but she should have talked to me instead of leaving my key and telling Valerie that she could have me."

"Well you know what, it's really hard not to assume the worst when your boyfriend's ex-fiancée is lying naked in his bed while he's in the shower."

Finley's words were like a punch to the gut, they stole his breath and for a minute he thought his heart stopped beating. Gabriel had no idea what she was talking about, but if it was true it would explain a lot of things. And really, he didn't have to wonder if it was true. He knew the kind of shit Valerie liked to pull. She'd probably snuck into his house and planned on waiting for him. The fact that Savannah came along when she did was just an extremely fortunate coincidence for her. Looking over at his ex, he knew he was right. The look on her face said everything. He was such a sucker, even though he knew she couldn't be trusted, he fell for her shit anyway. For a second he had even thought she might have changed.

"I'm sorry Gabriel, but I was waiting for you. Hoping that if you saw me the way you used to, maybe you'd be able to love me again. I've been so lonely without you and now without daddy…you're all I have," Valerie said, her bottom lip quivering, her eyes filling with tears.

"Oh cut the crap Val…that fake cry bullshit that you do isn't going to work on me. I've seen you do it too many times to know that it's not real. And don't you dare bring your dad into this. That man would be rolling over in his grave right now if he knew what you'd done to me. Not just today, but before our wedding. Your dad was the best fucking man I've ever known besides my brother and I lost time with him because you're a selfish whore. Now I might have lost the love of my life because you came barreling in, pulling the same old shit you used to. I let my grief blind me to the real you even though I knew better."

"But…"

"Shut the fuck up Valerie. I never want to see you again. Don't ever come into Arrow again or you'll be thrown out onto your plastic ass. And stay the hell away from Savannah or you'll regret ever knowing me."

Valerie tried to speak again, but Finley took a step towards her. "You better listen to him honey. I'm pretty fucking pissed right now and if you stick around much longer I doubt Dumbass here will be able to pull me off of you in time to save that face of yours."

With a huff, Valerie gave Gabriel one last pleading look before storming out of the office. Gabriel slumped over in his chair, his head hitting his desk with a loud thud. He had really let her ruin his life again and this time he had no excuse. It wasn't like last time when he was blinded by love and responsibility; when he didn't know the kind of person she was. This time his eyes had been wide open even if he was trying to hide behind the death of her father and the memory of his brother.

"Oh god, Finley, what have I done?"

Finley pushed some things out of the way on his desk so she could sit down next to him. "I don't really know what you were thinking Gabriel, but you fucked up. You hurt my best friend and none of us know why. Hell, I don't even know if you know why."

"I..."

"Dude, don't tell me. Tell her. If you love her half as much as you say you do, you'll fucking go to her and tell her. Make her see that you didn't do anything with that whore and apologize for being a jackass. Show her the ring you bought her. Let her know that you want forever and that you've wanted that for longer than you've been being stupid. Lay it all out for her and if your love is strong and real, then you'll be able to get past this. If it's not, well then it definitely sucks to be you. You'll let the best thing that'll ever happen to you slip away because you were too wrapped up in yourself to see what you were doing to her," Finley said before hopping off of the desk and striding towards the door.

"I like you Gabriel and I like the two of you together. As badly as I want to rip your balls off and feed them to you right now, I won't for her sake. But if you don't hurry up and get your ass out of this office, then you're going to miss your chance. Savannah won't wait around forever for you, not after what she saw this morning. The last time I saw her she was at home packing, I'm not sure what her plans are, but you better go to her. If you fuck up this chance, I won't feel bad for my homicidal thoughts where you're concerned."

Gabriel watched as Finley walked out of his office, he could hear the sounds of her heels clicking against the hall floor until they were drowned out by the sounds of the kitchen. She was right, he had fucked up so royally that the only thing he could do was go to Savannah and beg for her forgiveness. He had to get her to see the truth. There had never been anything between him and Valerie except demons of the past and a familiar grief. It was his fault that he let his insecurities and his fear get between him and Savannah and now he had to make it right.

With a renewed sense of purpose, Gabriel hurried to open the safe. The ring he had bought weeks ago sat untouched in the middle of the money and the paperwork, the black box covered in a light layer of dust. He hadn't moved it since putting it in the safe three days after he bought it. After Valerie stopped him and told him about her father, he had forgotten all about the ring until he found it in his pants pocket once he finally stopped crying. He had nearly thrown the pants, ring and all, into the washing machine, but for some reason he remembered to check the pockets, which he almost always forgot to do. At the time, he still hadn't thought much about the ring or what it meant, his head was in a messed up place, so he stuck the ring next to his keys hoping that he'd remember to take it to the restaurant so he could put it away. He had always meant to put the ring in the safe, but at the time he had to admit that he wanted it out of his sight. It was a reminder of the happiness he didn't think he deserved to have.

He had never been more wrong in his life. But now his stupidity might have set into motion his greatest fear. If he couldn't find her…if he couldn't fix it…there would never be another Savannah. There would never be another woman who made him feel the way she did. He would rather lose her like he lost the others, than lose her because he was an idiot. Fuck death and the fear that it had built inside of him and fuck himself for letting that fear take over. It wasn't just Valerie's fault that he was in this situation. Everything was his fault, although without Valerie's help he might have been able to salvage what he had screwed up, now he wasn't sure that Savannah would even give him the chance.

Not wanting to waste any more time, he ran out of his office and through the kitchen, narrowly dodging the chef who had a plate in each hand. He yelled out an apology before running through the dining room and past the host stand. This time he didn't bother to check in with any of the staff. By now they were more than capable of taking care of the place while he was gone. Someday, if he got his shit together, he'd get Arrow together too. Expand the business like he planned and give the staff that had been there for him more responsibilities and more money. But he couldn't do anything for them until he got Savannah to think about taking him back.

He ran to her house, dodging the people that strolled along the sidewalk, jumping over leashes of dogs that were in his way. Her house was only a few blocks away, but in that moment it felt like it was in another state. No matter how fast he ran he didn't think he'd ever get there. As he rounded the corner to her block, he stopped dead in his tracks as he saw her walk down her stairs carrying a suitcase in one hand and a briefcase in the other. Once down the stairs, she dropped the suitcase and pulled out a handle so she could pull it behind her. He couldn't let her leave. He had to stop her. He had to make things right.

"Savannah," he yelled out as he started to walk toward her.

He didn't want to scare her or seem over eager, so he didn't run to her and scoop her into his arms like he wanted. She stopped in the middle of the road and looked at him. When their eyes met, he lost his breath, his chest tightening like it always did when he saw her. The pain he saw in her eyes, even from that distance broke his heart. He had done that to her. Partially unwittingly, but he had done that to her nonetheless. He made her feel the way she did and he didn't know if he could forgive himself for that. The screeching of tires in a relatively quiet residential neighborhood broke Gabriel out of his thoughts. He looked around to see where the sound came from, but before he could really register what was happening a familiar car sped past him.

"Savannah," he screamed before breaking out into a hard sprint even though he knew he wouldn't make it in time to save her.

Gabriel watched helplessly as the car slammed into Savannah, her body flying onto the hood of the car, her head smacking into the windshield. The driver slammed on the brakes suddenly reversing which sent Savannah careening onto the cement. For a moment, the car stopped and Gabriel thought the driver might get out to check on Savannah. He thought that for a moment maybe the entire thing was really just an accident and not a total nightmare. But that passed quickly as the car continue to reverse back the way it had come. As the car passed him, he got a good look at the driver. Although he already knew who was behind the wheel of the red BMW, there was definitely no doubt now. Valerie had finally fallen off of the deep end and she had taken her crazy out on the one person in the world that didn't deserve it.

Without wasting another thought on the woman that he would see pay for what she'd done, he ran until he reached Savannah's side. Dropping to his knees next to her, he checked for a pulse and let out the breath he had been holding when he felt one. It was weak, but there. He lowered his head to her mouth, leaning his ear as close as he could to see if he could hear her breathing over the sound of Brooklyn frantically calling 9-1-1. He could hear a faint wheezing sound and could see the rise and fall of her chest with each small, sporadic breath she took. She was undoubtedly broken and while all he wanted to do was pull her into his arms and hold her, he was afraid to move her. There was no telling what kind of injuries she had; blood was everywhere.

"I can't lose you Savannah," he told her as he brushed a strand of hair off her face. "Please don't leave me. I'm so freaking sorry. I need you baby. I love you."

Tears flowed freely down his face as he reached down and grabbed her hand. He had to touch her and it seemed like the least damaged part of her body. While he stroked her hand, he kept telling her how much he needed her and how sorry he was. He talked to her like she could hear him, but promised to repeat it all when she was actually awake. By the time the ambulance arrived, Brooklyn had dropped to her knees beside him. She rested her head on his shoulder and sobbed while he continued to talk to Savannah. The last thing he wanted to do was let go of her, but he knew he had to let the paramedics work. He picked Brooklyn up and held her in his arms while the EMT's assessed the damage and put Savannah onto a backboard.

As they loaded her into the ambulance, they announced that they could only allow one of them to ride with them. Gabriel grabbed Brooklyn's keys and then helped her into the back of the ambulance. He promised to call her parents and Finley before they closed the doors and he watched them speed away with their lights flashing and sirens blaring. With Savannah out of his sight, he was finally able to take in the scene around him. Cops and onlookers covered the street as did Savannah's luggage.

"Can I..." he started turning toward the cop nearest to him. "Can I pick up her stuff...get it out of the street?"

"And you are?"

For a second, Gabriel didn't know what to say, but then he figured the cop didn't need to know about their dirty laundry. "I'm her boyfriend."

"Did you see what happened tonight?" the cop asked still not answering Gabriel's question.

"Yeah. I watched my crazy ex-fiancée rundown the woman that I love without a hint of remorse and then I got to sit here while the love of my life fought to stay alive. I'd love to give you a statement or do whatever it is you need me to do, but first I want to get her clothes and stuff off of the street and then I want to call her family so they can meet me at the hospital so we can all stand around and wait to find out if she makes it through this."

"Look sir…"

"No…don't look sir me. I obviously wasn't the one driving. Her sister can attest to that. I'm the reason she was standing in the middle of the street though, giving that sadistic whore a target, but other than that I had nothing to do with this. I know you need my statement, but you don't need it right this second and her belongings lying in the middle of the street aren't evidence of any kind. All you need to know is that Valerie Meadows is your driver and she owns a red convertible BMW with the license plate 2HOT4U."

"Sir all I was going to ask was what your name was so that I could have it for my report and so that we knew who to contact in the morning, although I do appreciate the information on the suspect."

"I'm sorry. My name is Gabriel Archer. I own Arrow restaurant in the Junction. I'm really sorry for my behavior, but I'm sure you can understand. I won't be leaving the hospital until she wakes up so you can find me there or here's my card with all my contact information on it," Gabriel said as he pulled his wallet out of his back pocket.

Pulling a card from the worn leather, he handed it to the officer who then gave him the go ahead to collect Savannah's things. As soon as he'd gotten everything loaded into Brooklyn's car, he climbed into the driver's seat and pulled out his cell phone. These were the last calls he ever wanted to make again and yet here he was. His first call went to the St. James'. Hearing Rebecca's hysterical cries through the phone tore him up. It reminded him of the night his mother heard about Jonathan's accident which had been one of the worst nights of his life.

After getting Michael's assurance that they would meet him at Harborview, he hung up and dialed Finley. She was more difficult to get a hold of since she rarely answered her cell phone when she was at the club given the shitty reception, but he knew he had to try because she would want to be with Savannah during this. After getting no answer at one number, he tried the other one he had for her. After five rings, she finally answered the club phone sounding out of breath.

"Fin…there's been an accident."

"Dumbass, what are you talking about?"

Gabriel sighed before going into the gory details. Finley swore and cursed the fact that she had let Valerie leave his office that day in anything other than a body bag. Gabriel felt the same way. There were so many ways he could have stopped this entire thing from happening. He had brought misery into Savannah's life and he wasn't sure that the love they shared was going to be enough to overshadow that. As soon as she agreed to meet him at the hospital, Gabriel started the car and maneuvered his way out of Brooklyn's parking spot. He had to work around the people that were still milling around the scene. He had a hospital to get to and he didn't want to let them waste his time. More than once he laid on the horn to get people out of his way, which he thought was a far better plan then nudging them with the car given what had happened.

Once he was free from Savannah's street he sped through West Seattle until he reached the West Seattle Bridge and then sped across that and the short span of I-5 that he had to be on. The drive that normally took at least fifteen minutes took him only eight. While he parked the car, Gabriel was more than surprised and very thankful that he hadn't gotten pulled over on his way to the hospital.

He ran full out from his parking spot to the emergency room entrance.

"Sir are you okay?" a woman behind the counter asked when he stopped inside of the sliding glass doors. She looked him up and down, her eyes lingering on his hands. He glanced down to see what she was looking at and that was when he realized that he was covered in blood. His hands, his clothes and god only knew what else.

"My girlfriend was just brought in. Savannah St. James. Her sister Brooklyn rode in with her. Where can I find them?" he asked as he wrung his hands together.

"The hit and run victim, right? She's been taken into surgery. Her sister should be over in the family waiting room," she told him, the look on her face had gone from concern to pity. "If you'd like to clean up, the bathroom is to the right of the waiting room."

"Thank you. Her parents should be here soon and her best friend. I don't think there was anyone else I was supposed to call," he muttered as he walked to the bathroom.

Shock started to set in while he scrubbed his hands with soap and the hottest water he could stand. Pink tinged water swirled in the bottom of the sink. Seeing Savannah's blood made his stomach lurch and before he could stop it, he was bending over the garbage losing every ounce of liquid he had in his stomach. His throat and eyes burned while he continued to dry heave and cry until he had nothing left in him. He sank to the floor, his head falling to his bent knees. He had to get a grip, get himself together before he could leave the bathroom. Out of everyone waiting for Savannah he had to be the strong one. Her family would need to lean on him. He needed to get everything out of his system before he could face them.

When he was able to control his breathing after a few minutes, he got up off of the floor and walked back over to the sink where the water was still running. He splashed water on his face and then gargled with some to try and rinse the taste of bile out of his mouth. When he looked at least somewhat presentable, he shut off the water and dried his hands. Taking one last deep breath, he left the bathroom and headed to the family waiting room. Brooklyn sat in a chair alone, her head in her hands, her body shaking with each loud sob. Gabriel was actually glad that he'd gotten himself together before her parents and Finley arrived. He wanted to be there for everyone from the beginning.

"Brook…" he said softly trying to get her attention before he sat down next to her. He didn't want to startle her or make anything worse so he walked to her slowly and said her name until she looked up at him. Her eyes were swollen and rimmed with smeared mascara. Black streaks trailed down her cheeks. There was blood on her clothes and hands, but nowhere near the amount that had covered Gabriel. Before sitting down next to her he waived down a nurse and asked if there were any wet wipes or anything that she could bring them so he could help clean her up. He knew there was no way he could get her to the bathroom, but the blood wasn't helping Brooklyn and it wouldn't help her parents either.

Sitting down next to his girlfriend's sister seemed strange. Wrapping his arm around her seemed even stranger. He pulled her against him and let her continue to cry against his shoulder. His shirt was soaking wet in no time, but he didn't care. She needed to cry until she couldn't cry anymore and Gabriel planned on being her shoulder until she no longer needed him. When the nurse returned with a container of cleaning wipes, he silently thanked her.

"Brooklyn, I'm going to clean some of this blood off of you okay? I want to get rid of as much of it as I can before your parents get here," he told her before removing his arm from her shoulders and grabbing her hands. He carefully and methodically scrubbed her hands and arms, then cleaned the make-up from her cheeks. By the time he was done, her parents were rushing into the room followed closely by Finley. He stood up, helping Brooklyn to stand; her legs were shaking as her parents barreled into her nearly knocking her over. The St. James family hugged and cried together for what seemed like forever while Gabriel stood awkwardly to the side. He looked over at Finley who had her arms wrapped around herself, her face also stained with make-up and tears.

"Have you heard anything yet?" she asked, her voice so quiet Gabriel barely heard her.

He shook his head before opening his arms and motioning for her to come to him. Finley didn't hesitate to rush into his arms allowing him to comfort her while she cried. Time ticked by while they waited for an update. Although, he knew that Finley was still pissed at him, she never left his side. Savannah's dad paced the . room, leaving his wife and other daughter to hold onto each other as they cried in the corner. Gabriel wasn't sure how they had any tears left by the time the doctor finally walked into the room asking for Savannah's family.

"That's us," Rebecca said jumping up from her chair and hurrying over to where the doctor stood. Brooklyn held her mother's left hand while Michael held her right. Gabriel and Finley stood off to the side, both unsure if they should join the family to find out Savannah's fate. Before the doctor started to speak, Brooklyn motioned for them to come forward reaching out to wrap her left hand in Gabriel's right.

"Miss St. James should have suffered considerable damage when she was hit by the car and then again when she was thrown to the ground, but she was luckier than most. She has a lot of scrapes and bruises and a couple of broken ribs which caused some serious internal damage. When she hit the ground, she hit her head which is where most of the blood came from. We don't see any swelling of the brain just yet, but we'll be observing her for the next few days as a precaution. It was the internal injuries that we had to rush her into surgery for. Both her spleen and her liver were lacerated and we had to go in to repair those," the doctor paused and looked at all of them, his face looking even more solemn then it had when he started.

"Just tell us, doctor," Gabriel said urging him to continue.

"When we did the initial ultrasound to see what was damaged and where we needed to go during surgery we discovered that Miss St. James was pregnant. From what we could tell she was about 7-8 weeks along. However, there was some bleeding in the uterus, not as much as in other areas of her body, so we triaged the uterus as the last place we would work after we stopped the bleeding elsewhere. About halfway through the surgery, her vitals dropped and we searched for the source of the crash and discovered that her uterus had started to hemorrhage. We patched her up as quickly as we could, but I'm really sorry, we were not able to save the pregnancy, she miscarried while we were trying to save her."

For the second time that day Gabriel felt like he had been punched in the stomach. Finley's hands tightened around his bicep and Brooklyn's hand tightened around his, but he barely felt them. His entire body felt numb as his mind tried to process the words that the doctor had just said. Pregnant...Savannah had been pregnant. Did she know? If so, how come she didn't say anything to him? How would she feel about him once she realized that not only had he broken her heart, but he was responsible for her losing her baby…their baby, as well?

"Oh god," Rebecca said, her sobs starting all over again as she curled into her husband's side.

"Miss St. James is resting now, she looks good at this point, but we are still keeping a close eye on her brain and her vitals just in case. We've moved her into her own room upstairs. There's a waiting room up there that's a little more comfortable. In a little while you can go in and see her, but please keep your visits short and to one or two people at a time. She needs to rest and may not be awake when you get up there, but I assure you, she was lucky and definitely looks a lot worse than she is."

The doctor gave them directions to Savannah's room and then left them huddled together in the waiting room. Rebecca was still sobbing into her husband's shoulder muttering about her baby and her baby's baby. Gabriel's heart hurt. He had done this to them and they didn't know it. They welcomed him into their family, shared their pain with him, yet they had no idea that he was the one that had brought it on them. He was sick to his stomach and he knew that if there was anything left to throw up, he would be crouched over another garbage can.

"I have to get some air," Gabriel whispered to Finley who was still holding onto his arm.

"Gabriel…"

"Just go up. I'll meet you up there. I just…this is my fault Fin. I need some time to process."

"I get it. Just don't be too long. I know, despite everything that's happened between you, she'll want to see you. She's not the only one who lost a baby today, Gabriel. You don't have to mourn that loss alone too. Please don't make that mistake again."

Finley sighed before squeezing his arm and then walked over to join Savannah's family near the door. They were heading up to the other waiting room and although Gabriel wanted to go with them, he couldn't bring himself to do it. Not yet. He might have lost something too, but it was entirely his fault and as soon as Savannah realized that, she would want nothing to do with him. Hell, he was pretty sure she wanted nothing to do with him already, given what had happened prior to the accident. He would go up and see her, but he needed some time to process what happened and decide on what

305

to say now that things had changed even more. The speech he had prepared after leaving Arrow would no longer work and it no longer mattered. Gabriel had to make her see that although he loved her more than anything, it was probably better that she left him behind since all he seemed to bring her was pain; even if getting her to realize that was going to break his heart.

Chapter 11

God she hurt. Every single piece of her body was bruised, broken or cut from the inside out. And her heart…her heart was torn into a million pieces that she wasn't sure she could ever put back together again. In a way Savannah was glad that with every millimeter she moved, her body cried out in pain. Physical pain overshadowed her wounded heart at least enough to almost ignore it, but every time someone mentioned what she had lost that day, the ache in her chest got worse. She hadn't just lost Gabriel; she had lost the life that they had created together. The life that she hadn't even known about until it was gone.

Savannah bit her lip, trying to hold back the sob that would only cause her more physical pain. She'd cry later, when it didn't hurt so much. Maybe by then all of the emotional pain would be lessened and she wouldn't need to cry, but she had a feeling that hoping for something like that was foolish. There was no way that the anguish that she felt now would ever go away, let alone become dull enough to ignore. Not if she had to face it all alone. She understood now what Gabriel had meant when he told her that she couldn't understand what he was feeling because she had never experienced the losses that he had. Now he was the only one who would get how she felt and he wasn't with her. Sure her family and Finley sympathized with her, but they didn't know how torn apart she felt.

She could never express to them the guilt she felt because they would never understand. To everyone else the accident was Valerie's fault. But Savannah felt differently, she felt responsible. She didn't understand how she never realized she was pregnant? If she had known, she would have done so many things differently. She would have fought harder for Gabriel. She wouldn't have let Valerie win. If she had only known, her baby…Gabriel's baby would still be growing inside her.

Savannah hated that it would have taken knowledge of the baby to get her to fight harder for her man. Gabriel should have been worth the fight on his own, but she let things go too far. She let the situation get away from her and it ended exactly how she knew it would. The fact that she failed Gabriel and their relationship just added more guilt to the pile that was resting on her shoulders.

"Sweetie, we're going to stay here with you tonight. Do you need anything?" her mother asked breaking her from her thoughts.

"I feel fine mom. You heard the doctor. Everything is looking good so far, they just want to keep me a bit for observation. You don't need to stay. Go home, get some rest and come back tomorrow. If anything happens, they'll call you."

"God, if anything happens, Michael…no, Savannah, we can't leave. I don't want to not be here if something happens. I don't want you to be alone."

"Mom, nothing's going to happen," Savannah tried to reassure her mother, but she wasn't sure it was going to work. The last thing she wanted was to have her family hovering over her. Even if visiting hours were over or the doctors made them leave the room, knowing they were right outside in the waiting room made her antsy.

"She won't be alone Mrs. St. James. I'll be here and I'm sure Gabriel will sit with her as soon as he's done straightening things out with Arrow and DD. You all look dead on your feet and Brooklyn needs a shower and a change of clothes. Go home, take care of yourselves, then come back in the morning. Your daughter will be fine, I promise."

Savannah was thankful for her friend's intervention and for her parent's obliviousness to the fact that Gabriel had been gone for hours. From what Finley told her, Gabriel had walked out of the hospital when they were given the all clear to come up to her floor nearly five hours earlier. She had no idea what he was doing, but using the restaurant and Savannah's business as an excuse was a brilliant idea. After another fifteen minutes of cajoling, her parents finally relented and agreed to go home for a few hours. At this point Savannah was willing to take whatever she could get. With any luck by the time they came back she'd be asleep and her worries about Gabriel would be over. She needed to speak to him, to see him. She needed to make sure he was alright.

"Why hasn't he come up here Fin?" she asked as soon as her parents were out the door.

With a sigh, Finley threw herself down into the chair next to Savannah's bed. "I don't know sweetheart. All I know is that he loves you so much and knowing that Valerie's the one that did this..."

"What if he blames me? What if me losing the baby..."

"You stop right there," Finley interrupted. "There is no way that man will blame you for any of this. And you losing the baby will not change the way he feels about you. I promise you that. You should have seen him this afternoon when I told him what happened with Valerie at his house. He said to me earlier that all of this is his fault. I don't think he was just talking about the accident, Savvy. He's being eaten up by guilt right now."

"So am I."

"You have nothing to feel guilty about. None of this was your fault. Not the accident. Not the baby. Not anything that happened before. All of this is on Valerie. She will get what's coming to her, even if I have to take care of it myself. You and Gabriel just need to hash things out, get everything out on the table. I know that you won't believe me until you hear this from him."

"God, I need to talk to him Fin. Can you go find him please? Make him come see me. I want to hear what he has to say, good or bad. I just need him."

"He's probably still sitting outside. I'll run down and see if I can find him, I just don't like leaving you alone."

"You're as bad as my mom Finley," Savannah said with a laugh that made her body throb with pain. "I'll be fine for the short amount of time it'll take you to find him. Call him if you have to; just make him come up here please."

Finley nodded and then left Savannah alone in the cold, sterile hospital room. The room was thankfully a single occupancy that had enough space for the bed and a few small pieces of furniture. On the left of the bed were two uncomfortable looking chairs and a maneuverable table that she could pull over her whenever she needed it. There was a tiny box TV bolted into the corner of the room across from her bed that she hadn't bothered to turn on. To the right of her bed she had a private bathroom and a small sink. The only noise in the room was the sound of her heartbeat on the monitor, although every once in a while sounds from the hall filtered into the room through the door that Finley had left slightly ajar.

Savannah closed her eyes, laying her head back against the pillows that had been piled up behind her. Finley had said that Gabriel blamed himself for what happened, but if he blamed himself, he had to blame her too. She should have trusted him, no matter what things looked like. He should have listened to her when she told him that she didn't trust Valerie. But neither of them could have foreseen what Valerie was capable of or what she'd do. They would both need to get over their guilt and realize that Valerie was to blame for everything that happened. It was her manipulation that pushed them apart and it was her behind the wheel of the car that had stolen the miracle they created.

No matter who was to blame, Savannah couldn't help but worry that Gabriel would think less of her for losing the baby. Not to mention the damage that was done to her uterus during both the accident and the surgery. There was a chance that she'd have difficulty getting and staying pregnant, something that the doctor hadn't told her family. She was damaged goods now, who would want to be with someone who might not be able to have children?

Gabriel wanted kids, at least two if what he had told her a few months earlier still held. There was no guarantee now that she could even give him one without more heartbreak. The doctor said miscarriages were a stronger possibility now, but not a certainty and that it could happen at any time during the pregnancy. There was always a chance that she'd have no problems at all in the future, but who would want to take that kind of chance with her knowing that at any time their hearts could be broken again and again? Gabriel didn't deserve that, not after everything and everyone he had already lost.

The tears she'd tried to hold back before seeped through her lashes and rolled down her cheeks. With her eyes closed she pictured Gabriel with the children that he always wanted, one boy and one girl that looked exactly like their daddy. She couldn't deny him that opportunity, no matter how badly she wanted to be with him. The man would be an amazing father and husband and it broke her that she likely wouldn't be the one to give him that. He wouldn't choose her once he found out just how damaged she was.

"Savannah."

Just the sound of his voice made her heart skip a beat and her stomach clench in anxious worry. She didn't want to tell him yet. Instead she wanted him to wrap her in his arms and hold her for a while so she could have that memory be the last of them together. She didn't want all of the bad things that had happened over the last few weeks be what she remembered about him and their relationship. But she knew she couldn't wait. He would hate her more if she waited to tell him, if she tried to hold on to him knowing that she was flawed.

She opened her eyes, immediately seeking him out. Gabriel stood at the end of her bed. His hair was ruffled and his eyes were red and swollen, his cheeks stained by tears. Savannah had never seen him look so horribly sad. Not even after Hank Meadows died or when he talked about his brother. This had broken him in a completely different way than it had her, but she wasn't sure he could be put back together any more than she could.

"Gabriel," her voice sounded hoarse as she said his name.

"God, baby…" he said, dropping into a chair next to her. He reached out to take her hand, holding it gently, like he was afraid she was going to break. He stroked his thumb back and forth against her palm. Tears started to fall from his eyes and it nearly ripped her in two. She closed her eyes, trying to keep herself from crying any more than she already had. Crying wasn't going to help her get through telling Gabriel what she needed to tell him.

"I'm so sorry Savannah. I'm so sorry all of this happened. I should have listened to you about Valerie, but I had no idea she would pull any of this. The stunt at my house this morning, I had no idea what you had seen until Finley came to my office. I swear I never touched her, even though she tried to get me too. God, I wish I had let Finley kick her ass this afternoon," Gabriel said.

"I should have trusted you. Hell, deep down I knew you hadn't done anything, but seeing her there, naked in the bed that we shared. It made me sick…literally by the way. I'm sorry about your bushes."

"Who cares about that, I should have come after you when I found out you'd been at the house. Even if the version of the story I got sounded like you were breaking up with me. I knew I should have gotten it all straight from your mouth, but I was so hurt and blind. And now my stupidity has cost you so much. I don't think I can ever make this up to you."

Savannah sighed as she looked into Gabriel's eyes. "It cost US so much. I'm not the only one here who lost something, Gabriel."

"I know, but how can I think of my loss when I did this? How can you ever forgive me for causing you so much pain?"

"I've never blamed you Gabriel. Not really. If anything we're both to blame here and I've already forgiven you."

"I don't want to lose you Savannah. You're everything to me."

"God...I don't want to lose you either, but there's something I need to tell you and that might change everything."

Taking a deep breath, Savannah told him everything about her diagnosis. She could barely look at him as she broke it down for him, the odds, the possibilities, the huge potential for heartbreak over and over. After she was done, they sat in silence, both of them processing what the other had said. It was obvious that Gabriel's guilt over what happened was eating him up inside. He wasn't going to take her word that she didn't blame him so easily. But she really couldn't blame him. She was feeling the same way about her new situation. While it wasn't her fault she was damaged, she still couldn't help but feel guilty about it.

"I don't care about any of that Savannah. There are other ways to have children if you don't want to take the risk. All that matters to me is you."

Her breath caught, unable to believe what he was saying was true. How could he get passed what she'd told him so easily? Most people would consider her situation a deal breaker. Sure there were other ways to have kids, but that wasn't the point. Her ability to carry their children was no longer a guarantee. How could he not care about that, unless his remorse over the situation was making him amenable to whatever she told him? And if that was the case their entire relationship going forward would be built on an unsteady foundation of guilt and tragedy.

"How can I know that you mean that, Gabriel? I don't want to lose you, but how can I know that you truly aren't upset by the fact that I may not be able to carry our potential children? How can I know that you aren't just letting your perceived culpability cloud your judgment?"

"God, Savannah…I don't see it that way. I love you. It doesn't matter to me if you can have kids or there might be miscarriages or any of that. All I care about is you," Gabriel tried to assure her. "But while we're digging into things, you say you don't blame me for this, but you should at least think about it. I did this to us and I want you to think about that now so that you can let it sink in. I don't want to lose you, but I would rather lose you now then weeks, months, even years from now when you realize I'm to blame for your condition. I don't want you to resent me, but better now than later once we've invested so much more time into each other."

"No…fine," she relented when Gabriel threatened to interrupt. "I will only think about you being to blame if you really think about me being damaged goods. Sure there's adoption or surrogates or trying to see if a baby will stick, but do you really want to go through all of that when you could find someone else who wouldn't have those problems? Love isn't always enough Gabriel and I don't want you to resent me either when we're tired of trying and tired of looking into our options; when it takes months, even years to get cleared to adopt a baby or to find someone willing to carry our child for us since I might not be able to."

Silence filled the room again as they both considered what the other had said. Savannah's heart was breaking. She didn't want to let him out of that room without assuring her that they were together forever, but it was obvious that they both had issues they needed to work on and things they needed to think about before committing to a future together. It had never occurred to her to blame him for what happened to her, all the way down to her now unstable uterus. And it had obviously never occurred to him that other alternatives wouldn't be any easier than the possibility of her getting pregnant and something bad happening.

"We need time, I guess. We both have things to think about and things to work out, but I'm not done with you Savannah. I want to be with you; to give you the engagement ring I bought for you before Valerie came tearing into our lives. I'm gonna leave everything in your hands. Take all the time you need, but when you've made a decision about us, please come to me no matter what you choose. Until then, I'll leave you alone. I want you to know though, that I will honestly think about what you've said even though I know it won't make a single difference in how I feel about you."

Without another word, Gabriel stood up. He leaned over the bed, gently kissing her forehead before swiping his thumb along her left cheek to catch an errant tear. She wanted to reach out for him, tell him that she didn't need to think about anything, but instead she watched as he walked out of the room. When she could no longer see him, she broke down, sobs wracking her battered body. Nothing could hurt as badly as her heart did in that moment, so she let the crying take over until she cried herself to sleep.

****

"You're 100% sure that this is what you want to do?" Finley asked her voice filled with her usual skepticism.

"I don't care about any of the crap that's happened in the last month. All I care about is Gabriel and being with him for the rest of my life. I need to figure out a way to tell him that and make him realize that I mean what I say."

Savannah sighed, looking around at the women that filled the back room of Delectable Delights. She had been out of the hospital for a couple of weeks and was slowly getting back to her old self. In the last few days, she'd been going into work, but was still taking it easy because Brooklyn wouldn't let her work too hard. With stuff at Delectable Delights working out, the only thing left to get her life on track was to get Gabriel back. She hadn't seen him or heard from him since he left her at the hospital and she knew that he was waiting for her to come to him. If it had been up to her, she would have called him the day after their talk to tell him that he was all she wanted, but she knew he wouldn't listen to her. He wanted her to really think about her feelings and what happened between them.

"You could always go all romantic on him and do something that is straight out of a movie or book," Sylvia suggested.

"Ooooh, you could totally pull a Lloyd Dobler at the restaurant. That would definitely get his attention."

Savannah laughed at the excitement in Meghan's voice as she threw out her recommendation. When Sylvia asked who Lloyd Dobler was, the entire room erupted in laughter. It had been too long since Savannah had been able to laugh and enjoy time with her friends. For this first week following the accident, they had all been very cautious around her. They didn't want to bring up anything that would hurt her either emotionally or physically. She really couldn't blame them for walking on eggshells around her, but she was glad that sentiment seemed to have passed. She needed her friends to treat her like usual so she could finally start feeling normal again.

"How about serenading him at the restaurant? That always seems to work," Sylvia suggested.

"Yeah, except, I cannot sing at all. Not even a little bit. I think that would end up scaring him away."

"You could fill his house with cupcakes and scones and every other pastry that you sell here. That's a hell of a lot better than flowers or balloons," Kerrigan said, throwing out her own grand gesture suggestion.

"Place an ad in the newspaper telling him how you feel and that you'll be standing in a certain place at a certain time waiting for him to come kiss you."

"I think you guys might watch too many romantic comedies. I need to do something that represents us. The date he planned for me for our first official date was ridiculously romantic. I need to match that, but in a grand gesture kind of way."

"You could always try sky writing or something," Finley said.

"Or you could just go tell him how you feel and not take no for an answer," Brooklyn finally put in. "I talked to him the other day Sav. He's miserable, but making due. I don't think you need the grand gesture or the over the top romantic ideas. You just need to tell him what's in your heart. That's all that matters."

"Brooklyn's right. I've never seen him so sad, yet he's functioning, which is more than I can say for his previous breakdowns. I think he's trying to be a better man for you, whether you take him back or not. It's really inspiring. I don't think you really need to do anything to get him back, just tell him how you feel."

Savannah let Meghan's words sink in. It was great to know that he wasn't sitting somewhere wallowing in his grief, but at the same time, she wished he wasn't so damn stubborn. Instead of spending the last two weeks sad, they could have spent them together, wrapped up in each other, leaning on each other.

Ultimately, she understood what he was asking of her and she knew they both needed the time, but she hated it; hated that they weren't together and that she was now sitting here trying to figure out how to make him realize that they should be.

"I know you're worried Sav, but Gabriel loves you. Just go talk to him," Brooklyn said as she stood up. "I gotta get back out front since my boss is a slave driver. You ladies please keep her from doing too much back here. She needs to rest more than anything else. And if she's not going to rest, she needs to get her ass out of here so she can get her man back."

Savannah smiled as her sister headed through the swinging doors that led to the front of the store. Brooklyn had been her savior during the time she was out of work after the accident. If she hadn't been around, Delectable Delights probably would have died a slow horrible death. There was no one else around that she trusted to oversee all of the locations. Brooklyn had even been able to keep up with the opening, which was still completely on schedule.

Her sister had also been a huge help in getting her to feel better too. For the first week after leaving the hospital, Savannah was instructed to stay in bed as much as possible. Brooklyn stayed with her during that week so someone was there to help her. With the broken ribs it was difficult for Savannah to move without pain and she couldn't lift anything over five pounds. While she was still limited physically, the pain was starting to subside and her doctor had given her the all clear to start easing her way back into her everyday routine. It had never been easy for Savannah to lean on other people, but she had learned really quickly throughout her ordeal that she had a really great support system in her family and friends.

The bell over the front door chimed, alerting them that someone had entered the store. The place had been pretty busy since Savannah'd come in that morning, but she had spent all of her time in the kitchen, mixing and baking and resting. Since being back at work, she hadn't worked the front of the store, but she was eager to eventually work her way back up to it. She missed chatting with her customers, encouraging them to try new things and watching the children's faces light up when their parents bought them their favorite flavor cupcake or pastry.

"Hey Brook, is Savannah here?"

The familiar voice at the front counter nearly made Savannah's heart stop. It had been weeks since she'd heard it in person, but it had been prominent in her dreams. She could barely keep from jumping up and running out to see him. Instead, she waited to see what he was doing there. She knew Brooklyn would tell him she wasn't available. Her sister was protective, not to mention nosey. There was no way she'd let Gabriel know she was around until she figured out what he wanted. Despite her assurances that he was ready to reconcile and that he loved her, Brooklyn always favored caution over anything else, especially love.

"She's at one of the other locations today, but I can let her know you stopped by."

"Could you give her a message for me? I know I put the decision on her and told her I would wait until she came around, but she needs to know I'm tired of waiting. I'm going to fight for her no matter what she decides. I'm not going to just let her go. I've got a ring with her name on it and I plan on putting it on her finger soon."

Silence filled the front of the store and the back where Savannah sat with her hand over her mouth. Gabriel wasn't going to let her go. He was going to fight for her and she was going to fight for him. They were finally on the same page, ready for the separation and sadness to end. Before she could get up to go see him, the bell over the door chimed again and Brooklyn was pushing through the kitchen doors.

"I hope you heard that."

"Every. Single. Word. I need to go after him."

"You'll have to wait. He's headed to the will reading for Hank which is going to take a while. He was all dressed up in a nicely tailored suit looking really fine sis. I think we need to get you back to your place so you can clean up and meet him after the reading. I have a feeling I know exactly where he'll be heading afterward."

To hell with grand gestures or romantic overtures; it was clear she no longer needed any of that. Gabriel wanted her as badly as she wanted him. She just needed to tell him. Her future, the one she had dreamed about since the trouble with Valerie started, was finally back within her grasp. Part of her wanted to rush out and find him, will reading or no, but she knew he needed the closure and she definitely needed to wash the flour out of her hair.

For the first time since the accident, Savannah was feeling like her old self. She had hope again and was looking forward to going out and winning her man back. He wasn't the only one that wasn't going to just let what was between them end. Gabriel Archer was her everything and it was about time she let him know.

Chapter 12

When he walked into Delectable Delights and essentially declared war, he thought that was going to be the most nervous he would be all day. He had forgotten, though, that he still had to go to his father's office for the reading of Hank's will. It had been years since he'd last stepped foot in the building. Thinking about the kind of person that he'd been back then, the things he'd done back then, made his skin crawl.

Richard Archer was a win at any cost lawyer. To be successful in his firm he expected his associates to lie, cheat and steal and to never get caught. They skirted the law as closely as they could and if they stepped over the line he fudged the details or swept them under the rug. He had powerful people in his pocket because of the favors that he'd been able to do for them. At one time, Gabriel had loved being a lawyer, loved the rush of the courtroom, but his dad barely let cases go to trial. Sometimes he even pulled strings to win cases before they ever reached a judge's desk.

Although some of the situations his dad put him in had bothered him, it wasn't until Jonathan's death that Gabriel realized how despicable of a life he was leading. He hurt people on a daily basis, often working with big corporations or the rich to nearly send innocent people into financial ruin. Of course there had been good things about working at Archer & Associates. They were all required to do pro bono work, which Gabriel always assumed was Richard's way of bending karma back in his favor. The pro bono cases were always Gabriel's favorite because they almost always ended up going to trial and he had been the only lawyer in the firm that could boast a 100%-win rate, the only thing he could be proud of regarding his time there.

But today everything was different, he was different. He wasn't there as a lawyer, but because Hank had left him something in his will. Gabriel has been shocked by the initial phone call letting him know about the will. It was odd that Hank would leave him anything considering the fact they barely talked in the end. They had kept in contact a little, but had definitely let the issues with Valerie keep them from being as close as they once were. Knowing that his actual father was going to be executing the will of the man who had always felt like more of a dad to him made the situation weirder. Not to mention the fact, that the other person that was likely to be there was the one person in the world that he couldn't be around. The entire situation was more than messed up and it made Gabriel wish he had someone with him; preferably the gorgeous blonde that he was in love with and couldn't wait to have back in his arms.

Realizing that the sooner he got the reading over with, the sooner he could get out of there, Gabriel headed into the building. Even though he hadn't been there in years, everyone he ran into knew his name. He tried to be friendly to each of them, but he really didn't want to make small talk with anyone. Thankfully, the receptionist sent him straight to the conference room instead of leaving him in the lobby to wait. He would have been a sitting duck, open to anyone who wanted to see how he was doing after all this time.

As he approached the conference room he saw that his father and his administrative assistant were already inside waiting for him. There was also one other gentleman in the room, but no one else. Either Valerie was late or she wasn't coming. Gabriel hoped for the latter. He wasn't sure what he would do if she showed her face in that room or anywhere else for that matter.

"Now that everyone is here, we can get started," the elder Archer said as soon as Gabriel entered the room. "Mr. Peters, we will go over Valerie's portion first so that you can report back to your client when you see her at her hearing this afternoon. She should be very familiar with this though since her father went over all of it with her when he changed it."

Gabriel sat in silence as his father went over Valerie's inheritance. He couldn't believe that this stranger and not his father was representing Valerie. The Meadows family had been clients of his father's since his father had started the firm. Long before any of the kids were ever born. The elder Archer had a hand in everything that Hank had done over the years and by extension had represented Valerie in her dealings as well. Even when Gabriel had called off his wedding, his father sided with Valerie, making sure that she got restitution for anything she had put into the wedding and their relationship.

"To my daughter Valerie, I leave the house and a lump sum of money equaling 20 million dollars. I have also made investments in her name that she is allowed to use as she wishes with the full acknowledgement that once the investments and the lump sum of money are gone, she will be getting nothing more from my estate. She is fully responsible for the payments needed to keep the house functioning, including any staff members that choose to work for her. All of the staff members have been given sizeable severance packages and are free of any contracts that held them in my service."

"To Gabriel, I leave the remainder of my estate, properties and holdings which equal somewhere north of half a billion dollars at this time, although it may have changed by the time of the reading of this will. Richard Archer should be able to provide the actual figures when needed."

Gabriel's father paused to hand him a thin stack of papers, their eyes meeting for a second before Gabriel grabbed them. He didn't know what to say or do. He couldn't believe that Hank would leave almost everything to him. Hank Meadows had been a wealthy man; an extremely wealthy man. Nothing could stop Gabriel from expanding Arrow now. And money would not be a problem when it came to adoption or finding a surrogate or whatever it took to have a family with Savannah. They could have whatever they wanted because of Hank's generosity.

"I also wanted to apologize for letting my daughter get in between us. I have always thought of you as the son I never had, even in the last few years when we weren't close. You were better to me than my actual daughter ever was and you deserved better than me sticking up for her when I knew what she had done. I appreciate that you took the fall for your relationship ending when she hadn't been faithful to you for the majority of your time together. I have tried to get her help over the years, but she has refused and unfortunately you cannot force someone to take care of their issues. Please be careful after I'm gone. I have no doubt that she will come after you to get to my money. It won't take her long to go through what I've left her and while I worry about her, no one can make her be a better person. Please do not feel responsible for her. I don't. I am sorry it took my death to bring us together. I hope that you have found happiness in your life and that you are finally being the man I know you can be."

Blinking back tears, Gabriel watched his father put the will back into a manila folder. He was shocked and sad knowing now that Hank had known about Valerie the whole time. They had lost years of friendship because of her. Hank had obviously felt like he had to take care of Valerie, but now he was done with her. And so was Gabriel. It was obvious that his father had also washed his hands of her. Hopefully, the situation that Valerie was in now would make her get help, but he doubted it. She was delusional and narcissistic and spoiled. If she got away with what she did to Savannah, he knew she would go out and find some rich man eager for a trophy wife. It was the only thing she was really good at in life.

His stomach roiled, bile rising in his throat. He needed to get out of the conference room. He needed fresh air. Hank had known the entire time what a horrible person his daughter was and his father was looking at him with concern and pity in his eyes. The last person he wanted to deal with was his father and his condescending, hypocritical ways. He knew his father well enough to know that he would want to talk before Gabriel left the building. This was likely the last time they would see each other and Richard Archer would not let the occasion pass without causing his son more anguish.

There was so much he needed to think about, deal with and not for the first time he wished he wasn't alone. The entire situation would have been easier with Savannah by his side. Having her there would have grounded him, calmed him down so he could focus on what was important. Her hand in his would have made him feel better about dealing with his past and his future. Pushing his chair back, he started to stand knowing that the sooner he could leave, the sooner he could see Savannah. He was making things right with her today no matter what she said. They were meant to be together and he knew that she realized it too.

"Gabriel, I'd like to speak to you before you leave," his father said breaking through his thoughts of Savannah.

Speaking to his father was not on the list of things he really wanted to do, but he couldn't just get up and run away like a child. Instead, he stood and walked to the end of the table where his father now stood. If they were going to talk, he was going to be ready to walk out if his father tried or said anything that pissed him off. They hadn't talked in years, but the last time they did, Richard Archer had made sure that his eldest son knew that he was a giant disappointment to him and his mother.

"I don't have a lot of time," Gabriel said trying to give himself an out.

"That's fine. I'll be quick. I just wanted to apologize for the way I treated you. I didn't realize that you were covering for Valerie. I should have never cut you out of our lives because of her or because you decided to respect your brother's wishes. And I never should have made you live a life you didn't want. I know it's all probably too little too late, but I hope that someday we can try to mend what I've ruined."

Gabriel reeled, grabbing for the chair next to him so he didn't fall to the floor. To say he was shocked by his father's admission would've been an understatement. An apology wasn't what he'd expected to hear. He didn't think he had ever heard his father request forgiveness for anything his entire life. And while most people would probably feel good about what they heard, it made Gabriel angry. His father had years to make amends. It seemed odd that he would want to fix things now.

338

"Why? You've had years to figure this out; years to trust your son over some woman. You had to have seen how miserable I was before and after Jonathan's death, but you didn't care. Why do you want to suddenly make amends now?"

"Since I was still representing her at the time, I was called down to the precinct when Valerie was arrested. She came clean about everything, what she did when you were together, what she did to end up in jail. I heard about what she took from you and realized that it could have been you she decided to run down. I didn't want to lose another son, especially with the way things are between us. At least your brother knew that I loved him when he died."

Gabriel wasn't sure what to say. This was the most his dad had said to him about his feelings his entire life. At times, he wasn't even sure his dad actually had feelings. He always acted like a robot, hell bent on making people's lives miserable. There was never anything soft about him, not even when Gabriel and Jonathan were children. He never gave them hugs or told them that he was proud of them; at least he never gave those things to Gabriel. It sounded like he had a different type of relationship with Jonathan in the end, which should have made Gabriel angry, but didn't. Of the two of them, Jonathan had always been the one that needed their father's approval.

"Look, I appreciate what you're saying and that you dropped Valerie as a client, but I don't know if we can repair what you've destroyed. I have to think about it and right now you're gonna be the low man on my list. I've got other things that are more important. My life is in ruins thanks to that woman and I need time to repair that before I can even think about this."

"All I can ask is that you think about it. Your mother misses you and we would love to meet this woman of yours someday. I'm sorry about everything that has happened and I promise that until you're ready we'll only speak in a professional capacity. It'll take time to get Hank's assets passed over to you and then perhaps we can discuss what you'd like to do with the money."

Gabriel sighed, realizing that the money was now another thing he had to add to his list. There would be more to it than what he wanted to spend it on. It came with responsibilities and paperwork; all things he didn't really have time for.

"That works. I don't even think I've fully processed what happened today, but I'll let you know once I do. Give my regards to mom."

Gabriel excused himself, needing to get out of the building more than anything. He was feeling nauseous again and he hoped that the fresh air would help calm him down. There was so much he had to do, that he had to think about; the possibilities were overwhelming. It was a good thing he was already planning on visiting his brother's grave because now he had even more he had to get out in the open. He just wished Jonathan could talk back because he needed advice in a desperate way.

Could he forgive his mother and father for abandoning him when he needed them most? Could he get Savannah to start again even with everything that had happened between them? Would she care about the money or think that it was just another strike against him since it came from Valerie's dad? His head pounded and his chest ached. His world seemed to be spinning out of control and he needed to decide if he wanted to spin with it or get the heck off the ride.

****

Twenty minutes later, Gabriel sat in the grass, his back against his brother's headstone. He had stopped at the store to pick up a few miniature bottles of whiskey on his way to the cemetery. He hoped the booze would help clear his mind, but so far, the two that he'd drunk had done nothing to dull the ache in his chest. When he'd woken up that morning, Gabriel knew that it was going to be a weird day, but he had not been prepared for what actually happened.

In a matter of hours, he laid things out for Savannah, but hadn't actually spoken to her, become a millionaire, and had a decent conversation with his father for the first time in his adult life. He didn't know what to make of any of it, except for Savannah. There was no way that they weren't getting back together. He would do whatever it took to make sure that by the end of the day she was his again.

He wasn't sure what to think about his father's apology. Did he even want to make amends with his family? Was it worth it? Or would it do him or Savannah more harm than good to be associated with people who were that horrible to their own children? What would that mean for any children that he and Savannah had? Was it possible that his father had changed enough that Gabriel didn't have to worry that he would treat his grandchildren the way he had treated his own son? That wasn't a risk that Gabriel was sure he wanted to take anytime soon. And he knew that ultimately, it would be up to Savannah. His life was hers, if she thought it was a good idea, he'd go along with it. If she voted against it, then he would back that too.

Then there was the money. He didn't know what Savannah would think of it or how she would react. She was a self-made woman who worked her ass off for her home and the businesses that she owned. He had money that Jonathan left him, not to mention the money he made from his years at the firm and the profits from Arrow. Neither of them was hurting in the financial department, but Hank had left him millions. They could do a lot with that kind of money. Travel, adopt a ton of children, buy a house big enough to have a roof over that ton of children's heads. The possibilities were endless and frightening, yet exhilarating as well.

Once Savannah was his again, he hoped everything else would fall into place. He could use the money to expand Arrow and buy a home that they could raise a family in. He could take Savannah away from Seattle on a vacation around the world. But without Savannah, the money would mean nothing…his life would mean nothing. He would go back to the man he was before her; going through the motions, barely enjoying life while working too hard and too much. He would still expand Arrow because he owed it to Jonathan and the staff, but it wouldn't be the same as doing it with Savannah by his side.

"I knew I'd find you here. I heard you had an interesting meeting today," a familiar voice said from behind him.

Whipping around, he took her in, seeing her for the first time since the hospital took his breath away. She looked good, great actually. Her cuts and bruises were almost all faded on the outside. By the way she limped a little, he could tell that she still wasn't 100% better though, which he supposed wasn't surprising given that the accident had only been a couple of weeks earlier. He stood quickly, but stopped himself from rushing to pull her into his arms. He didn't want to seem too eager, especially since he didn't know why she was there. While he didn't plan on letting her leave without her agreeing to take him back, he was still worried that she had come to tell him that they were through for good.

"What are you doing here Savannah?"

She kept walking toward him, her eyes never leaving his. "I got your message and I wanted to give you my response in person."

Gabriel's breath caught, his heart pounding frantically in his chest. This was what he'd been waiting for; the moment of truth. Of course, he was preparing for the worst. She was here to end things, not that he would let it stop him if she was. If she told him to take a hike, that she was better off without him after all that he had done, he would make her change her mind. Gabriel waited for her to continue, but she didn't speak again until she was standing in front of him, her hand resting on his.

"Nothing matters to me but you Gabriel. I don't care about what's happened. I don't blame you for any of it and I don't want you to blame yourself either. From this point forward, I want to wipe the slate clean. I love you and I want to spend the rest of my life with you, but only if we can do it untainted from our past issues."

"I can put it all behind me, the guilt, the grief, but we're going to have to deal with some of it. We'll have to talk about what we want for the future and we're going to have to deal with Valerie if she goes to trial. And I have some news I have to share with you that could change things immensely, but I'm ready to do whatever it takes to be with you. I told you before, you're my everything and that hasn't changed. I love you, Savannah, more than I've loved anyone or anything in my life and I will continue loving you even after I die."

Savannah's eyes filled with tears, one of the huge smiles that he loved so much graced her beautiful lips. She leaped into his arms, nearly catching him off guard. He caught her around the waist, pulling her against him until there was absolutely no space between them. Looking down at her, he wiped a tear from her cheek and smiled. Wrapping her arms around his neck, she pushed onto her toes until her lips met his.

The kiss was anything but tentative. It was weeks' worth of pent up love and sadness. It was all the words that they wanted to say to each other, but hadn't been able to. Kissing her was something he would never get tired of and he planned on doing it every day, multiple times a day, for the rest of their lives. Slowly, he pulled back, ending the best moment he'd had in nearly a month. Savannah smiled up at him, her lips swollen, her eyes filled with love.

"Let's go home. We've got a lot of time to make up for and some things we need to talk about and I'd rather do all of that somewhere other than my brother's grave. It's not really the best place for make-up sex," Gabriel said with a wink.

Savannah's laughter filled the silence around them. After being starved for weeks, it was the greatest sound he'd ever heard. Grabbing her hand, he twined his fingers with hers. Together they headed toward the parking lot; toward their future.

Finally, his life was starting to look up even though there were still so many things up in the air. As long as he had Savannah by his side, he knew he could conquer anything...they could conquer anything. With her back in his arms, he just had to get his ring on her finger and he felt like everything else would fall into place. There was nothing else that mattered to him as much as Savannah. He had been restless without her, but now that nothing separated them, a sense of calm filled him. He was finally back where he belonged.

Epilogue

"Dude, what the hell do you have in this box?" Declan yelled from across the lawn where he struggled with one of Gabriel's overstuffed boxes.

"I think that one might be my box of rocks."

Declan grumbled as he readjusted his grip on the box. Gabriel smiled at his friend, and then turned to watch Savannah grab a box out of the back of her moving truck. It had taken four months, but they were finally officially moving in together. Once they had discussed the issues that had broken them up, they went over the news of his inheritance and his father wanting a relationship again. When they were on the same page, they decided that they needed to start over and date again for a while. Of course that decision lasted all of a month before he was down on one knee at the opening of the newest Delectable Delight location getting his entire proposal caught on the evening news.

Savannah refused to step foot in his house, which he couldn't blame her for, so he spent every night at her place because he refused to be away from her even for one night. Early on, they decided that they wanted a fresh start; a house that was new to both of them that wouldn't be filled with ghosts of the past. A month after the proposal, they started looking at houses to buy using the money that Hank had left him. Savannah decided to let Brooklyn rent her house with a rent-to-own condition while he used Jonathan's house as another rental property. They hadn't been too picky when it came to the house, although they knew they had to stay in West Seattle, it had to have a large kitchen for Savannah and it had to have enough room for the litter of children that they planned on raising.

While searching for their perfect home, they got the news that Valerie had decided on a plea bargain which meant there would be no need for a trial. Savannah had been grateful to finally be able to put the entire situation behind them and didn't care what happened to Valerie. Gabriel's dad made sure that he was kept up to date, so he knew that she'd been charged with vehicular assault for hitting Savannah. For the baby, she pled down to vehicular manslaughter. Her lawyer had been able to get her sentence down to five years in a women's minimum security facility, with the condition that if she willing subjected herself to psychiatric treatment there was a chance that her sentence could be reduced further.

All Gabriel really cared about was that Valerie stayed away from him and his family. She tried contacting him, but he ignored her calls. He wanted nothing to do with her and had even talked to his father about getting a restraining order against her. Part of him wondered if she would ever get the help she needed or if he would have to worry about her coming back into their lives somewhere down the road. He never mentioned it to Savannah, but he knew she occasionally worried about the same thing.

"Could you whine a little bit more please? The rest of us aren't miserable enough already," Brooklyn said, hefting her own box up a little higher.

"I'm sorry princess. Are you sure you should even be helping out? We wouldn't want you to break a nail or anything."

Gabriel tried to hold back a snicker, but ended up snorting instead. Declan grunted as he shifted the box again, the look on his face saying everything he didn't want to say out loud. Watching Brooklyn and Declan interact was hilarious. The tension between them had gotten worse. It was noticeable to anyone who happened to be around them, even strangers, but they fought it by fighting with each other. Sometimes Gabriel liked to put them together just to see what kind of inane thing they could fight about next. One night, it had been about some TV show neither of them watched, another night it had been about the color of shirt Declan had been wearing. If they were in the same vicinity, they never failed to provide the entertainment.

He was just thankful that Declan was back in his life. After getting Savannah back, Gabriel spent a lot of time mending the relationships with his friends that he had once again damaged because of Valerie. It had taken a lot to get them to forgive him, Declan especially. Gabriel had done the one thing he had promised Declan he would never do again and that was push his friends away. He said things to his best friend that were horrible and to most would have been unforgivable. Gabriel was lucky that Declan understood him enough to know that he didn't mean any of it. He had been lashing out in the only way he knew how.

"Tell me again why Finley got to get out of helping you guys move?" Brooklyn asked from the porch of his new house.

"She's down in California at her childhood best friend's wedding," Savannah said as she walked by her sister. "Just remember the sooner we get these boxes inside, the sooner we get to eat pizza and get drunk."

Gabriel laughed at his fiancée before grabbing a box of his own. They had been through a lot in the year that they'd known each other and he knew there was still a lot more that would likely be thrown at them. No matter what, he was even surer now than he had been before that they'd be able to conquer it as long as they were together. This was the start of his forever and he couldn't wait to see what happened next.

Acknowledgements

Writing a book and publishing it has been a dream of mine since I was a little girl. The road to get here has been long and winding. It's been rough and there have been times when I didn't think I was good enough; that I would never write a book that other people would want to read. Thank you for buying this book and making my dream come true. Thank you for proving me wrong by reading my book. You will never understand how much it means to me.

Thank you to my family, Lori Hansen, Randy Hansen, Desmond Hansen, Melissa Linscott and Izaiah Hansen for being so supportive of my dream and for encouraging me at every turn. Without them, I don't think I would have gotten this far. Thank you for being my rock, my inspiration and my safe haven.

To Christina Ross, Alana Reeves, Sami Jacober and Jennifer Huntington, thank you so much for loving Savannah and Gabriel as much as I do and for all of your amazing feedback on how to make their story better. Thank you for being there for me when I had a ton of questions and when I needed a creative team to help me pick a cover. I wouldn't have been able to do any of this without you guys.

To Taracina Zebley, thank you for letting me bounce ideas off of you in the early stages of the book and for giving me your input on the finished product. I appreciate the support you've shown me through this journey. It means a lot to know you've got my back.

Finding Love Series

Restless (Book 1) – Out Now
Powerless (Book 2) – Coming Soon
Speechless (Book 2.5) – Coming Soon
Breathless (Book 3) – Coming Soon
Priceless (Book 3.5) – Coming Soon
Timeless (Book 4) – Coming Soon

About the Author

Paris Hansen was born and raised in Seattle, Washington. She started telling stories at a young age, garnering invitations to writing conferences while in elementary school. Aside from a writer, she also aspired to be a lawyer and an actress as a child, but as a teenager realized she was far better behind the scenes than in front of a crowd. She earned a Bachelor of Arts degree with an emphasis in English from Washington State University in 2000.

When not writing, Paris devours as many books as she can get her hands on. After a long day at work, unwinding with a good book, a glass of wine and a decent TV show is her idea of a great evening.

She also loves cupcakes, sexy heroes and popcorn, but not always in that order.

To Contact Paris:
E-Mail: pa.hansen13@gmail.com
Facebook: https://www.facebook.com/AuthorParisHansen/
Twitter: @ParisAja13